CORPUS DE CROSSWORD

CORPUS DE CROSSWORD

NERO BLANC

BERKLEY PRIME CRIME, NEW YORK

CORPUS DE CROSSWORD

A Berkley Prime Crime Book / published by arrangement with the authors

PRINTING HISTORY
Berkley Prime Crime trade paperback edition / July 2003

Library of Congress Cataloging-in-Publication Data

Blanc, Nero.
Corpus de Crossword / Nero Blanc.
p.   cm.
ISBN 0-425-19021-8 (alk. paper)
1. Polycrates, Rosco (Fictitious character)—Fiction.   2. Graham, Belle (Fictitious character)—Fiction.   3. Crossword puzzle makers—Fiction.
4. Crossword puzzles—Fiction.   5. Massachusetts—Fiction.   I. Title.

PS3552.L365C67   2003
813'.54—dc21
2003045336

Berkley Prime Crime Books are published by The Berkley Publishing Group, a division of Penguin Group (USA) Inc., 375 Hudson Street, New York, New York 10014.
BERKLEY PRIME CRIME and the BERKLEY PRIME CRIME design are trademarks belonging to Penguin Group (USA) Inc.

PRINTED IN THE UNITED STATES OF AMERICA

10 9 8 7 6 5 4 3 2 1

A Letter from Nero Blanc

Dear Reader,

Once again, we auctioned off a character in our novel to benefit a charity we support. The organization we chose is ECS (Episcopal Community Services) in Philadelphia, Pennsylvania, a social services agency that has been assisting needy folk of all faiths for over 130 years.

Giving a fictional character the name of a real person is a fun and intriguing challenge. In life, we are named as infants; how we are called molds us—and vice versa. In fiction, the character and his or her place in the story is the first decision; the name is secondary and is selected because of associations it creates. We're all aware of the power of words!

As always, we look forward to hearing from you and invite you to send your thoughts and comments to us through our website: www.crosswordmysteries.com where you'll find information on other Nero Blanc books as well as some clever puzzles.

We hope you enjoy our fifth crossword mystery. There are more tales of Rosco and Belle in the works!

Happy solving,
Cordelia and Steve
AKA
Nero Blanc

P.S. To learn more about ECS's programs, please visit their website: www.ecs1870.org.

In Memoriam Nina and Slim

Nina, whose gentle prodding and subtle sighs reminded us when it was time to eat, take walks, sit in the sun, share our abundant love with each another.
Fifteen and a half years: puppy to adult to wise old lady.
Slim, who liked to type with his beak and tiny bird feet, who was fearless and raucous, and had free and delighted reign of our home.
You two are greatly missed.

C H A P T E R

1

"What if you had something to hide . . . ? Or maybe you already hid it?" The speaker stood, hunched and frail beside the room's wide window, then lifted a veiny, blue hand to touch glass grown greasy from institutional cooking: glass that now reflected an early autumnal night, a fog-wet roadway, the diamond-bright lights of trucks and cars and minivans roaring past—roaring away. The hand stroked the window's surface, leaving a smeary mark on the cold pane.

The response to these questions drifted across a hospital-style bed, and came from a nurse's aide who huffed and puffed with exertion as she lifted the mattress and tucked in sheets. She was a large and cherub-faced woman, dressed in a lilac cotton smock and matching drawstring pants printed with teddy bears and balloons—a peculiar choice for a home for the elderly, but one intended to bring cheer into declining years. "You mean an object—like a purse or piece of jewelry or some such . . . ? Or do you mean something hidden from yourself? Like an emotion?" The aide wheezed, stood up straight, and tugged at her print top. She was long accustomed to these verbal guessing games with her patient. "Or like a lie? Something like that, you mean?"

No reply came from the aged body at the window.

"Playing twenty questions tonight, are we?" The aide chortled and punched a bedraggled pillow into shape.

"Can't see anything from up here," was the grumbled retort.

"Sure you can! You look down, you see the highway, the supermarket off at the right—"

"There's no people out there. No people at all."

"You want people, you come downstairs and join the others in the recreation lounge . . . game hour . . . activities hour . . . TV . . . mealtimes . . . I keep telling you—"

"Just a lot of old folks drooling in their sleep."

"Not when they're eating," was the cheery comeback. "Besides, you're gonna go stir-crazy if you insist on staying up here for the rest of your born days." She grabbed another pillow, turning her back on her charge, and so failed to notice the reaction to this reference to incarceration.

The shoulders grew stiff and hostile; the head with its paltry covering of hair ducked as though anticipating a blow. "I don't like it downstairs. Never have—"

"Tell me something I don't already know." The bed finished, the aide turned to the single dresser, a shabby affair with a top crisscrossed by water rings and deeply etched scars. She sighed, but the sound was indulgent. "Why you keep all them books stacked up here, I'll never understand."

"Don't you touch them."

The aide ignored the familiar directive, instead tidying up a storm while her patient helplessly scowled in protest.

"I don't like my things—"

"Touched, I know . . . You'd be happy rolling around on the floor with a bunch of dust bunnies . . . Oh, dear, you spilled your juice again, didn't you? Cranberry, too, which is real sticky . . ."

A dismissive shrug greeted the complaint.

"And down the wall . . ." The aide bent, flicking a damp rag over the gummy spots while two old and weary eyes followed every bustling movement.

"What if . . . ?"

"You back to hiding things again?"

". . . What if you had a horrid secret?"

The aide straightened her bulky body and looked long and hard at her charge. "Horrid? How horrid?"

The patient didn't answer while the nurse's aide kept up her searching gaze. "You mean something you did a while back? Something that makes you feel unhappy now? Or guilty, even?"

A brief nod was the sole reply, and the aide's round face crumpled in empathy.

"Why, everyone on this earth has feelings like that! Honest! Things we wish we hadn't done . . . unkind words we shouldn't have said to loved ones . . . mean thoughts . . . selfish notions . . . If I was to pay you a penny for all the times I—"

"I mean something worse . . . something evil." The words ceased, but the frightened stare bored holes into the aide's eyes.

"Are you asking to see a priest maybe?"

The denial was far more forceful than the aged voice seemed capable of. "No!"

"Sounds to me as if you're—"

"I'm not . . . I'm just . . . I was just . . . talking."

The aide cocked her head to one side. In the ten years she'd worked at the nursing home, she'd learned that almost all the patients had secret worries and sorrows they'd hidden away. The older the residents grew, the more anxious they became to unburden themselves. Mostly the stories were common-place tales: long-forgotten sibling rivalries, family arguments needlessly begun and never resolved, estranged children, unforgiving mates. Once in a while, though, the situation was worse.

"There's the priest who comes to—"

"I'm not talking to any priest!"

The wet rag was folded with a noisy slap; a chair was yanked back against the wall. "I'll fill your water pitcher and bring in some more straws . . . He's an Episcopal priest . . . The religious preference you indicated on your—"

"I don't want any priests in here."

"But your admission card says—"

"I won't see him!"

"Okay, okay. You needn't bite my head off."

"And I don't want anyone else coming into my room . . ."

"I know—"

"No one!"

The aide's expansive chest released a weary sigh. "I'll be bringing your supper in about half an hour. You want I should put one of your books beside the bed before I go?"

"No one else—"

"I said, I heard you."

CHAPTER

2

" 'The way of transgressors is hard.' Proverbs 13:15." The voice of the man making this pronouncement was stony, a no-nonsense tone that brooked no equivocation—or argument. As he spoke he thumped calloused fingers on the long Formica table while his aging yet wiry physique and bristly white hair quivered with outrage and indignation. " 'If thou faint in the day of adversity, thy strength is small.' Proverbs again . . . Well? I'm still waiting for an answer. Are we going to make them cease this reprehensible activity?"

It was Curtis Plano who answered. Unlike the first speaker, his fingers were not visible on the tabletop. The reason being that Plano had lost his left hand in the early days of the Vietnam War, where he'd served as a medic. And although his prosthetic hook had long been accepted by his peers, he wielded it with discretion; the rest of the time it remained out of sight: in a jacket pocket, under a table; in church, the hymnal or prayer book rested upon it. "Wars are better off forgotten," Curtis liked to repeat, with a been-there-done-that shrug. "The past is the past, and nothing's going to change it," Now his speech was equally pragmatic. "I agree with Warden Stark, something needs to be done—"

"Something needs to be done, and right *quick,* Curtis," was the fiery retort. "The damage is already—"

"*Potential* damage, John; it's only *potential,*" Milton Hoffmeyer interjected. Like Stark, he was in his early seventies, but where John was a dictatorial bantam rooster, Milt was yielding and placid, a bear-shaped man with a tranquil and shambling air. "Because like it or not . . . and I admit, I don't like this situation any better than you . . . I cannot, at this point, say that they're—"

John Stark snorted. "So you're advising we just let them get away with murder up there—?"

"No. That's not what I'm saying. And murder isn't a word I'd—"

"It's the term I'm using! Unlike you and all the other nervous Nellies who live around here . . . closing your eyes to every problem that comes down the pike. But then, you always have—even when you were a kid." Stark rocked rapidly back in his folding chair while Hoffmeyer's tall body bent forward, precipitating another stalemate among the two top-ranking vestry members of Trinity Episcopal Church in the hamlet of Taneysville, Massachusetts.

Senior Warden Stark and Junior Warden Hoffmeyer, life-long neighbors and polar opposites. Month after month, year after year, decade upon decade: allies one moment, adversaries the next. Before his retirement, John had spent a life out of doors, first as a house painter, then as a self-employed general contractor. He held little truck with those whose trade consisted of "punching cash register keys." This dictum naturally included Milt, who still worked "six days a week, sunup to sunset" at Hoffmeyer's General Store, an emporium established by his father during the late 1930s; and little had altered since that bygone era.

"I take 'nervous Nellies' amiss, John. I have to tell you that."

"Well, I take it *amiss* that you're waffling on this issue."

"I'm not *waffling*. I'm merely suggesting that your approach is extreme—"

Curtis Plano stepped into the breach. "It's more than 'potential damage,' Milt. Like John says: Every time those damn—" He checked his speech, scowling with the habitual frown that raced across his square, sixty-year-old face every time he—or a neighbor—stepped beyond what he considered the "bounds of decency." Now the owner and proprietor of the village pharmacy, Plano felt it his duty to maintain a conscientious and ethical attitude in all dealings—whether at the shop or at home. "Sorry, Father," he muttered to the priest at the table's far end. "But you know what I think about those machines. And working all hours on Sunday, too! It's simply not right. We're a law-abiding community. A good community. We've worked hard all our lives, and we've earned the right to have our share of peace and quiet."

As if awaiting their cue, the machines in question, the relentless earthmoving apparatus that the vestry was now discussing, increased their thunderous rumblings; and the meeting room in the church's undercroft vibrated with the din. Cooling coffee danced in the mugs; the steam radiator in the room's far corner hiccoughed and hissed while the waning late October light that filtered down through the basement windows jumped and shivered as though it had also been affected by the noise.

"You're forgiven," said Father Matthew with a quick and grateful smile. He was a young man, just out of seminary and so eager and helpful as to seem hopelessly naive. He preferred to be called plain "Matt"—had tried from his first day at

Trinity to be on a relaxed, first-name basis—but the vestry members, all older, all fastidious about church "niceties," insisted on time-trusted honorifics. "Father" he was, or "Father Matthew"; and on the rarest occasions "Father Matt."

John Stark cleared his throat and prepared to speak again. "My fellow members of the vestry," he began, using the magisterial mode he employed for reading Scripture lessons on Sunday mornings. "It's our building I'm worried about . . . Now, we all know that backhoe shakes the living daylights out of the hillside every time it bites up another scoop of dirt; and I'm telling you right now, I think it's damaging Trinity's foundation. We can hardly afford minor repairs. What are we going to do with major ones? We'd have to shut down. And I mean that. We'd have to find another space in which to worship."

A murmur of dismay buzzed around the table.

"But we've got a good, strong structure here, John," Hoffmeyer countered. "It's stood in this spot a long while . . . almost as long as Taneysville has been a community. Besides, unless we hire ourselves a lawyer, I don't see how we can—"

"Money, money . . . that's all it is with you, Milt . . . Well, believe it or not, that's what I'm talking about. Trinity may be strong enough to withstand Massachusetts winters. And it may be strong enough to cope with the occasional 'big blow' that moves up or down the coast, but I guarantee this place can't take all that infernal shaking and shimmying every time one of those monsters starts tearing up the landscape. What we've got here is stone and wood construction and, as you pointed out, *old* construction. We're not talking steel beams and reinforced concrete. So, if you're trying to tell us that—"

"No one's questioning your expertise when it comes to foundation work, John," Curtis Plano interjected.

"More coffee anyone?" This was Sylvia Meigs speaking up

at last. She was the town's librarian, a normally loquacious librarian as well as the newest member of the vestry. Fifty-seven, plumper than she wished, Sylvia was also the vestry's youngest member—as well as the only woman present at this emergency meeting. An awareness of her gender, age, and role had conspired to keep her cheery demeanor in abeyance, but such constraints couldn't last for long. "I made enough, and it's still hot. And there are some doughnut holes left from Social Hour . . . I fried them up myself so I can promise you they're tasty. That is, if you didn't sample them already . . . Which most of you did . . ." She stood and smoothed her skirt over amply padded hips. "Well? I'm awaiting your orders, gentlemen."

Sylvia's sunny offer failed to alleviate the standoff between the senior and junior wardens; and she repeated her question, adding a chirpy: "How about you, Father? Care for a refill?"

Matt didn't want more coffee; his stomach was jumpy enough—just as it was every Sunday since he'd come to Ta-neysville. He wasn't comfortable with preaching yet, let alone with the nail-biting anxiety of producing sermons that sounded both relevant and innovative. But following every service was Social Hour, and close on its heels on this partic-ular Sunday, an emergency meeting of the vestry. "Thank you, Sylvia. That would be nice."

"And a couple of doughnut holes, too, Father?"

"Sure. Why not?"

"He won't be so free and easy in twenty years' time, will he, Curtis?" Sylvia laughed.

Curtis smiled; Matt smiled; Sylvia continued to chuckle; but John Stark and Milton Hoffmeyer remained unmoved by the levity surrounding them.

At length, another member of the vestry weighed in. It was Gus Waterwick, the church treasurer. Gus was approach-ing Stark's and Hoffmeyer's age, and his hair—or what few strands remained—was a pale and watery gray. Gus stood for Gustavus; Waterwick was anyone's guess. When his grandfather had arrived from Poland to work in the paper mills of New England he'd been too young to argue with immigration officials who couldn't understand his native tongue. "Waterwick" had been the name hand-printed on his entry card; Waterwick the new-minted American became. Gus inclined his nearly bald head. When he spoke his words wrapped themselves around the remnants of an accent that still turned "w" into "v." "What are you proposing we do, John?"

"Simple enough; get them to stop."

"And how do we do that? The man bought the entire property fair and square. Fifteen acres . . ." Gus paused, his demeanor that of a presiding judge rather than the former owner of Taneysville's filling station and auto repair. ". . . He has the right to build an addition—"

"You're correct," interrupted Curtis. "However, to my way of thinking—and John's—that addition is—"

Gus shook his head. "We can't just march up there and shout, 'Stop it right there!' Why, we'd be laughed right off the property. Taneysville should have considered new zoning years ago. Now it's—"

"Which brings us back to the issue of hiring ourselves a good lawyer—" interjected Hoffmeyer, but Stark paid no heed.

"Addition?" he demanded. "What about the proposed horse barn, the guest house, the Olympic-sized swimming pool? They're probably planning some kind of fancy beach cabana, too—"

"There aren't no beaches in our little sector of the state, John," Sylvia soothed.

"You know what I mean," Stark grumbled. "And didn't you say you were getting us coffee?"

"Testy, testy . . . It won't do your heart any good to talk on so, John."

"Mrs. S tells him the very same thing," offered Father Matt with a peaceable grin.

The senior warden glowered him into silence.

"John, let me repeat my question," protested Gus in his old-world accent. "How do you propose to halt this construction? From what I hear, the owner's got more money than G—than is good for any man. Something to do with making magnets, I've heard, although how that would—"

Stark interrupted. "He doesn't need to build on the hill above our—"

"Yes, but that's where the old Quigley place *is,*" was Hoffmeyer's reasoned response. "The house and the—"

"Well, why did he buy Quigley's property in the first place? Why start there if all he wanted to do was gut the original home and 'remodel' it into a make-believe castle? Five thousand square feet! That's what the addition's going to be. Five thousand square feet! Do you know how much bigger that is than the old house?"

"That's the way it is nowadays, John," Hoffmeyer said as he bowed his large and shaggy head. "People want bigger, better . . . These farmhouses that you and me grew up in, that we've lived in all our lives . . . They're—what's the word . . . ? They're *stylish* all of a sudden. Summer homes, winter homes, *weekend* homes . . . Folks like our new neighbor—"

Stark waved an impatient hand, but Milt continued on his course. "Folks like our new neighbor buy up these homes because they admire that old-timey look—and then they change them around because they want all the modern conveniences. Nothing wrong with liking comfort, John—"

"They don't even bother using local builders," Stark argued hotly.

Hoffmeyer regarded him, recognizing that the importation of outside laborers irked Stark as much as anything else did. "You and me can't stem the tide, John. All we can do is try to welcome the newcomers in, try to make them—"

"Try to sell them fancy bottled water, is more like it! I can hear your cash drawer now; ka-ching . . . ka-ching . . ."

"Gentlemen! Gentlemen!" Sylvia murmured, but Trinity's senior warden ignored her.

"What's the fellow planning to do up there anyway? Sit in his fancy glass palace and stare down his nose at us when we come to worship?"

Father Matthew raised four tentative fingers. "If that's one of your concerns, John, why don't you and I simply invite the new owner to join—"

"I want to know why the man can't take his damned fortress and put it on the other side of his land!" was the outraged response. "Why can't he leave us in peace before our roof caves in and the foundation cracks—"

"But you don't know for certain we're sustaining any damage—" Hoffmeyer tried to interpose, but the incipient argument was drowned by the sudden wail of the backhoe, and the tumultuous crash of a tree pitching into the ravine that separated church property from what had once been the Quigley homestead. Sylvia Meigs screamed. A wooden cross hanging on the wall leapt from its nail and fell while a coffee mug jittered off the table and shattered on the linoleum floor.

"Hell and damnation," John Stark roared. "I'm going up there right this very minute. I won't see us threatened like this!"

CHAPTER

3

Despite his outburst, John Stark wasn't a violent man, and his strong reaction had stunned the others into a sheepish and embarrassed silence. One by one they filed up the basement steps and into the encroaching autumnal dusk. The scarlet and gold–hued foliage for which New England was famed had vanished into the fallen, dead leaves of the days approaching November while the air carried the chill and dank of a not-too-distant winter. Except for the steady drone of the earthmoving equipment working the hillside, the fading Sunday afternoon would have provided a perfect time for introspection and reflection, a few quiet moments in which to think back on the past year—or years—of rural existence in the sleepy community of Taneysville.

Instead, the noise increased the group's consternation; and, locking the church door behind them, they began scattering across the parking area like loose marbles.

"Can I give you a ride, Sylvia?" Curtis Plano asked.

Both widowed, it was generally accepted by the locals that

the two were "keeping company" although neither had as yet admitted to a relationship.

"Why, thank you, Curtis." Sylvia sounded duly surprised and grateful. "Going to be a cold winter, according to the Almanac," she sang out to the other vestry members as she approached Plano's car. With a polite flourish, he opened the door with his right hand while the left remained buried in his coat pocket.

"And early," was Milton Hoffmeyer's agreeable response.

"We've had 'em before," Gus Waterwick added.

"And doubtless we'll see many more." This was Father Matt's offering, and it was greeted—like many of his ruminations—with the kindly benevolence of a grandparent patting a child on the head.

"*You* will, Father," Sylvia chortled, "but I don't know how many decades the rest of us old-timers have—"

"One . . . maybe two, if I'm real lucky," Curtis interposed with a good-natured laugh.

"Then you'll have to make the most of them," she rejoined.

John Stark didn't speak through the entire leave-taking. Instead he eased himself into his station wagon in silence and drove up the lane toward what had been the Quigley place.

"I hope he don't get himself in trouble," Gus observed in a worried tone.

"Or us," was Milton Hoffmeyer's pensive reply.

Stark's car climbed the tree-lined and twisting village lane toward the dirt drive that had once been the approach to Hiram Quigley's farm; a home that had remained an unobtrusive neighbor to Trinity Church through generations of Quigleys and generations of parishioners. The modest woodframe house with its low-slung doorway, introspective windows, single chimney, and antiquated kitchen covered by a sagging rear roof had been such an accepted part of the Ta-neysville landscape that no one could have imagined it wouldn't always be so.

"Old-timey," Stark muttered, *"stylish . . ."* His lips were pinched white and his chest pounded with feelings he couldn't quite name. Without intending to, he remembered Sylvia Meigs's warning about his heart, and thumped a hand against his breastbone as if willpower alone could calm him.

He stopped the car and climbed out. The rutted drive was jammed with vehicles: workmen's pickup trucks, a bulldozer, a chipper, a stump grinder. Numerous felled trees littered what had once been a kitchen garden.

"Hell and damnation," Stark swore. Normally, he wasn't a swearing man any more than he was a violent one, but the circumstances were working powerful changes on his psyche.

He strode in the direction of a person who seemed to be the foreman. "You've got to stop this! People can't hear them-selves think!" Stark shouted above the noise of the backhoe.

The man merely turned and peered down at him. He was far bigger than Stark, and thirty to forty years younger. His hair and face were the same color: a tawny, reddish pink. "Who the hell are you?"

"I'm the senior warden of—"

"A warden, eh? Well, we ain't got no escaped prisoners here, warden." The man also raised his voice above the din, but it was clear from his posture that he was the one on solid ground and not his visitor. "I only hire top-notch workers. Can't afford not to. Not with the time schedule we're on, and all . . . You know, I would have took you to be retired there, warden—"

"No, you misunderstood. I'm—"

"You gotta speak up—"

"Of the church! I'm the warden of a church, not a prison!" Stark bellowed. "Of the church down there!" He pointed in-sistently. "The one your machinery is—"

"Take it easy there, mister——"

Stark's blue eyes flashed with rage. "Don't you know that this is the Sabbath day! It's Sunday!"

The foreman's face broke into an easy smile. "This could be Independence Day and New Year's rolled into one, and my crew would still be working. We've got to get these foundations dug before the November freezes set in or we're toast; and right now we're behind schedule . . . Architects! You gotta love 'em . . . They give the owner a pretty picture, and bing-bang, you've got a whole new hole to dig . . ." He made to move off, but Stark grabbed at his arm.

"Your machinery's damaging our church!"

The man stared hard at the hand clinging to his arm. Stark released his grasp, but maintained his confrontational stance. "Sue the owner if you want, fella, but don't go hollerin' at me. I don't make the rules. I just follow them . . . And that's the same thing I told all the other folks who've been barging in here with complaints. You want a stable; you want a pool, a pump house, guest house, summer kitchen, you name it . . . just call me up. But don't come here and start yellin' about destroying the community, or not giving local laborers a chance to work—or ruining a neighboring building. Or history—I don't know nuttin' about history." Again, he began to walk away, then stopped himself and gazed curiously at Stark. "I never heard of a church that needed a *warden* . . . What kind of a place is it anyway? Like a rehab house?"

"It's an Episcopal church, a very old church, and you——"

"Yeah, I know . . . I know . . . We're wreckin' the neighborhood. Talk to the owner, if you want, fella . . . But right now, I'd suggest you leave before you get hurt. This here is a construction site——"

"I can see that," Stark countered testily. "That was my line of work before——"

"Well, there you go then, pops. You know exactly what I'm up against. Winter setting in and a homeowner breathing fire . . . Architects! Yeesch. And there's more rocks in this ground than I got in my head for takin' on this friggin' job in the first place." He walked off before Stark had time to respond.

It was dark by the time Milton Hoffmeyer pulled into his own narrow lane. His hands clutched and reclutched the steering wheel as he stared unhappily at his home. White shingles, a freshly swept porch, light streaming from the ground floor windows, the curtains hung just so. Milton's wife was far more fastidious than he; and he knew when he walked in the door he'd smell the familiar aroma of Sunday night supper: a soup with dumplings she'd made by hand and an apple crisp with fruit picked from their own trees. The apples would be the strongest scent, winey and redolent of autumn. The linoleum floor would be immaculate, the tea towels beside the sink pressed and clean, the countertop spotless as though no one had been chopping or peeling or slicing.

Another spasm of misery attacked him. Although he hadn't expressed the opinion as vociferously as John Stark, he was just as upset about the changes being worked on the Quigley house. *Why does "progress" need to barge in here?* Milton thought. *And why now—just as I'm thinking of retiring? How come we let big spenders from Boston or Newcastle buy up our land and change it? All they do is make us feel small, make us feel old and useless.*

"Is that you, hon?" he heard as the kitchen door swung open. "Whatever are you doing skulking out there in the car? Come in before you take cold." Backlit, his wife appeared featureless, but her shortish hair fluffed around her face like a fuzzy white halo, and her entire persona seemed to emanate good.

Hoffmeyer dragged himself from the car.

"That vestry," his wife sighed goodnaturedly. "It'll be the death of you."

"It's not the vestry this time, May—"

"Not one of your regular rows with John?" She stood aside to let her husband pass through the door. His long back was bent and dispirited. "I swear, I don't know why you two like bickering so much. You'd think you would have had enough of it by now. Enough of it several decades ago. Maybe enough of it when you were young—"

"It's not a disagreement with Stark this time, May. It's all that mess up at Quigley's—"

"Uh-oh . . . That sounds like John talking—"

"I hate to admit it, May, but I think he's right . . ." Hoffmeyer shook his bearlike head.

"Nothing you can do, Milton. Besides, that church has been around a mighty long time—"

"John's concerned about structural damage. He went up to the site—"

"Oh dear, I hope he doesn't get himself into mischief. You know how bullheaded he can be." She closed the kitchen door behind them, and returned to her place at the stove. "What do they say? *If it ain't broke . . .*" May stirred her soup, adding a pinch of salt, a pinch of thyme, a generous pat of yellow butter. The problematic issue of the senior warden disappeared in a cloud of scented steam. "We had a call from young Milt while you were gone. He sounded real happy, real upbeat. He said his campaign's going great guns. The latest polls said he was holding his lead." She smiled as she worked, all troubles banished. "Just think of that . . . a grandson who's almost in public office. Public office! I still can't believe it . . . Milton Hoffmeyer the Third, United States Congressman. Don't those words have the grandest ring. He said he'd see us on Election Day . . . Now, you go and wash up. Supper's almost ready."

CHAPTER

4

By five past seven Sunday evening the regular customers at Eddie's Elbow Room—the nearest workingman's drinking establishment to "downtown" Taneysville—were in a jovial, almost celebratory, mood. The Patriots had just upped their record to 6 and 2 by beating the Buffalo Bills 15–14. They'd accomplished this by kicking their fifth field goal of the day with three seconds left on the game clock—a forty-seven-yarder that literally bounced on top of the crossbar before dropping to the turf on the plus side. Eddie's ten or so patrons had responded to this last-minute triumph with the expected whoops and hollers and more than a few elongated sighs of relief. A round of beers had been purchased by Big Otto Gunston, a fifty-something electrician renowned for the size of his walrus mustache, his arm-wrestler's forearms, and his equally obvious paunch—and conversation had become a boisterous analysis of the game just won.

"What we need is a quarterback who can run the damn football," Gary Leach groaned at Eddie Apollo as the taproom's owner punched the TV remote, darkening the set and silencing the professional analyzers. "The old ticker can't take too many games like this. What are they trying to do? Murder me before Christmas?" For effect Leach pressed his cold beer to his chest, but everyone knew the gesture was purely for show. Unlike Big Otto, Gary was proud of his physique; he kept a set of dumbbells in his basement, and was always ready to try out a new high-protein or high-carb diet—as long as it didn't mean eliminating the day's closing ration of brewskis. "I mean, come on! Is this pro ball or what?"

In answer, the other patrons merely hoisted their drinks, and the taproom drifted into momentary silence.

The establishment was standard fare for rural Massachusetts: a collection of neon Budweiser, Coors, and Miller signs decorating the walls and windows; a parking lot within easy view; and queued up on the gravel, a small line of pickup trucks. The bar at Eddie's Elbow Room seated fifteen, but was never filled to capacity—except for the World Series, Super Bowl, and Stanley Cup. Beyond the bar sat eight tables with checkered plastic tablecloths and beyond that, the kitchen. Laminated menus were wedged between shakers containing salt, pepper, and red pepper flakes. The menus offered up hamburgers, French fries, grilled cheese sandwiches, et cetera—all prepared and served by Eddie's wife, Tina, a woman with coal black hair and the kind of figure not normally found in Taneysville.

Nearly every man, no matter his age, upon his first visit to Eddie's would misinterpret the relationship, and make a pass at Tina. This was a great source of entertainment for the regulars, since Eddie stood well over six feet tall and was no slouch when it came to muscle. Occasionally the regulars would draw straws to determine who would get to enlighten the neophyte as to his imminent demise. And Eddie would play into the game by standing with his massive arms folded across his chest and a brutal expression on his face. In reality, he was a bit of a "gentle giant" and would enjoy the show as much as anyone.

"The Pats need a QB like that guy Philly's got," Gary continued. "What's his name?" It was a rhetorical question; no one bothered to answer.

Like most of the customers at the bar, Gary Leach was a local craftsman—a mason—who'd been unable to secure work on the renovation of the old Quigley place. The same held true for nearly all the men at Eddie's on this particular evening, and the subject of the renovations and additions was a sore topic with every one of them—but a subject that was bound to come up sooner or later—and more often on a football night, because the Patriots' current placekicker just happened to be named Quigley as well.

"Run the ball?" Stu Farmer laughed. "I'd be happy if the bum learned how to *throw* the ball. Four intercepts? Come on, where's that come from? If it wasn't for the Toe and his three-pointers, we woulda been shut out fourteen–zip." Like Big Otto, Stu was also an electrician. He was twenty-one years old, gangly as a string bean, and had lived in the environs of Taneysville all his life. His source of pride—as well as a good deal of needling from the denizens of Eddie's Elbow Room—was a blond ponytail that fell halfway down his back. Technically, Stu was Big Otto's assistant, but that was only when work was good; when it wasn't Stu picked up what odd jobs he could—and slept in his truck when he couldn't make rent. By referring to the Patriots' placekicker as "the Toe," rather than Quigley, he'd hoped the conversation would stay with football for a while longer. No such luck.

"Speaking of the Toe, i.e., Quigley," Big Otto said in a tone designed to include only Stu Farmer and Gary Leach, "I understand old man Stark tromped up to the Quigley work site this afternoon and gave those scabs a piece of his mind."

They're not exactly scabs, Stu considered observing, but instead opted for the less inflammatory: "I thought we were talking football here."

"Game's over, Stu. Time to stop *stewing.*"

"Yuck, yuck."

"You're the one's always yammering about his hairdo . . . 'Scuse me—'hairstyle.' Maybe we can spend the next few hours talking about your ponytail?"

It was Gary who interrupted this familiar exchange. "I heard the same thing about Stark," he grumbled while he polished off his beer. "Who woulda figured? But it's gonna take more than one creaky old man to set those bozos straight."

"Maybe," Gunston answered, "but don't forget he was in construction for a long time. He knows what it's like to lose a gig to out-of-town contractors."

"Out-of-town?" Gary demanded. "How about out-of-the-damn-country? That crew is all from Italy or Germany or someplace like that."

"That, too . . . but the general contractor's American. From up north somewhere. A Mainiac, or something . . . I tried to score the electrical on that addition after they get it up . . . All I got was a snooty, 'I'll keep you in mind' . . ."

"Bum," Stu and Gary groused in unison.

"You got that right, gents . . . But what I'm sayin' is, Stark's as steamed as we all are about this setup, and he can be a tough old dog. You guys are too young to remember him in the old days."

"Hah, that's a laugh," Stu countered. "All he cares about is that little church—and the fact that they're runnin' backhoes on Sundays and that he can't hear himself sing the songs . . ."

"Hymns," Big Otto said.

"Whatever."

"Another round?" Eddie asked as he removed the three empty Miller Lite bottles.

"Yeah, sure . . . This one's on me." Gary tossed a ten-dollar bill on the bar, and waited for Eddie to move off toward the other customers. "So, what are you sayin', Otto? That Stark's aimin' to throw a monkey wrench—?"

"I'm just telling you that there's a lot of folks around here that wouldn't be too heartbroken if those clowns at the Quigley place disappeared—and some locals took over their jobs."

"Whoa . . . whoa . . . whoa," said Stu. "What do you mean by 'disappeared'?"

Gunston gazed at him; his bushy mustache quivered with droplets of beer. "What I'm sayin' is this: If you and me and Gary here was to decide to do something that 'persuaded' the contractor up there that he should be hiring local folks . . . well, I don't suspect we'd be gettin' too many complaints from the goody-goods at the church. Don't forget that our good 'constable' goes there, too—sometimes."

Stu studied the bottle in his hands. "What are you thinkin' of doing?"

Big Otto looked down the bar before answering. "Like I said, *Stew,* I'm not talkin' about *me,* so forget the *you* stuff. I'm talking about *us.* This has got to be an 'all for one, one for all' deal. I'm not stickin' my neck out unless I know you guys are with me on this."

Gary nodded his head, and after a quiet moment said, "Okay, I'm in."

"In on what?" Eddie asked as he sauntered over. "You guys starting a pool for next week's game?"

"Ahh . . . Not exactly. We were just talking about the geeks working on the old Quigley place," Stu said.

Gunston rolled his eyes.

Eddie folded his arms over his chest, taking a stance much like one he might take if someone made a pass at Tina—but there was no twinkle of humor in his eye. He gave Stu a tight-lipped smile and said, "Greeks."

"Huh?"

"They're Greeks, not geeks."

"Greeks, geeks, what's the difference?"

"You want to tell him, Otto, or should I?"

Big Otto shook his head. "Stu, Eddie's last name is Apollo."

"Yeah . . . ? So? Who doesn't know that?"

"His family comes from Greece."

Stu stared at Eddie, then looked back at Otto. He was no more enlightened than he'd been before. "So?"

"So, Eddie is telling us the guys working the Quigley job are from Greece . . . like Eddie."

A light bulb finally flashed on in Stu's brain. "Well, hell, Eddie, you don't talk weird like they do. How was I supposed to know you came from someplace other than the good old U.S.A.? Anyway, I thought those guys were from something like . . . like Italy or something . . . Well, hell, now that I think on it, Apollo sounds like an *I*-talian name . . . Ends with an 'o' and all . . ."

A gravelly groan sounded deep in Eddie's throat. "Keep an eye on your friend here, Otto." He made a point of hitting the "o" at the end of Otto; then he moved down to the other end of the bar.

"You know what, Stu?" Gunston said. "You're about as brain-dead as that bottle of beer in your hand."

"Come on, big guy, how was I supposed to know Eddie was Greek?"

"Greek, schmeek, that's besides the point. If we're going to make some 'adjustments' in personnel on that Quigley job, we've got to keep it to ourselves. You can't just go blabbin' about what we're up to here. Get it?"

"Absolutely," Gary piped in. "You gotta learn to keep your mouth shut, Stu."

"Okay, okay . . . What's the plan?"

Big Otto took a long, slow swig from his beer. It served to get the undivided attention of the other two men. After setting the bottle back on the bar, he glanced right, then left, to be certain he wouldn't be overheard. "Alright . . . Now . . . these guys are working on Sundays, right?"

Stu nodded. "Where are you going with this?"

"Why do you think that is, *Stew?*"

"They don't go to church," was Stu's triumphant answer.

"Are you a churchgoer, Stu?"

". . . No."

"Do you work on Sundays?"

"Ahhh . . ."

Being a mason, the answer to Otto's question was a simple one for Gary. "Look, Stu, these guys are behind the eight ball; they have to finish digging those foundations before the ground freezes. Actually, they need to get their cinderblock or stone set in there before the real cold weather sets in. Mixing mortar in twenty degrees isn't happening."

"Right," Otto said. "Now, all we have to do is stop that backhoe from digging for . . . say a week, maybe two . . . three at the outside . . . and that job's on hold till spring. Nobody's doin' nothin'."

Stu seemed to give this some very serious thought. Finally he said, "And that gives us all winter to figure out what our next move is."

"Now you're cookin'."

"So, the way I figure it, there's two ways we can go with this," Gary said. "We can either incapacitate the backhoe . . . or we can incapacitate the backhoe operator . . . right, Otto?"

"I think we'd better pick up this conversation back at my place."

CHAPTER

5

The Taneysville post office was housed in what had originally been built as a combination dwelling and commercial property. Except for the blue and red government lettering above the door, the ramped access for persons with disabilities, and the steel letterbox outside, it still retained its homelike feel: weathered brown shingles, windows with white trim, shutters also painted white, a steeply pitched roof from whose eaves snow and icicles draped themselves each winter.

The interior was nearly as eclectically cozy as the exterior. A wall divided what had been the original parlor of the house. Cut into the wall was a lockable door (rarely even closed) behind which the two postal workers labored, a single window for picking up mail, and a bank of personal postboxes with antiquated combination locks and brass numbers—the largest being 193.

If there was community news to share or spread, Taneysville's post office was the place to do it. And on this Monday morning, as was natural, it was overflowing with gossip. The babble of voices almost overcame the sound of construction blaring down upon the town from the Quigley place. Almost, but not quite.

". . . they say that John Stark went up there and confronted the contractor. Got real het up——"

"That's old John all right . . . Well, he wouldn't be the first one to complain, and he darn sure won't be the last——"

"And——?" A third voice joined the discussion.

A fourth speaker weighed in. "You hearin' anything different outside than you did yesterday—or the day before that? Whatever Stark did or said, they're still busy diggin'. They should be in China in a few days!"

"What really gets my goat," a fifth person ventured in a tense and edgy tone, "is that none of the site work is goin' to us here in town. It's all out-of-state——"

"If you don't count the lunchtime sandwiches served up at Hoffmeyer's——"

"Well, what good does a bunch of takeout do the rest of us?" was the aggrieved rejoinder. "Those sales just fill Milt Hoffmeyer's big pockets——"

"Hey, c'mon, now. Milt's not the problem. He's just earnin' a livin', same as——"

"I'm not sayin' Hoffmeyer's wrong to take their money . . . and I'm not sayin' he isn't. Alls I'm sayin' is that we're gettin' diddly from this. Plain diddly." The speaker's mood was turning uglier by the second. He thrust a slip of yellow paper toward Clarice, the postmistress, as he spoke. "This was in my box, Clarice . . . Item too big, the notice says."

She didn't bother to look at the yellow paper or at the man staring through her window. The postmistress sorted the mail and placed it in each box; she knew every resident of Taneysville and nearly every facet of their lives: whose kids were writing home, whose weren't; who kept being suckered into magazine subscription lotteries, and who gave away their hard-earned dollars to every charitable request that came down the pike; she even knew whose bills were paid on time—and who required supplemental warnings. "Your wife picked it up already, Frank. It wasn't a single item, but that's the only official card we've got. Nope, it was a whole bunch of catalogs. Gift-type stuff and clothes. I couldn't squeeze 'em all into the box."

She took the yellow card, and looked beyond him to the next person in line while Frank started stalking away, head lowered in sudden rage, his slim black beard working around unspoken oaths. "Where does she think the cash for that junk comes from?" he demanded of the floor. "Aren't I doing the best I can . . . ? Don't she know money don't grow on trees . . . ?" He slammed a greasy baseball cap on his slicked-backed hair and stormed out the door while the others, who were already crowded into the room, moved quickly out of his way.

"Well!" one portly woman announced in the silence that followed his departure. "I always said that girl shouldn't have married a Bazinne. Frank's been a bad apple all his life, and age hasn't mellowed him a lick."

"And his father before him," another woman responded.

"Amen to that."

Additional comments on the Bazinne family began filling the room.

"Never were good neighbors . . ." one elderly man intoned. "You remember that old hound I kept—"

"The one that never shut up?"

"That's the one. A good old dog. Kept away strangers—"

"Really? What kind of strangers do you get out your way, Hugh?" one speaker teased.

The owner of the dog pointedly ignored the jibe and resumed his tale. "You remember? All of a sudden, she up and died—"

"Now that you mention it, I do recall that. You said you thought that dog had been given poison—"

"Still do. And I think the culprit was Frank—"

"Well, his wife never does look well . . . pinched and gray around the eyes—"

"*When* she even shows her face—"

"*When,* indeed—"

"Well, all I can say is that she was a pretty girl before she took up with Frank. I always thought she could have made something of herself. She and my daughter were—"

"And how is your daughter doing, Annie?"

But this conversation was also interrupted by the arrival of May Hoffmeyer, who smiled at the assemblage as she always did: rain or shine or snow or summer drought.

"I heard John Stark went up to the Quigley place yesterday," the person nearest her said. "They say he was mighty peeved. Aimed to make them stop all the digging, is how I heard it."

May shook her head; her smile turned rueful. "Milt told me the same thing. He can be a stubborn man, John can. Once he takes to a notion, you can't stop him. Never could."

"Does Milt have any idea what happened up there?"

"Not a one . . . But my guess is that they're going to keep digging on Quigley's hill come hell or high water. I guess we're just going to have to learn to cope with—" May's words died in her throat. Every head spun toward the windows; no one spoke; instead, they were all busy listening.

"What's that . . . ?" a voice finally ventured.

"They've stopped digging. That backhoe at Quigley's, it's stopped. Goodness, you can hear a pin drop!"

"Kinda like the old days, ain't it?"

CHAPTER

6

"What is it?" Nikos shouted in his native Greek the moment the roar of his backhoe subsided.

"Bones. It looks like bones," Taki replied, also in Greek but in a far more subdued tone. He was on his knees digging with his hands in the freshly turned dirt.

"Hey, hey, I told you guys to speak English when you're on this site," the foreman and general contractor, Sean Reilly, barked as he approached the backhoe. "You know how many looky-loos we've been getting up here . . . that old guy yesterday, those other clowns last week. So, let's remember to use English, okay? We're going to end up with some serious accidents if we don't know what the heck we're saying to each other . . ."

Nikos and Taki stared at their boss but didn't answer.

"Okay, what's the holdup, Nikos? Who told you to shut this baby down?"

"Taki thinks he saw something." Nikos pointed toward the

backhoe's bucket, where Taki was carefully removing small stones from the earth beneath it.

"You'd better be looking for gold down there, Taki, that's all I can say," Sean grumbled. "We've got rain coming in tomorrow and I can't afford any more delays around here." He jumped into the shallow pit and shook his head. What was intended to be the basement for the addition was less than four feet deep. The combination of inclement weather and the rocky New England landscape had forced the excavation to take three times as long as Sean had anticipated—a fact that had strained to the limit his relationship with the property's new owner.

"Come on, Taki," he said, resting a forearm on the backhoe and peering around the bucket, "what the hell are you doing down there? Let's let Nikos get back to work."

"There's bones down here, Sean."

"So what are you? A dog, all of a sudden? Who cares?"

Taki lifted a bone, about ten inches in length, and handed it to Sean.

"So?" Sean said, looking the bone over. "Probably a deer or something." He waved the bone toward Nikos. "Fire that backhoe up. Let's get back to work." He placed the bone under his arm, clapped his hands three times, then clawed his way out of the pit, holding the bone in his left hand.

"I don't think it's a deer, Sean," Taki called back to him.

"Then a horse, a cow. Who cares? It's ancient. I mean look at it. Probably been down there for a hundred years . . . This was a farm, for pete's sake. There's probably lots more animal skeletons lying around—"

Suddenly Taki let out a small, startled yelp, stood quickly, and genuflected.

Nikos jumped from the backhoe and trotted toward him. "What is it, my friend?" Again, he spoke in Greek.

"In English . . . in English . . . Come on, you two. You know the rules."

Nikos placed his hand on Taki's back and glanced at the cleared area. "You better take a look at this, Sean. This is no horse or deer."

Sean slid back down into the hole and joined the other men. When he saw what they'd found he dropped the bone he'd been holding like a hot iron. He then walked around them and bent down to get a closer look. What he saw was the top half of a human skull sticking out from the loosened dirt. The backhoe seemed to have crushed a portion of it. "Damn," he said as he stood. He turned to face Nikos and Taki. They both took a step backward.

"Probably an Indian . . . Native American . . . whatever," Sean said as he dusted his hands off on his jeans. "No telling how long he's been down here." He sat down into the bucket of the backhoe. "Whoa boy . . . I've got to think for a minute. This could mess up everything . . ." He rubbed a dirty hand across his forehead and the three men were silent for several long minutes. "Okay," Sean finally said, "here's the plan: Taki, I want you to go keep an eye on the other guys. I don't want any of the crew to know about this besides the three of us. I don't care what you tell them, just don't let them come down here for twenty minutes or so, okay?"

Taki nodded and climbed out of the dig. Sean turned his attention to Nikos.

"Alright, Nikos, we've got to get rid of this stuff. And we've got to get it out of here without anyone seeing us. I want you to finish digging it up with the backhoe. Then smash the bones with the bucket as best you can—enough so that no one can figure out what the hell it is. Especially the skull—that's the first thing these guys will recognize. One of 'em might even want to take it home for Hallowe'en . . . I'll bring my truck around; you can drop the load into the bed; and I'll dump it in the lake or somewhere tonight."

Nikos looked down at the skull, then toward the backhoe, and eventually back to Sean. "I can't do that, boss."

"What do you mean, you can't do that?"

"This is a person. This is the skeleton of a person. It is sacred. He must be given a proper burial."

"What? Are you nuts? He's an Indian. That's who lived around here originally . . . All those tribes, hunting and stuff . . . living in the woods. He already had a proper burial. That's why he's here in the first place . . ."

When Nikos didn't answer, Sean continued in what he hoped was a rational explanation. His pink-red hair bristled, and the skin of his ruddy face glistened with sweat and nervous exertion. "Look, Nikos, if anyone finds out about this thing we're going to be shut down for weeks. Maybe longer. Maybe a lot longer . . . We could get archaeologists in here, tribal representatives poking around . . . Maybe the site is declared off limits for building . . . Maybe they start uncovering more stuff . . . a burial mound, stuff like that. Hell, they could even find an entire Indian village up here. And you know what that would mean? It would mean you, me, Taki, everybody on this site will be out of work—and even worse, we'd have one really angry homeowner on our tails. And I bet our Mr. Gordon knows from lawsuits: breach of contract, stuff like that. If he's got the kind of dough he's throwing into a place like this . . . ? Hell, I could be out of some major bucks—"

"You don't know the skeleton belongs to an Indian."

Sean let out a long, exasperated sigh. "Oh, man, what am I talking to here, a wall? The point is: *Whoever's* skull this is is dead. A long time. And if our anxious homeowner's *real* lucky and the skeleton *doesn't* belong to a Native American, the police are still gonna come in here with tweezers and spoons and yellow crime scene tape. Do you have any idea how long that could take?"

"It's still not right."

Sean placed his arm over Nikos's shoulder. "What's the problem here? Do you need a raise? Is that it? A little bonus, maybe?"

"This man must have a proper burial."

"Dammit, Nikos, he's already had one. You found him in the earth, right? Well, that's where people get buried."

Nikos walked over to the backhoe, removed the keys, and dropped them into his pocket. "We need to call the authorities, boss. It's the only way."

"You do that and you're fired, buddy. Do you hear me? You'll never work for this company again. I swear, Nikos, your name will be mud from Rhode Island to Maine."

Nikos shrugged. "So be it."

CHAPTER

7

"You've got to be kidding me," Sean Reilly snapped at Lonnie Tucker. He took a step closer to Lonnie, making his superior size and strength all the more conspicuous. "If you think you can close down this site, you've got another think coming, buddy. Mr. Gordon will have every lawyer in Boston down your throat before the sun sets."

Lonnie Tucker owned the Chevron station that had once belonged to Gus Waterwick. Besides providing Taneysville with gasoline, car oil, an air pump, and numerous laconic remarks from the various folks who manned the place, the filling station was the only auto repair shop in the vicinity. Tucker, a master mechanic, did double duty as the community's elected constable. It was a job he took very seriously, even though its sole requirement, as of late, seemed to be helping the volunteer fire department search for missing dogs and cats. Lonnie was a short five feet two inches tall, but solidly built for his age—an age revealed by a receding hair-line and the deeply sun-etched lines of his perpetually tanned face. A fading reminder of his twenty-two years in the navy was visible in a tattoo of an anchor on his left forearm.

Taneysville's constable didn't bother to look up at Sean, but instead kept his eyes fixed on the skull that protruded from the ground near his feet. "Well, first off, Mr. Reilly, when I was stationed down in Groton—that's in Connecticut—I had the opportunity to visit an archaeological dig. See, I can trace my family tree way back, and some Pequots show up here and there, so it's always been a kind of interest of mine—Native American culture, that is."

"Come off it. This is no damn burial ground and you know it." Sean moved closer to Lonnie, but the intended intimidation had no effect.

"I wouldn't be too sure there, Mr. Reilly . . . but, then, I'm no expert, not by a long shot . . . However, in support of *your* theory, I'd have to agree that this skull doesn't look nearly as aged as the ones I saw down in Connecticut. Actually—"

"Look, buddy, if you're lookin' for some casino deal up here like the one they got themselves in Connecticut—"

Lonnie lifted his hand and Sean fell silent. "You're not helping your case by calling me 'buddy,' Mr. Reilly. You've been presented with my I.D.; and until we're drinking beers together over at Eddie's Elbow Room, I suggest you try calling me Constable . . . or Mr. Tucker. Understood?"

Sean groaned slightly, resisting the temptation to mutter, *Short guy with way too much power.*

"Now, this can go one of two ways," Lonnie continued. "I can either call the state's Council on Native American Indian Affairs—"

"Hold it. Stop right there," Sean barked. "These local yokels have put you up to this. I'll place money on it." He pulled his cell phone from his work belt. "I'm calling Mr. Gordon. We're getting some lawyers out here . . . You can't get away with this."

"You're not hearing me out, Mr. Reilly. The other option I have—at this point—is to assess that these skeletal remains do not belong to a Native American. Which, believe it or not, I'm inclined to do."

"Meaning . . ."

"Meaning, I do some digging . . . see what else I unearth before that nor'easter blows in. Then I send my findings over to the forensics specialists in Newcastle for analysis."

Sean smiled, sensing a glimmer of hope. "And then I can get my men back to work . . . ?"

"As long as their work doesn't involve any more digging, sure."

Sean exploded once more. "What the hell are you talking about?"

"Until the Newcastle lab confirms that this skull is not that of a Native American, or that this is not a crime scene—meaning that no criminal activity has been committed on these premises—I want nothing disturbed. No further work can be done in this vicinity until I get the okay from Newcastle. That goes for the interior of the house, as well. We've got to be careful here. After all, we might be talking homicide. I'm not saying we are . . ."

"Are you crazy?"

"That's my position."

"How long is that going to take?"

"I don't know. Depends on how busy the forensics lab is. It's a city, know what I mean? They got homicides like any other urban population . . . So it depends on what kind of priority they put on it. Shouldn't be more than three weeks, a month at the most . . . that's my guesstimate—"

"A month? You can't do this. I'm calling the lawyers."

"Call whoever you like." Lonnie walked back to his truck. He returned with six wooden stakes, a small sledgehammer, and a roll of yellow Caution tape. He then began cordoning off the area where the skull had been found. "I'm going to block this section off. I only have Caution tape, but inform your men to read it as 'Police Line, Do Not Cross.' I don't want anyone, and I mean *anyone,* to enter this area until I return. If I find anything moved, people are going to be arrested, and I mean that. Yokel or no yokel, it's within my authority, so don't push me. I'll be back in an hour . . . If I were you, Mr. Reilly, I'd dismiss my crew. Just a suggestion, but no point keeping them on the clock."

Lonnie headed back toward his truck. Before he climbed up into the driver's seat he called out to Sean, "Tell your lawyers to rustle up a restraining order if you want to stop me. If they can't get one before five P.M., they're wasting their time because I'll be driving those remains to Newcastle myself."

True to his word Constable Tucker returned to the old Quigley property an hour later. He brought with him a large plastic bin he'd purchased from the hardware store, two shovels—one with a pointed tip, the other flat nosed—and Amanda Mott, a grade-school teacher and volunteer EMT with the Taneysville Fire Department. Amanda was in her late thirties, and taller than Lonnie by a good eight inches. Her demeanor was of the sunny, apple-cheeked New England variety that made strangers immediately think of fresh powder skiing, white-water rafting, and day-long hikes on unmarked mountain trails. She was also the type who insisted on looking at the bright side of things—at all costs. She liked to laugh, liked to see other people laugh, and wasn't opposed to taking a caustic jab at those she felt deserved it. Pretensions—whether social, physical, or intellectual—didn't sit well with Amanda Mott.

"I appreciate your leaving your classroom to help me with

this, Amanda," Lonnie said as they approached the pit, back-hoe, and yellow tape. "I didn't know who else to call, but I figured you had some good knowledge of anatomy." Then fearing an unattached and good-looking woman might take this statement the wrong way, he added, "I mean, you know . . . how bones fit together?"

"Ah, it's so nice to know that my reputation as a bod-person precedes me . . . Anyway, this breaks the routine. What's more exciting for a bunch of fifth and sixth graders than an emergency? And a dead body? The eighth grade English teacher's taking over till I get back."

"The new guy ?"

"One and the same . . . Mr. English Lit from Andover . . . He'll probably have them quoting Longfellow by the time I get back . . . 'Listen my children, and you shall hear . . .' "

"Hey, I remember that one . . . 'Paul Revere's Ride' . . . What comes next?"

"Sorry, that's the end of my literary party tricks. I fare much better with the bod thing."

"I didn't mean it the way it sounded . . ."

Amanda raised a disbelieving eyebrow. "I'm a healthy fe-male. Nothing wrong with that."

Just as he'd been when Tucker had last seen him, Sean Reilly was leaning against the backhoe, arms folded aggres-sively across his chest, legs locked in defiance. The only dif-ference to the scene was that he'd apparently taken the constable's advice and dismissed his crew, making the hilltop eerily empty and quiet. But when Sean saw Amanda he straightened and his face took on a guy-sizes-up-good-looking-woman grin. "Well, well, things are certainly start-ing to improve around here." He extended his hand to Amanda. "The name's Sean Reilly. I'm the one who found the body . . . er, skull."

Amanda gave him a quick once-over. Rather than shaking

his hand, she tossed him her shovel as she ducked under the yellow tape. "I guess I heard the story somewhat differently, Mr. Reilly. Constable Tucker told me one of your workers found it. A gentleman by the name of Taki, was it?"

"Well, technically, yeah, sure, Taki did find it . . . but I phoned it in."

"Now, I heard something else there, too—like, another worker made the call. Nikos, was it?"

"Sure . . . Nikos. But under my directive."

"Well, you must be very proud of yourself. Being able to give important 'directives' like that." She gave Sean a disingenuous smile. "I don't think you'll be needed here any longer, Mr. Reilly. Actually, I've been told some men can find this sort of thing nauseating—especially if the flesh hasn't decomposed. We wouldn't want you to get ill, now, would we? I can take my shovel back now."

"Hey, doll, I can handle anything."

"Doll? Doll? Did you say *doll?*" Amanda placed a finger in her ear and wiggled it. "Am I hearing correctly? You did say doll, didn't you? As in Barbie . . . that kind of doll? Do I look like a doll to you?"

"Ahhh . . ."

Amanda turned toward Lonnie. "Do you need Mr. Reilly for further questioning, Constable? Or should he also vacate the premises? As was suggested only a moment ago."

Lonnie suppressed a chuckle. "No, I don't think I'll be needing him, Ms. Mott."

She turned back to Sean. "Well, then, I guess it's *adios, doll.* Be careful you don't slip and hurt yourself climbing up the embankment."

The muscles in Sean's face twisted and pinched as he tried to develop a snappy comeback. Nothing came to mind, so he stormed off and clawed his way out of the hole.

Lonnie laughed. "Don't say I didn't warn you, *buddy.*"

Amanda stared at Sean's departing figure and shook her head. "That kind always gets my goat. I wonder why?"

"Ahhh . . . too full of themselves?" Lonnie said, lacing it with a dose of facetiousness.

"By a long shot." Amanda looked down at the skull. "So. Where do you want to start?"

"Head to toe, I guess. I want to get it all out of the ground and give this area a good once-over; especially with this nor'easter coming in . . . I don't want to miss a thing. It's either that or tarp over the entire site, and hope to keep the rain from turning this into a mud pit . . . which I don't think's gonna work." Lonnie rubbed the back of his neck. "There's no way Newcastle's going to get someone out here before that storm rolls in, so I think this is the best approach."

"We'll do what we can."

"That's why I wanted you along . . . As an EMT, I'd hoped you'd be able to tell if we were . . . well, *missing* anything— i.e., parts."

"I'll try . . . but I've got to tell you, Lonnie, this isn't anything I've been trained for . . . I'm pleased to say that all the bodies I've dealt with in the past have been alive and kicking." Amanda studied the skull for another minute. "Now, assuming this *was* a grave, and that nothing else has been disturbed, my guess is that the rest of the body should be lying in that direction." She pointed.

"Sounds about right . . . So, what do you say we dig a trench along the perimeter, then slowly remove the dirt as we move to the center where the skeleton should be." Lonnie pushed his shovel into the earth. "Surprising how loose this soil is. No rocks at all . . . You'd think the earth would have compacted by now—"

"That's *if* the remains were buried a long time ago." Amanda tossed a shovel load of dirt off to one side. "I'm guessing we're only at a depth of five feet here . . . Sort of belies the old 'six foot under' concept, doesn't it?"

"Maybe people didn't used to be so choosy back then . . . whenever 'then' was."

"Maybe. But I'll tell you this, bad news travels just as fast nowadays. I heard about the discovery up here long before you called me. It was all anyone could talk about in the teachers' lounge . . . same down at the P.O., I'd guess."

"And Eddie's bar . . . Small-town living."

"One thing's for sure, there's not one resident of Taneysville who isn't happy about that backhoe being shut down. It was even driving me up a wall."

Lonnie chuckled slightly. "Yeah, but it's gonna pick right back up again as soon as we get an okay from the honchos down in Newcastle. I don't know why people can't see that. They're only putting off the inevitable."

They continued to dig for another ten minutes, until they'd excavated the area adjacent to where they suspected a body might lie.

"I guess this is it," Amanda said. "Let's move in and see what we find."

"Wait, hold on, I almost forgot: I want to shoot some photographs as we go along. I want to make sure we're covered. I picked up a disposable at Hoffmeyer's. It's in my truck."

He returned with the camera and two pairs of work gloves, then snapped a quick photo before continuing where the excavation had left off. They were working now at a much slower pace and using their hands more often than the shovels. Lonnie photographed the site as they moved along.

Eventually, what appeared to be a complete skeleton was revealed, the bones arranged somewhat intact, except for the arm bone and skull Taki had previously unearthed.

Both Amanda and Lonnie straightened up, then stood staring down, momentarily silenced.

"Wow . . ." Amanda finally murmured. "I feel like . . . well, I don't know what . . ."

"Yeah . . . me, too . . . kind of speechless . . . And if this *is* legit—a proper burial of some long-forgotten Quigley, or a Native American Indian—then we're—"

"Grave robbers," was Amanda's muffled response.

Lonnie nodded. He took a deep breath. "We're not robbing the site. If anything, we'll be moving these remains to hallowed ground."

"Right . . . Unless they're Native American." Amanda tried to smile.

"In that case we'll see that they're repatriated." After another quiet moment Lonnie asked, "What do you think? Do we leave the dirt that's in the chest cavity? Or do we shake it out?"

"Leave it there, I think—if it doesn't fall out when we lift that portion. I'm not sure what these forensics people look at, but we should probably give them as much as we can."

"Right. Let me get one last picture before we put him in the bin." Lonnie lifted the camera and pressed the button. The flash left a stark and bleak image in their minds.

Amanda released a slight sigh. "It makes me kind of sad . . . looking at this poor guy . . . I wonder who he was."

"We'll have to wait and see what Newcastle discovers." Lonnie checked the camera. "One shot left. I'll get one for the newspapers."

"What for?" She made no attempt to hide her surprise.

"It seems like sensationalism, I know. But how else can I handle that side of it? I mean, if I don't inform the press that skeletal remains were discovered . . . What I mean is: It might seem like a cover-up . . . And what do we have to hide? Nothing that I can see."

"I guess you're right." Amanda looked down as Lonnie snapped the final photo. She wrapped her arms around herself.

"Cold up here," he ventured.

"Autumn in New England . . ." She tried for another smile; the effort failed.

"Okeydoke," Lonnie said with false heartiness. He removed the lid to the plastic bin, and he and Amanda placed the remains in it, doing their best to keep the body in the position in which it'd been found, but it was a futile effort. Finished, Lonnie covered the container, and they both carried it to the bed of his pickup truck.

"Is it okay if I give your name to the press . . . as a witness?" Lonnie asked as he climbed into the cab.

"Is that really necessary?"

"Your name's going to appear in my official report. Sorry, but I really want to play this thing entirely aboveboard. If there are secrets hidden here, I don't want it to look like I was a party to it."

"So, I have no choice."

"Sorry. I just wanted you to know I'd be passing your name along."

Unconsciously, Amanda sighed again. "You know, I started off the day feeling on top of the world." She grimaced. "Well, no time to mope . . . got to get back to my kids . . . Sure, Constable, of course you can supply my name. What have I got to lose?"

"It'll give your students a thrill."

"Oh, you betcha . . . Hallowe'en's going to take on new meaning this year."

CHAPTER

8

Snow hadn't yet been predicted, nor had the days begun to take on the relentless cold of winter, but they would. They would. And when the first storm came (mid-November, most likely), rural Massachusetts would turn its back on progress and the dismaying march of time. Villages and hamlets would be cut off from one another; farms would become inaccessible; mountain roads would turn into lethal slopes of ice. At least, that's the way it had been once.

Once upon a time. When the world was a different place. Once upon a time, when a boy and his girl . . . The old eyes closed; the head sagged toward the sunken chest while a hundred dreamland pictures began cavorting through the sleeper's aging brain. Some of the images were joyful; some were not; and some were—

"Ready for your lunch, now, hon?" The door banged as the nurse's aide nudged it open with her foot. In her hands she bore a brown plastic tray covered with containers of white Styrofoam and plastic. "Oopsy-daisy, you plumb fell fast asleep on me again, didn't you? You know that wouldn't happen if you were downstairs in the lounge with everyone else. Shared activities, a little chitchat with your pals . . ." The aide plopped the tray on a rolling table and bent toward the floor to retrieve a fallen newspaper. "And look, there's that paper I brought you yesterday . . . I don't believe you've even read—"

"I did," was the irritable answer, followed by a stubborn: "I don't have 'pals.' "

The nurse's aide retained her professional good humor. "And whose fault is that, I'd like to know? You're not winning the congeniality award, that's for sure . . ." As she spoke she fussed over the meal tray, removing the lid from the soup, the Saran Wrap from a yellow-colored pudding. "Tea, like always, toast without butter, banana custard . . . Oh, don't go making a face like that! You know you like bananas. Everybody likes bananas . . . And today's soup is clam chowder . . . Real New England-style, not Manhattan . . . You want I should help you spoon it up?"

"I can manage." The tone was now slow and hollow.

The aide cocked her head and pursed her lips. "I'm happy to sit here and jaw, if you'd like." She hefted the newspaper and opened it. "You did the crossword—and perfect, too. Not even one letter out of place. They say these puzzles will keep your brain real sharp . . ."

A dismissive shrug greeted the compliment while the aide turned the page, searching for further items for conversation. Naturally the news of skeletal remains accidentally unearthed on a farm in rural Taneysville was high on the list of attractions. "Did you see where they found a body on some old property out west of here?"

Again, a noncommittal shrug.

"Well, you're just a bundle of gab today, aren't you?"

"An Indian, probably—"

"Native American," the aide corrected.

"Humph. I'm a native American," her charge insisted. "I was born in the same America as everybody. I'm as 'native' as anyone else."

The aide sighed; the paper was folded. "You're right about that, I guess . . . Tell you what . . . Maybe you'd like . . . Well, remember that problem you were fretting over the other day . . . the bad thing . . . Maybe you'd like to talk about—"

"I don't have any problems."

"A secret, you said—"

"I don't have secrets, either! Not anymore."

"You needn't bite my head off." The nurse's aide turned on a professional smile. "Tell you what. You finish all your lunch like a good little baby—"

"I'm not a—!"

But the aide brushed aside this new complaint. "Then we'll see about a game of checkers. Or cards, if you'd like. I seem to recall that you're partial to gin . . ." She bustled toward the door, a cotton pantsuit exuding purpose. "But don't you go dozing off on me again . . . or start up on one of your kooky rants . . . You know I don't like it when you get peculiar like that . . ." The aide turned, her expression hopeful, almost beseeching. "You want I should leave the door open this time?"

"No."

"You're gonna go nuts keeping all to yourself. No one else does it."

"I like being by myself."

"Old age can be fun, if you make the most of it."

There was no response to this platitude. The aide shook her head. "I'll be back in a while with those checkers. Don't you run away now, you hear?" Then the door shut behind her.

The lumpy chowder was swallowed, the cold toast perfunctorily nibbled, the tea sipped at, the offending neon-hued pudding pushed aside. Then the work of the day took precedence. From a drawer came a sheet of graph paper, already densely decorated with boxes of black and white; a list of numbered clues was painstakingly printed at the paper's edge.

A thin and sinewy hand took up a pencil; the heavy heart gave a quick leap of hope. The envelope to whom the crossword would be mailed was already stamped, addressed, and waiting. Maybe the truth could finally see the light of day.

Across

1. Pitches
4. Honey or spelling add-on
7. Like some windows
13. Bump into
14. "... out like a_____"
16. Look up to
17. "Suspicion" producer
18. "Sayonara" setting
19. Visit
20. Hard wood
21. Struggle
23. Reeve role
24. Struggles
26. Vale of_____
28. Amb. crew
29. Burden
30. Quick, in music
34. 1-Down, e.g.
36. Beat
37. Early video game
38. Magic device
41. Some hatters
42. Movie locale
43. Nigerian coastal town
44. Nutty
45. Wise one
46. Ieoh Ming_____
47. "Who, me?"
49. Some laughter
52. Mr. Crosby
55. Like most "i"s
57. Day-_____
58. "Now!"
60. Chilly
61. Roscoe
62. Slots spot
63. See 56-Down
64. Certain Shoshonean
65. Shirt sizes
66. Buck's kin?
67. Mr. Beatty

Down

1. Cupid's missile
2. Capital of Senegal
3. Posse ploy
4. Lays into
5. Bridge positions
6. Turkish title
7. Witch town?
8. "Much_____About Nothing"
9. False front
10. March
11. Leprechaun's land
12. Fender-bender
15. Sleazy sales move
22. Provoke
25. Airy announcement
27. Early "Tonight Show" host
29. 2,000 pounds
31. Proof positive
32. Bern's river
33. Part of MIT
34. Allotted; abbr.
35. Roman 2,051
36. Had been
37. Cherry stone
39. God of love
40. Mr. Torme
45. Certain Siouan
46. "Up a creek without a _____"
48. Inklings
49. Stringed instrument
50. Buoy
51. Adored
52. Blocks
53. Memo point
54. Unpredictable star
56. With 63-Across, Grahame setting
59. CM ÷ II

A BURNING QUESTION

CHAPTER

9

Belle Graham pulled the envelope from the mailbox on her porch. The accompanying bills and junk mail she tucked under her arm as she examined the small, precise lettering and the almost arrogant determination with which her name had been spelled out in full: MRS. ANNABELLA GRAHAM. Not the ambiguous Ms., and not simply Belle, as everyone in Newcastle seemed to know her. Whoever had sent this missive had done their research and wanted the fact known.

Without opening the envelope, she knew what it would contain. As the now nationally celebrated crossword editor of Newcastle's *Evening Crier* as well as an equally publicized amateur sleuth, Belle had become a target for both practical jokers and the marginal types obsessed with the famous— none of whom she took as seriously as she'd been advised.

"What do you think, Kit?" she said to her multicolored dog frisking around her feet. "Hallowe'en in the offing . . . ? I'll bet we get a lot of these kind of cryptic messages before

October thirty-first . . . Clue: *On the graveyard shift . . . A skel-eton in the closet . . . Ghost writer . . . Oooooo.*" Belle laughed and shook her head. Her pale blond hair danced; her gray eyes shone. "What people do with their spare time! It's certainly not as productive as playing with a puppy, is it, Kitty?"

Belle chuckled again, strolling the length of the porch to look out on the peaceful view of Captain's Walk in Newcas-tle's refurbished historic district: a congenial street lined with nineteenth-century homes originally built by sea captains and whalers. The city's early wealth and prominence, its role as a seat of the Massachusetts county that bore its name, was due to its harbor and ocean trade.

Kit kept her "mom" company. The puppy was a "Heinz 57," a foundling and a serendipitous addition to Belle's life. Rosco, her husband, was the other happy improvement, and as unstinting as Kit in his love. Together, these three crea-tures, two with two legs, one with four, made a devoted fam-ily.

Belle bent down to pick up a fraying tennis ball. Kit yipped in anticipation. Belle made a toss, but the projectile didn't go where either she or Kit had anticipated. Instead it skittled back along the porch, caroming hard against a window pane. Belle winced. "One of these days, I've got to learn how to throw . . . I'm a danger to myself. I'm a danger to our home."

The dog made the rapid and necessary adjustments in at-tack, retrieved the ball, and dropped it at Belle's feet. "I think we'll wait for Rosco to get back from work, Kitty. I'm not in the mood to replace windows."

A quick bark of protest.

Belle shook her head no. She then wrapped her sweater tighter against the cool air, breathed in the refreshing scent of sea air, lifted her face to the golden New England sun, shut her eyes, and whispered: "I'm so lucky. I'm so, so lucky . . ."

Then she and Kit walked or romped—depending on foot shape and energy level—back inside.

Belle preferred to construct the *Crier*'s daily cryptics at home, where she was surrounded by her collection of reference material: the O.E.D., of course, but also two antiquated—but much beloved—sets of Encyclopædia Britannica, a number of foreign language dictionaries, a book of song titles, the plays and sonnets of William Shakespeare, and another shelf devoted entirely to poetry. The latter wasn't necessarily part of her current craft; Belle had once intended to become a poet. It was after exposure to the compendia now lined up in her home office that she'd decided her poems would never measure up. Better to admire from afar.

She and Kit walked into the room, a converted rear porch that had been crossword-themed to within an inch of its life. Black and white squares (scuffed by puppy claw marks) were painted on the floor, the curtains (slightly askew) mirrored the motif, the canvas covers of the two deck chairs were white and black—to say nothing of the in-the-works puzzles that covered the desk, the empty plate with a crossword design, ditto a calendar, a notepad, a lamp shade, a coffee mug. Belle took such surroundings for granted; newcomers were startled, to say the least.

Reflexively, Belle reached her hand into a tall white jar containing licorice sticks (second to deviled eggs as her favorite comestible) and began munching while dialing the phone with her free hand. She plopped herself down on her desk chair, tapped her feet, then cradled the phone against her shoulder, stroked Kit's ears, kept nibbling (Belle was a consummate multitasker), and when the answering machine at the other end of the connection picked up with a brisk male: "Polycrates Agency. Leave a message and we'll get back to you," she mumbled a mouth-filled:

"Hi, Rosco, it's me . . . Just calling to say I love you heaps . . . Kit, too . . . Actually, she's not saying anything. But she looks as if she could . . . Well, that's it . . . See you later . . . Oh, it's Belle . . ."

She slid the phone back into place. "Darn, Kitty . . . I guess I'll have to get serious about work today . . . Your dad obviously is . . ." She pulled the mystery crossword from the envelope again and studied it for a long moment, squinting at the clues and silently mouthing a couple of the more obvious answers. Then she sat up straight, muttered a surprised: "Oh, I get it . . ." and almost simultaneously reached for the phone.

This time the voice at the other end was not recorded. "Briephs residence."

"Hi, Emma. It's Belle. Is her nibs around?"

Only Belle—and maybe Rosco—could have gotten away with this irreverent tone when referring to Newcastle's grand dame, the illustrious (some might say imperious) Sara Crane Briephs.

"Indeed she is, Miss Belle." Emma was as old-fashioned as her starched maid's uniform. "In fact, Madam was just about to phone you . . . She wondered if you'd do her the favor of lunching with her today."

Belle grinned. "You bet. Tell her I've got something to show her."

"We're having deviled eggs," was Emma's calm reply.

"You certainly know how to weasel your way into *my* good graces." Belle looked at her watch. "The usual time?"

"The usual time . . . Oh, Madam adds that if you wish, you may arrive earlier."

"I'll be there in two shakes of a lamb's tail."

This answer was relayed by the dutiful Emma, who concluded with a pleasant: "Madam asks me to tell you that 'your timing suits her to a T.' "

Belle again replaced the receiver, started to slip the envelope and crossword into her jeans pocket, then suddenly reassessed her wardrobe. Something more formal than tattered jeans and her favorite thrice-darned sweater was in order when visiting White Caps for luncheon.

In a blindingly white apron and a rustling black taffeta uniform, Emma ushered Belle through the White Caps foyer just as she'd always done, parading past the formal sitting room and dining room hung with portraits of long-vanished Crane family members as well as a plethora of other oil paintings: romantic and verdant landscapes, moody seascapes, and a number of depictions of Crane-owned clipper ships plying the oceans during the lucrative era of the eighteenth-century China trade. The surface of every highboy, every mahogany table, and every chair glistened; unlit, the matching crystal chandeliers that hung at the center of the two rooms still managed to infuse the air with a shimmering glow.

The first time Belle had seen the house, she'd decided it looked just like a museum. Now she knew the home for what it was: an anomaly. A wonderful relic from another era—a little like its mistress.

"Madam is in the garden," said Emma. "She's having a spot of trouble with an espaliered pear tree."

"Not behaving this summer, was it?" Belle asked.

"Apparently not."

"Poor tree."

In answer, Emma merely smiled.

*   *   *

I t wasn't until hostess and guest had gathered in a cozy and chintz-filled sitting room for after-dinner coffee that Belle produced the crossword. She and the doyenne of White Caps sat together on a camel-backed settee; before them was a table upon which rested a silver tray set with the items Sara deemed necessary for serving a hot liquid refreshment: an antique silver coffeepot, silver sugar bowl and creamer, silver spoons, two gold-rimmed porcelain cups. Mugs, whether crossword-themed or not, were unknown at White Caps.

"This came in the mail today," Belle said as she produced the envelope.

Sara slowly put down her cup, folded her hands in her lap, and turned to balefully regard the young person beside her. Sara's white hair, although impeccably coiffed as always, shook with disapproval. "Belle, dear, you promised me—and you promised your husband—that you would be more cautious with these anonymous messages. You remember what happened before? That odious person who—"

"What's the chance of lightning striking the same place twice?" Although Belle's tone was playful, her manner was less so. No one—whether of the plant or animal world—liked receiving a scolding from Sara Crane Briephs.

"A promise is a promise, dear girl."

Belle squared her shoulders and set her jaw. "I thought you'd enjoy helping me work through the cryptic . . . There's an intriguing through line"—she pointed, although the gesture had a defensive and palliative air—"here: 9-Down; the answer to the clue is SMOKESCREEN . . . and here at 31-Down: SMOKING GUN . . . and at 38-Across . . . Well, never mind . . . I guess I was mistaken about your interest." She began to refold the puzzle.

Sara's stern demeanor softened slightly, but her tone remained assertive. "Stubbornness never helps a person advance in life, young lady—"

"Oh, right!" was Belle's equally energized reply. "You're one to talk."

"Touché," said Sara. "But being old and set in my ways shouldn't inspire the same behavior in you."

"You're not set in your ways, Sara. That would mean you can't accept change. Stubbornness is a far different quality."

Sara sniffed even as a private expression of pleasure began creeping across her face. "It takes one to know one, I suppose."

"Stubborn," Belle chided. "Synonyms: obstinate, headstrong, inflexible, willful, pigheaded—"

"Mulish," was Sara's rapid reply. "Bullheaded, hardbitten—"

Belle laughed full out. "I've never heard that one before."

"It refers to horses that are difficult to manage."

"That's right. I forgot. You're so 'old' you remember an era in which there were no automobiles."

"Don't you get fresh with me, young lady."

"I'll stop only when you stop referring to yourself as an obsolescent antique."

Sara was silent a moment. Then she took the younger woman's hand. "I have every right to worry about your safety, dear girl . . ."

"And I'm grateful for your concern, Sara—"

"But you'd like me to butt out."

Belle laughed again. "I wouldn't have used that precise term."

"I like to keep *au courant* with my lexicon," rejoined White Caps's regal owner.

"In all seriousness, Sara, I *am* careful. But you can see as well as I can that this puzzle was created for fun . . . Which is too bad, because if the constructor had remembered to add a name and contact number I would have been tempted to publish it—"

"I remain apprehensive about your receiving anonymous messages, my dear—"

"And *I* remain uneasy—"

"With a worried old lady breathing down your neck." Sara lifted her head, pulling her ramrod straight spine even straighter. "Now, let's look at 38-Across . . ."

CHAPTER

10

Abe Jones had been with the Newcastle Police Department for slightly over ten years. He was the department's chief forensics expert—a position that had more responsibilities than Crayola had colors. He'd fallen into this line of work by accident—having had every intention of becoming a medical doctor, as his father had hoped. But as an undergrad at BU he'd dated a woman who just *happened* to be a member of a Boston undercover unit. She'd convinced him that police work would be a more exciting and rewarding career choice, not to mention risky, exhilarating, and action-packed: all the elements that appeal to young men. Later, he'd suspected that the lovely policewoman's function with the department might, in fact, have been that of a recruiter: Go out and seduce college students and sign them up. Nevertheless, she'd certainly won him over, and his career path was set.

But Abe was quick to discern that he was a lover and not a fighter, and had absolutely no desire to walk around for the rest of his life with a gun strapped to his side—or to get shot at, for that matter. A compromise was in order, and he'd decided to divide his studies between medicine and forensic science.

After all was said and done, he'd finished school with both a medical degree and a Ph.D.; and his work with the New-castle Police Department often called upon the entire spectrum of skills that his studies provided: whether it was determining what bullet came from what pistol, if an assailant had been left- or right-handed, whose blood was on what shirt—or what DNA samples lifted from a set of truck tires might indicate.

Abe sometimes imagined running into the female who'd inspired his life in crime—although he knew from long experience that the relationship hadn't been destined to continue. She hadn't been the first woman to seduce him, and she wasn't likely to be the last. Abe was an exceptionally good-looking man; standing an inch over six feet, with dark skin and a winning smile, he resembled a young version of Harry Belafonte. He never, *ever* lacked female companionship—a fact that garnered a fair amount of envy as well as a steady dose of ribbing in the Newcastle PD, from the beat cops all the way through to the detectives.

This modern-day Lothario now sat on a metal stool in the forensics lab in the basement of the NPD headquarters. Before him, on a stainless steel examining table, rested a group of human bones that had been painstakingly rearranged by Abe to form a complete skeleton. The task had taken him three days, and after all was said and done, he was left with more questions than answers.

Abe set his clipboard on the table beside the skeleton, folded his arms across his chest, and sighed. "What can you tell me, darlin'?" he asked. The inflection and expression were so sincere that any visitor entering the lab would have half-expected the skeleton to sit up and answer him, hand over a life story. Obviously, no response came.

There was a knock at the laboratory's entrance. Out of habit, Abe checked his watch, then crossed the room and unlocked the door. Standing before him was Lt. Al Lever, Newcastle's chief of homicide, a balding, overweight chain smoker with a gruff exterior that hid an intrinsically sentimental heart. Al was also known as a fair cop; he was diligent, honest, and hid a sneaky sense of humor that took strangers by surprise. It just didn't seem to match the no-nonsense facade.

With Lever was a shorter man who appeared apprehensive and edgy, a fish out of water whose shoulders almost quivered with tension. Jones pegged him to be mid-fifties—about Lever's age—and deduced that this was none other than Lonnie Tucker, the part-time constable/mechanic responsible for the jumbled set of bones that had been delivered to his lab three days earlier. The three men exchanged handshakes and walked toward the remains. Tucker seemed to take two steps for every one of Lever's.

"Never seen a place like this," Lonnie Tucker said a trifle breathlessly. "Not in all my years—"

"A good thing, too," Lever observed in his wry and even tone. "Only kooks like Dr. Jones here enjoy year-round Hallowe'en." He nodded at Jones. Enough of the polite chitchat. "Okay, Abe, I want you to run through what you've told me. I think Mr. Tucker should hear it from the horse's mouth." Lever reached for his cigarettes as he spoke.

"Don't smoke in here, Al."

"What? You're serious? You can't be serious."

"New rules." Abe smiled his signature smile. It didn't impress Lever.

"Since when?"

"Since now. I've got a date later. I don't want my hair smelling like a pack of Luckys."

"So what's that supposed to mean? I can't smoke just because you have a *date?* When *aren't* you hooked up with some luscious lady?"

Abe raised his hands over his head. "Guilty as charged . . . Maybe you should think about quitting. You know what they say about cigarettes—?"

"Oh, please! You and my wife . . . yap, yap, yap—"

"I keep telling you, Al: You gotta listen to these women. They have a unique ability to make your life more enjoyable."

Lever only grumbled and shoved the cigarettes back into his shirt pocket.

"You pay attention to the ladies, Al, you'll be all right. If you want to stay happy—"

"Please . . . Spare me the helpful hints, *Doctor.*"

Jones shook his head, but he was still smiling. "Okay, to begin with: Thank you for taking the time to drive all the way back into Newcastle, Mr. Tucker—"

Tucker held up a nervous hand. He was clearly trying to reestablish his equanimity. Jones recognized the behavior: a small-town, part-time government employee suddenly facing a big-city problem. "Call me Lonnie."

"All right . . . But thank you just the same. I'm sure you have work to do . . ."

"Yeah . . . I do have a couple of guys who pump gas for me, but they're not mechanics, so if anything of an emergency nature pops up back at the station . . ."

Jones looked past the two men. "Wasn't there a woman who helped you with this?" He glanced at his clipboard. "A Ms. Amanda Mott? I was hoping she'd be with you to help answer some questions."

"She couldn't leave her classroom today. She's a teacher. Elementary school."

When Abe Jones didn't respond to this information, Lonnie forged anxiously ahead. "She's also an EMT. That's why I brought her in on the situation."

Jones gave Lever a look that clearly said, *Spare us from novices messing with crime scenes,* but opted for a less cutting: "EMT. Right. Good thinking."

Lonnie accepted the assessment as tacit approval. He stared at the skeleton. "He sure looks different all put together like that."

"All in a day's work," Jones answered, "or three in this case . . . Now, what I want you to understand, Lonnie, is that everything I say, at this point, is based strictly on a preliminary visual examination of the remains. Other tests will take time . . ." Abe paused, waiting for Tucker's response, which came in the form of a silent nod. "Now, from the hip and pelvic bones we know that this was most definitely not a male, but a female. At this point, I place her age somewhere between eighteen and twenty-one. Determining her age was a fairly simple exercise. Some of her bones are completely developed, where others, like her sacrum, for example, are not yet matured . . . Of course the most important fact, and the reason I alerted Lieutenant Lever, is that this woman was definitely murdered."

Tucker drew in a breath, although he didn't utter a single word. It seemed a lot for him to take in all at once.

With his pen Jones pointed to a small section of the skull that had been crushed inward. "This type of trauma to the rear of the skull would cause almost instant death . . . in most cases."

"Jeez," Lonnie finally said, "Amanda and I thought maybe the guys with the backhoe did that . . . Actually, we kind of hoped they had . . ."

"No. The fracture would appear quite different if that had been the case . . . I'm surprised Ms. Mott hadn't made that assessment, given her EMT *experience.* Anyway, you'll note that the woman's bones have a dry and brittle appearance. If the backhoe had come into contact with the skull it would have cracked—like an eggshell cracks—while scrapes and nicks, easily recognizable as recent disturbances, would have then been introduced . . . The skull of a living person is much more flexible . . ." Again, Jones looked to Tucker for signs of comprehension. "My initial read on this, Lonnie, is that the damage occurred when our lady here was alive—and was definitely the cause of death—"

"You still don't have any idea when she died? Or how long she was buried?" Lever interrupted.

"Not yet . . . As I said, Al, tests like that are going to take some time." Jones returned to Tucker. "Is there any way you could fill in some blanks for us?"

"I can try . . ." Lonnie squinted his eyes, then muttered an unhappy: "Murder . . . This ain't lookin' good." He blew out a breath and rocked back and forth on the balls of his feet.

Lever again reached for his pack of cigarettes, then, remembering Abe's request, groaned and dropped his hands into his pockets. "I guess the big question is: Who was this young woman? Any ideas, Constable?"

Tucker shook his head. " 'Fraid not . . . Taneysville's always been a real sleepy place. A big crime is breaking the speed limit. And we've had our share of DUIs, but that's it."

Lever returned to Jones. "How long do you think she's been dead?"

"Like I said, I've got to run more tests. Definitely over five years, I'd say, judging by how little remains of her flesh and clothing. But beyond that—maybe ten years? Maybe thirty? Maybe fifty? It's a shame she didn't have any dental work done. That could help us a lot. Technology's changed over the years. Even a good clothing sample can give us an indication of dates." Jones shrugged. "Considering a section of what was clearly an elasticized clothing material, we're not talking ancient history, but at this point, it's really up in the air. Soil conditions vary, meaning that states of preservation vary . . . also decomposition rates." He turned back to Tucker. "As I mentioned, I picked up very few other textile samples in what you brought in . . . I took the liberty of driving out to the site yesterday evening, but it's completely compromised. That storm's turned everything into a huge mud pit."

"That's why I thought it was important to get the bones out of there as quickly as I could."

Lever and Jones exchanged another look that indicated they didn't agree with Tucker's decision.

"What's done is done," Abe said as politely as he could. "So . . . Did you—or Ms. Mott—notice anything that might have been a larger clothing sample? Anything in the surrounding soil?"

Tucker thought. "Nothing at all. But the dirt was very loose. The backhoe seemed to have scooped out underneath where the skeleton was and then a whole clump of earth sort of slid into the work site. The photos I brought don't really show that very well."

"I'd like to have those negatives. Maybe we can get better prints than the one-hour photo place."

"Ahh . . . sure," Lonnie said. "Maybe you want to talk to the guys who were working the backhoe . . . They might be able to tell you how it ended up in the position where we found it."

"Right." Al Lever coughed and cleared his throat. "Let's get back to the *who* . . . Taneysville's a small place. In your recollection, have there ever been rumors of a young woman going missing? Even old-time rumors?"

Tucker shook his head. "I was born and raised out there . . . Well, I was gone for my twenty-two years in the navy, so I guess maybe then someone might have . . . Nah . . . I would have heard all about it. I always came home on leave. Christmas, Thanksgiving when I could. My pop would've told me about anything like that. We're too tight-knit a community . . . News travels faster than folks can create it. You can't step outside without a neighbor wondering where you're headed."

"When did you finish with the navy?" Lever asked.

"Twelve years ago. And I've been back in Taneysville ever since."

"It wouldn't be the first time someone dumped a body a good distance from the murder site," Jones said. "If our lady here isn't a local, then her killer probably isn't local either."

Lever rubbed at his forehead. "Lonnie, can you recall what was on that particular site before the crew started digging the foundation for that addition? Was it similar to the way you described the rest of the property—just empty land?"

Lonnie smiled. He was ahead of Lever on this one. "Right, I thought of that, too, Lieutenant. The body turned up exactly where the Quigleys used to keep their vegetable garden. Just behind the house there . . . If any dirt had been disturbed— somebody using it for a dumping ground, for instance—no one would have noticed . . . Aside from the growing season, of course . . . But late fall . . . this time of year when they'd turn the soil over . . . or early spring before the new crops are put in . . . you could have had a field day out there—"

"Where are the Quigleys now?"

"Old Mrs. Quigley died eight or nine years ago; her husband ended up in an old age home here in Newcastle somewhere. I heard he'd died, too, although he was never buried in the graveyard next to his wife and I never read an obituary anywhere. Their house has been vacant for five years, easy."

"No heirs?"

"Nope. No kids. No relatives. Kind of a shame . . . But they were private people, the Quigleys. Not mean, necessarily, but not friendly either. You didn't want to be caught cutting across their land to get into town." Lonnie allowed himself a small laugh. "Especially if you were a youngster."

Lever folded his arms across his chest, then sat on the stainless steel stool. He studied the skeleton for a long moment and finally said, "What's the feeling about this in Taneysville, Lonnie? I guess folks must be pretty upset?"

"I'd say *curious* is a better term, Lieutenant . . . We've got rumors, sure . . . Indian burial mound, that kind of thing . . . But what Abe's sayin' makes sense: Someone unknown in the community could've dumped a body, and then skedaddled out of there . . . I guess the next story to circulate is that we've found Jimmy Hoffa." Tucker attempted another brief chuckle. "And that sure wouldn't sit well in Taneysville. People out home don't like a lot of fuss—or press."

"Trust me," Abe said with a thin smile, "this lady's not Mr. Hoffa."

Lever stood. "There's not much I can do on my end until you give me a place to start, Abe. And I'll admit I've got more pressing business on my plate right now than trying to track down a mystery murderer of an unknown woman . . . If you can narrow down the year she died, I'll get someone started on the missing persons records . . . Until then, I'm afraid this is going to get 'cold case' classification."

CHAPTER

11

"Polycrates Agency." Rosco stared out the window of his downtown office as he spoke into the phone. The afternoon had turned suddenly squally and grim, the sky a leaden color that presaged a storm rapidly moving in from the sea. He hoped Belle hadn't taken advantage of the day's earlier sunny weather to bring Kit out to Munnatawket Beach. If she had, it looked as if she and the puppy would be soaked through in about five minutes' time. For the briefest of seconds he considered trying to phone her, then caught himself and shook his head. Belle didn't appreciate cautionary advice any more than he did. In fact, she probably liked it less. "Hello?" he repeated into the telephone, "Polycrates Agency. May I help you."

"Yes . . . I'm trying to reach Mr. Polycrates." It was a female voice, young and vacillating between insecurity and pushiness.

"This is Rosco Polycrates. May I help you?"

"Um . . . yes . . . I'm calling on behalf of Milton Hoffmeyer the Third, the candidate for—"

Rosco interrupted what he assumed was a solicitation job, scaring up contributions for Hoffmeyer's congressional bid. It seemed a little late in the game to Rosco—Hoffmeyer was holding a nice lead in the polls. "This is an office you've reached. A work number?"

The woman at the other end of the line uttered a sharp, "I realize that—"

"Well, phone solicitations to office numbers aren't—"

"Phone sales?" The tone was shocked, almost outraged. "I'm not engaged in phones sales."

Rosco sighed; he leaned back in his swiveling chair, letting his eyes sweep across his office: two unmatched chairs facing the desk, a small round table between them, a coat rack, three filing cabinets, and the necessary electronic equipment his private investigative agency required. Bare bones stuff, and unchanged despite his modified marital status. Belle's home office's unusual appearance notwithstanding, she had little interest in interior design. The decor of the Polycrates Agency was the same as it had been when he and Belle had first met. Although there had been a few additions to the office closet that contained an assortment of apparel, i.e., disguises which could help Rosco pass himself off as anything from banker to busboy—items Belle had "discovered" at various thrift stores.

"Look, miss . . . ma'am—"

"It's Ms. actually."

"Right . . . Ms. . . . ?"

No name was forthcoming. Rosco suppressed another sigh, and pushed ahead. "I know Milt Hoffmeyer's a good guy . . . an excellent candidate, in fact, and I understand that political campaigns need money—"

"I'm not calling in reference to contributions," the voice

snapped back, then added an equally peppery: "I'm not a fund-raiser. Please hold for Mr. Hoffmeyer."

Rosco had only a second to gaze ceilingward in surprise before another voice appeared on the line.

"Mr. Polycrates? Milt Hoffmeyer here. Thanks for taking my call."

Rosco sat up straighter in his chair. Although his career had at times brought him into contact with the rich and famous, his encounters with men like Milton Hoffmeyer III were rare. Perhaps that was because the Hoffmeyers of the world were honorable folk who didn't have nasty secrets they wanted to suppress—or enemies who wanted to expose them. "What can I do for you, Mr. Hoffmeyer?"

Hoffmeyer hesitated for the briefest moment before proceeding. The tone was expansive and open—the genuine article. At least that was Rosco's read, and he was usually correct when it came to intuition. "I don't know if you're aware of this, Mr. Polycrates, but skeletal remains were found on a construction site in Taneysville."

"I did see something about that in the paper, yes."

"Taneysville is where I grew up, Mr. Polycrates. It's where my grandparents still live."

Rosco recalled the story the media spouted about Hoffmeyer, although he hadn't remembered the locale. Small-town boy, raised by hard-working grandparents after both his parents had been killed. DUI, the cause of death had been ruled, if Rosco remembered rightly. DUI—as well as a series of prior arrests and numerous other scrapes with the law. Milt III had worked hard to overcome his father's unhappy history and follow his paternal grandfather's virtuous example. In fact, his campaign literature stated that he "owed his life and his love of his nation to his granddad and grandma." The statement could have seemed insincere and cloying, but listening to the candidate's voice, Rosco suspected that it wasn't.

"I remember reading about your grandparents, Mr. Hoff-meyer."

Hoffmeyer allowed himself a brief laugh. It was a warm sound, intimate and inviting, the kind engendered by a joke shared with a friend. "And do they ever hate reading about themselves . . . ! Those two are New Englanders through and through. 'Don't you go calling attention to us, now, Milt. We're simple people, in a simple community; you go off and do what you need to do; we're happy being quiet.' . . . And that's precisely why I'm calling you, Mr. Polycrates. This . . . unfortunate discovery happened near the old Quigley house—on the hill just above Taneysville's church—and I was hoping that you—"

Rosco interrupted. "You're not suggesting you want to retain my services are you, Mr. Hoffmeyer?"

"I am."

"I assume the police are already on the case."

A pause. "They are, yes. In a way."

Rosco sat straighter; a brief frown crossed his face. "Taneysville is part of Newcastle County, if I'm not mistaken; and Newcastle has a homicide detective. An excellent one."

Another pause, though briefer this time. "I realize that Al Lever was your partner when you were with the NPD."

"You've done some homework."

"I believe in dotting the i's and crossing all the t's, Mr. Polycrates. It's what's gotten me where I am. I don't like conflicts of interest, and I don't like secrets . . . You were NPD, considered a good cop, maybe *too* good a cop, because you inspired a certain level of mistrust—I'll call it envy—with one or two of your fellow officers . . . You're of Greek descent; your father was a commercial fisherman, now deceased. You've got a mother, two sisters, and a brother living in the Newcastle environs. You've been a PI for eight years; you're thirty-eight years old, married to Annabella Graham, who's employed by one of Newcastle's newspapers—the *Evening Crier* to be exact. Together you've cracked a number of local crimes, which has gained you both some national notoriety. Lieutenant Lever served as your best man at your wedding—"

"That's more than homework. That's a thesis. Maybe you should have my job."

"As I said, Mr. Polycrates, I like everything open and aboveboard."

"Then it's no secret what I think—that I *know* Al's a good cop, Mr. Hoffmeyer. One of the best there is."

"I'm not suggesting otherwise."

"Then what do you need me for?"

"Lieutenant Lever has classified this as a 'cold case.' "

"I hadn't heard that."

Milt III paused again. "I'm sure you're aware that I'm facing a tough fight against the incumbent, Mr. Spader . . . Even with the campaign coming down to the wire, Spader's still got a significant war chest; I'll be lucky if I can throw a beer and pizza party if I win. And that, in itself, is a big *if*—"

"You've got youth on your side," Rosco threw in. "You're up in the polls."

"Which doesn't go a long way against a well-oiled political machine."

"I'm trying to read between the lines here, Mr. Hoffmeyer . . . I hope you're not inferring that the police are part of that machine."

"No, I'm not. Definitely not. At this point, I think Lever has no choice but to label this situation a cold case. No one knows where this body came from . . . There isn't even a remote lead as to the victim or perpetrator's identity . . . But we all know that Taneysville's a small place—an *insignificant* place except to those who live in it . . . And that's why I'd like to have you working on this. I want to see attention paid to the little people. That's what my campaign's been about."

Rosco ran a hand through his dark hair. It was a reflexive gesture, and probably added to his slightly rumpled appearance. That and his choice of attire: scuffed boating shoes worn without socks, chinos that had been pulled directly from the dryer, a gray canvas work shirt that had never known an iron. "Going undercover" for Rosco was a stretch only when it required a suit and tie. "I appreciate your thinking of me, Mr. Hoffmeyer. But I've got to be honest: barging in on Al's turf is the last thing I want to do."

"I'm not asking you to 'barge in.' I'm just asking for an additional point of view . . . You're being honest with me; I'll share something else with you. My guess is that my opponent will attempt to use this situation for political gain. Now, I know he can't stonewall on an investigation; and that the police would never permit such a directive—whether articulated or implied. But rumors can be created . . . a body dumped following a mob hit in Boston . . . maybe *collusion* with the constable or a former constable—"

"But there's been no such incident . . ." Rosco's response was more query than statement.

"Not on your life! Oh, sure, Taneysville's got its share of malcontents; and it's got a few neighbors who enjoy nursing grudges against each other. But it's also got some of the most decent and kindly people you'll ever hope to meet. And that's what bothers me, Mr. Polycrates. If my opponent decides to attack *me* by attacking my hometown . . ." The words trailed off, then the positive and optimistic tone that was Milt Hoffmeyer's signature style returned. "Look . . . the way I see it, if this is all still up in the air on Election Day, people may get the idea that Taneysville and/or I have something to hide. I'd like to see it settled more quickly than that so we can all concentrate on the business at hand—which man would be best suited to represent this district and go to Washington in January."

Rosco drummed his fingers on his desk and stared at his calendar. The election was three weeks away. "There's another way of looking at this problem, Mr. Hoffmeyer, and it bothers me. You're running against an incumbent—wouldn't it behoove your cause to insinuate that our present congressman was putting pressure on Newcastle's homicide division to slow the investigation down? And if that's your strategy, I have no interest in dragging a very good friend, Al Lever, through the mud in the process."

"I'm not asking you to work against Lever. If anything, I'm asking you to work *with* him. I completely understand his rationale for placing a low priority on this situation. There's no next of kin; basically, nobody cares about this dead woman. But as a citizen, I'm asking you to work with me, and place a higher priority on it. I'm asking you to go out there. Take a look around, ask some questions. If you're uncomfortable and want to call it quits, I'll understand . . . But if not . . . well, I sure would appreciate your help . . . A good place to start would be with my grandmother . . ."

Rosco thought it over for a long moment. "All right, I'll see what I can find out. If you have a fax number I can send you a breakdown of my fees."

"Sounds good. And thank you . . . I don't suppose you'd like to make a contribution to the Milt Hoffmeyer Congressional Campaign Fund? It could easily be arranged as an in-kind contribution."

"That depends on what I find out."

CHAPTER

12

"So . . . when do we go?"

"Whoa, whoa, whoa . . . Hold up, my lovely. What do you mean by 'we'?" Rosco said as he and Belle passed through their sparsely furnished living room and into a kitchen that retained a staunchly retro feel: glass-fronted wood cabinets, an antiquated apple-green Formica countertop, a deep porcelain sink. None of these details were calculated or contrived, however; they were simply left over from the kitchen's prior owners and last refurbishment—circa 1957. Belle loved the room. She insisted it made her feel nurtured and secure, as if she were visiting a mythical relative who was fond of concocting angel food cakes.

Dangling from one of Rosco's hands was a grocery bag containing the makings of supper. Both of Belle's hands were free, and they flew around in the air as she tried to illustrate her point.

"Well, aren't I going with you? To Taneysville, I mean? Didn't Hoffmeyer mention my name?" She perched on a chrome and vinyl bar stool while Rosco went into serious cooking mode. It was fortunate for her—fortunate for them both—that he had been working toward amateur chef status. If the newlyweds' diet had been Belle's responsibility, a lot of cans of soup would have been needlessly sacrificed. One cannot survive on deviled eggs alone.

"Yes, he mentioned your name. He also referred to my mother, sisters, and brother . . . and we're not renting a van and *all* heading out there." Rosco pushed sliced onions into a frying pan, turned on the gas, and reached for a spatula. "Wait a minute. Did I give you a kiss when I came home? I don't think so."

Belle slid off her perch, crossed to Rosco's work area, and wrapped her arms around his shoulders. "Let it not be said that you have a one-track mind."

"I'll have you know that I can handle two tracks simultaneously."

"Sometimes . . ."

"Definitely one and a half."

"One and a quarter. And that's as high as I'll go."

She smiled. He smiled back. Then their lips touched and their noses touched; and for a moment the couple were lost to the world of criminal investigations—and even of onions browning. That is, until the onions began to send up a small smoke signal.

Rosco yanked the pan away from the flame. "Arrgh. Great! There goes my white marsala sauce."

Belle peered at the blackened contents of the pan. "We'll just separate those out . . . the black ones. The others are okay. Leave it to me. I'm a pro at rescuing ruined dinners."

Rosco chuckled. "Like the meat loaf you made on our first date?"

"How was I to know that red pepper flakes aren't the same as diced bell peppers?"

"It was definitely a new experience—and *rescue* came nowhere near it."

"They eat food as hot as that in other parts of the world."

"I'm not so sure about that . . ."

Belle counted places off on her fingers: "Mexico, Africa, India, Asia—"

"Hah! Stop right there. India is *in* Asia. It only counts as one. You can't cite both areas."

"Jeez . . ."

"Go ahead, name some other location where people eat food hot enough to remove automobile paint."

Belle raised an eyebrow but didn't immediately answer. Then she returned to her previous train of thought. "But if Hoffmeyer suggested you start by meeting his grandmother, wouldn't you want to take me with you?"

"I'm not certain I'm following the logic of that notion . . . Oh, wait, I get it . . . You're discreetly hinting that I can't hold my own with elderly ladies—"

"That's not *exactly* what I meant . . ."

"Uh-huh . . ." Rosco grinned; it was the expression of a man devoted to his bride. "Just remember who Haughty Mrs. Sara calls a 'prince.' "

Belle cocked her head. "And Al Lever goes all squishy when she refers to him as 'darling Albert'—and that's despite his efforts at creating that hard-nosed, cantankerous-cop image." She put down her spoon, her face pensive as she abruptly switched topics. "Do you think there's something else going on here?"

"I take it you're not referring to my burnt onions."

She gave him a look. "Hoffmeyer suggested a mob murder . . . Was he serious with that notion? A body dumped in a secluded place, albeit years ago, and then inadvertently discovered—"

"A fairly logical assumption—"

"Well, what I'm getting at is this: What if someone *intended* that the skeleton be found? What if it's part of a larger plan—?"

"Like what?"

Belle thought. "I know this is going to sound like a conspiracy theory . . . but what if it's the work of Hoffmeyer's opponent?"

"Spader? He's a U.S. Congressman, Belle."

"What? These guys don't play dirty pool? Grow up, Rosco."

"I don't buy that. I admit I'm leaning toward voting for Hoffmeyer, but I have no real problems with Spader either. We've certainly had worse."

"And better . . . Okay. Maybe some underling's trying to make certain their man remains in office? After all, he is a thuggish kind of guy. Who knows who he's hired—"

"That's a word? Thuggish?"

"No, I just made it up. *Thugs, Thuggees:* An ancient confederacy of professional assassins preying on wayfarers in India. They were worshipers of Kali, the Hindu goddess of destruction—"

Rosco slipped his arm around her waist. "I love you, but you're still not coming out to Taneysville with me."

"Maybe the mob has nothing to do with this—"

"Belle, are you listening to me?" Rosco chuckled as he spoke.

"You mean the part about me being excluded from this investigation?"

"Yup."

"Absolutely." She handed Rosco the pan of resuscitated onions. ". . . On the other hand, if the skeleton turns out to be the remains of a long-lost heiress—"

"Belle!"

She looked up at him, her eyes wide. "Okay, okay, I won't say another word."

"Is that a promise or a threat? Actually it doesn't make any difference, because I don't believe you for a second."

"Har, har . . ." She returned to her place on the bar stool and remained quiet for the merest of seconds. "What's certain is this: If the village of Taneysville gets a black eye because mysterious remains were discovered, then the town's favorite son will get one, too. Spader won't leave this alone. Mark my words."

"I'd like to think the voters are smarter than that. I honestly believe Hoffmeyer may be overreacting to this situation."

"Well, you just wait and see what the press does with this story. Don't forget I work for a newspaper. The concept of 'innocent until proven guilty' doesn't hold much water at an editorial meeting."

"I guess that's where I come in."

CHAPTER
13

A slippery darkness stared back from the window, once again reflecting the room's sparse furnishings: the hospital bed, the dresser, the rolling table upon which sat the requisite plastic water pitcher, the contents of which were intended to keep the room's occupant "hydrated." Hydrated! Like a vegetable sprouting up in a garden.

There were so many modern words and phrases the room's resident decried: *disabuse*—as in righting an erroneous judgment; *present*—as in displaying medical symptoms; *lifestyle; stress management; significant other*—as if everyone else a person held dear were reduced to *in*significance. There were other terms equally discomfiting. All seemed designed by a battery of attorneys; they were guaranteed not to disturb or provoke. Or, perhaps, they were simply designed to be emotion-free. *Compatible* replacing the mortal conditions of *love, ardor, yearning,* and even *lust.*

A sharp sigh curtailed these rueful meditations while the eyes drew away from the mirrored blackness of the window, coming to rest on the newspapers scattered around the slippered feet.

A cane jabbed them; another angry sigh erupted; the thin lips tightened in frustrated disbelief.

The body had been found—"unearthed" as the reporter noted—but that had been on Monday and no further mention had been made in two solid days! Wednesday's paper and Thursday's contained not so much as a boo. Nothing! No speculation about what had occurred in Taneysville. No concern as to where the skeleton had come from. Or why it had been interred near a now-abandoned farmhouse.

No mention of police involvement, either. Which didn't seem right. In fact, it was downright disturbing. Weren't the police always on hand to call press conferences and such? Assuage the public's fears. Assure them the department was doing its "level best"? Shouldn't there be a homicide detective spouting a theory or a battery of media "personalities" milking the moment? Or what about an interview with the town constable, or photos of the pair that had unearthed the body— even a description of the house and property? Didn't anyone care?

The cane jabbed the useless papers. It was lucky the hour was so advanced, and the residents of the home and their "caregivers" (another odious term!) retired into either sleeping or wakeful silence. It was easier to think without all the foolish bustle of daylight hours. The constant interruptions. The chirpy, saccharine chat. The pleading recommendations to join the rest of the old-timers at their silly games.

This time it was a foot that slashed at the newspapers, sending them sliding across the floor accompanied by a clump of grayish fluff that the nurse's aide referred to as an inconsequential "dust bunny" but which earlier generations had condemned with the decidedly more censorious "sluts' wool."

Another tirade attacked the aged brain. You "minded your

p's and q's" back in those rigorous times! You "toed the line." You didn't "lollygag"; you didn't "cooter around." No, indeed. Instead you did your "level best" to be "whole-footed" and conscientious.

At least, *some* people did.

A final grim sigh broke the pervading silence. It was time to send that Graham girl another hint. She needed direction, needed to recognize the seriousness of the situation.

The arthritic fingers began to move across the gridded paper, creating clues in a surprisingly facile hand.

Exposed was 1-Down . . .

CHAPTER

14

Rosco drove his aged and beloved red Jeep along the narrow and winding road that led to Taneysville. The city of Newcastle and its outskirts were long past, as were the wealthier suburbs with their homes and schools and shopping complexes. What lay before and around the car was either wooded or cultivated land, and the rare home and barn glimpsed through countless trees or across a naked stretch of recently harvested field.

Rosco noted that what houses he saw were simple affairs: two slim stories, a couple of dormer windows, maybe a porch, maybe an outbuilding with a stack of split logs to warm the residents in winter. Several of the dwellings appeared to have newer windows—the type with storm protection built in. Other homeowners had nailed up plastic sheeting to keep out the bitter New England winds. The route to Taneysville was not lined with the edifices of the rich and famous.

All of which made him curious about the man, Gordon, on whose property the skeletal remains had been found. Why had he chosen Taneysville for an obviously expensive second home? Why Taneysville, rather than one of the tonier hamlets in the Berkshires; a place where the Boston and New York newspapers could be purchased on Sunday mornings—along with fresh-baked bagels and high-priced jams and jellies, Dijon mustard, and cold-press olive oil: the lifeblood of non-natives.

If Taneysville gets a black eye, Rosco thought, remembering Belle's comment from the previous evening, *so does Milt Hoffmeyer.* Which would mean that Gordon's name wouldn't be spared either.

Mᵃy Hoffmeyer opened her door the moment Rosco stepped from his Jeep. "Young Milt phoned," she called out. "I've been watching for you—and your Jeep." Then she hesitated. "You *are* Mr. Polycrates, aren't you?"

Rosco approached the porch on which she stood. "I am." He smiled.

"Milt Senior tells me I'm too trusting . . . Doesn't want me taking strangers into the house. I don't know what he imagines could happen to an old lady like me. And way out here! The next thing you know he'll be telling me to lock the door even when I'm home—"

A sudden gust of blown leaves interrupted her. They rose from the lawn and neighboring woods, swirling and taking flight like a flock of small brown birds while the sun momentarily appeared then vanished again into the slate gray air. "If I didn't know better, I'd say that was a snow sky."

Rosco glanced upward. "I don't think so . . . Too early. Too warm."

"Oh, that's for sure. But I've heard they've already had a few dustings up in Vermont. We're never far behind . . . Please do come in, Mr. Polycrates."

"Rosco's just fine, Mrs. Hoffmeyer."

"When Tree was a boy he had a goldfish he called Roscoe—because of those bug-eyes, I suppose."

Rosco couldn't quite make the bug-eye/Roscoe connection. He simply said, "Tree?"

"Young Milt."

"Ahh . . . Because of his height, I take it?"

May let out a laugh and closed the door behind Rosco. "No, no, everyone makes that mistake. Young Milt didn't get his nickname of Tree for that reason at all—though he certainly did grow into it . . . You see, back when he was born, my husband decided to avoid confusion by calling himself Milt *One,* our son Milt *Two,* and of course the baby—Milt *Three.* Well, the poor little guy couldn't pronounce 'three,' so he became 'Tree' around Taneysville."

"He didn't mention that."

May laughed again. "Oh, no, I guess he wouldn't . . . Now that he's on his way to Washington, D.C., he's no longer going to be our little Tree, is he?"

"There is the slight matter of the election," Rosco said, figuring May was astute enough to see he was teasing. "A famous man once said, 'It ain't over till it's over.' "

"I'm not worried about *that* in the least. I feel it in my bones. He's going to win. 'Course, he probably won't take Taneysville . . . Most folks around here are registered with the other party."

Rosco said nothing. He wasn't here to discuss politics. At least, he hoped he wasn't.

"It was good of you to see me, Mrs. Hoffmeyer—"

"Call me May . . ." She led the way across the living room through mismatched and cozy furniture that looked as if it belonged in a display on home style through the decades: two ornate late-Victorian side chairs thrown together with an Arts and Crafts bench sitting between a couple of blond end tables, one of which held a sleek fifties-styled chrome and porcelain lamp. The couch was straight sixties, the fabric a nautical motif in steely blues and maroons. It didn't have a speck of dirt or a stain upon it. Neither did any other surface. May was clearly a thorough housekeeper.

She chose the couch's center and gestured for Rosco to take a large, overstuffed easy chair—which he guessed to be Milt Sr.'s favorite spot as it was surrounded by a magazine rack and a basket containing a number of library books. A pouch for reading glasses was clipped to the chair's arm.

". . . If Tree says 'Jump,' I jump," she added. "I guess I'm what you'd call a doting grandmother. I was a doting ma for him, too . . . But I'm sure you know that story." She leaned back—slightly. It was the gesture of a woman attempting to appear relaxed and unconcerned. "Fire away." She frowned. "Well, maybe that's the wrong word . . . seeing as how we're discussing a murder . . ."

Rosco removed a small notebook and pen from his windbreaker. "Do you mind if I take a few notes?"

"Not at all. Tree wants to get to the bottom of this. So do I; so does his grandfather. Tree told us he was worried that the incumbent might try to use the situation to his advantage . . . which would be a downright shame. We've got a nice little village here, Rosco. Nice people. *Good* people—for the most part. It would be sad if the rest of the world sees us as something we're not."

Rosco nodded. "What I'm trying to do is get a sense of the community. You said 'good people—for the most part.' Can you be more specific?"

Instead of responding directly to the question, May shook her head, her lips tight with unhappiness. "A terrible thing isn't it, murder?"

"It is."

"And here, of all places . . . No one's stopped talking about it . . ."

"Can you tell me what people are saying?"

Again, the quick frown, but deeper this time and longer lasting. "I don't hold with speaking for others. And I'm plumb against any kind of gossip . . . But I guess I can say I don't know why anyone was surprised to learn that the young woman had been *murdered* . . . After all, it's only logical. If she'd died of natural causes and there'd been nothing suspicious about her death, then she would have been given a proper funeral and buried in a proper cemetery . . . instead of the Quigleys' old vegetable patch."

"That's a very good point, Mrs. Hoffmeyer."

"May."

"May." Rosco smiled again. "A very good point." He jotted words in his notebook while May appeared duly proud.

"Of course we didn't know it was a girl until your medical specialist in Newcastle figured it out. It's interesting, isn't it? We all jumped to the conclusion that the body just had to belong to a man." She looked toward a bay window. Another troubled expression crossed her face. "Why do you think that is?"

"Maybe we don't like to think that this type of crime could be perpetrated on a woman."

"I guess that's it . . ." May sighed while Rosco glanced at his notes and reread the sketchy information he'd picked up from Al Lever and Abe Jones.

"Apparently it's going to take Dr. Jones three to four weeks before he can determine anything very specific with regards to when the victim might have died . . . Now, I'm sure you've given this a good deal of thought over the last few days, May, but can you think of anyone, anyone at all, who may have gone missing? And we could be looking back as far as fifty years. Maybe longer."

"No one in this village ever disappeared." The voice was assertive, even a trifle aggressive. "Because, if that had been the case, I guarantee, we'd still be talking about it . . . I guarantee it."

Rosco tried a new tack. "Can you tell me anything about the Quigleys?"

May didn't respond for a moment. Rosco could tell she was struggling with her rule of not trading in gossip or speculating on the motives of others.

"I guess I could say they were unusual. Kept to themselves. They weren't what you'd call unfriendly . . . but they sure weren't neighborly. They'd look down on the church every single Sunday, but they never stepped in, not once, to my recollection. It upset Milt something fierce; but I say let people get their religion where they can."

"And the Quigleys had no children, from what I understand?"

"Nary a one . . . Which was hard; a farm needs plenty of extra hands." She paused, thinking. "They did have a young man working for them once. It was a long time ago, maybe in the sixties . . . kind of a chunky kid with odd hair; that's what makes me think it was back in the sixties or seventies. He was from Newcastle, as I recall, inner city . . . I got the impression it was part of a plan to help troubled youth . . . I also got the impression that Mrs. Quigley liked him a heck of a lot better than her husband did . . . But that was just my observation." Again, May hesitated. "I'm sorry to say the community wasn't very friendly to the poor child . . . I wasn't, I can tell you that, and it's not something I'm proud of. I mean, I didn't have reason to see the young fellow that often because Quigley kept him pretty tightly reined . . . But still . . . I guess I was just nervous on account of his being different, maybe even dangerous. Boys in big cities grow up so fast, and if they're running around with the wrong crowd, well—"

"You wouldn't recall his name?"

"No . . . I'm not sure I ever knew it . . . All I can tell you was that he had really white skin—kind of unusual in a boy, though I suppose that's what comes of living in an apartment complex—and very blond hair. A real towhead." Her mouth turned downward in self-criticism. "We should have reached out . . . the church should have reached out . . . I mean if he was a young man in trouble . . . That's what churches are for, aren't they?" She paused again. "Maybe Lonnie Tucker knew the boy's name. They must have been about the same age . . . And Lonnie did his share of raising Cain when he was a teenager."

Rosco noted the information and said, "The Quigleys never took in another boy for the summer?"

"No . . . but like I said, Hiram didn't seem to cotton to him. It's hard mixing city folk and country folk. He stuck with hiring local kids from then on."

"You've lived here your entire life then, I take it?"

May gave a light laugh. "Oh, no. Only since I married Milt. But that's nearly sixty years now. I'm from Rhode Island originally . . . I'd planned to go off to college after finishing with the Hobson School. I worked summers as a chambermaid at an inn in Narragansett. Worked there since I was fourteen . . . I don't know what brought Milt out there. He's not a seaside sort of person . . . But he plain swept me off my feet. I was sixteen at the time. Milt was older, of course. I'm happy to say that Taneysville's been my home ever since." She smiled—beamed almost.

"So all of your relatives are in Rhode Island?"

The smile flattened. "The Hobson School was an orphanage. It's all closed up now."

"I'm sorry . . . 'Tree' didn't tell me that your parents were . . . He didn't give me any of that background."

"It's not something young people tend to remember about

their grands. And since Tree's father and mother are gone as well, it's a subject we didn't dwell on when we raised him. Besides, the three of us made as loving a group as you'll find anywhere. We just didn't have the *extended* part of a family— as they say nowadays."

Rosco tapped his pen on his pad of paper. "If you were me, Mrs. Hoffmeyer . . . if you were going to start asking questions about our mysterious skeleton, where would you start?"

"Not the way you're doing it."

Rosco raised his eyebrows in surprise.

"I'm not saying I mind your brand of snooping . . . but a lot of folks around here might resent it. Some might even get downright mad—"

"Those would be the characters who you suggested were less than—"

May raised her hand. "Outsiders aren't popular in Taneysville. You go poking around someone like John Stark and you'll find yourself juggling a hiveful of grouchy wasps. And John's not the only one—"

"Stark would be—?"

But May wasn't finished. "And then there are the Bazinnes . . . you don't want to tangle with them—" She interrupted her own speech by leaping to her feet. "Oh, my goodness, I can't believe I've been so rude. Can I get you a cup of tea? Coffee? I should have asked the moment you walked in. I don't know what's gotten into me."

"Nothing, thank you. I'm fine."

"The coffee's fresh ground. Milt does it up nice at the store. And I have a pound cake. Made from scratch. Nine eggs . . . the old-fashioned way . . . Tree likes to tease me about cholesterol—"

"Thanks, May, but I'm okay."

"You sure I can't get you some cake?"

Rosco made a show of patting his stomach. "It's not that

I wouldn't love some, but I'd notice it the next time I put on my running shoes."

"You young people. So health conscious. Just like Amanda Mott . . . she's big on *hiking*. In my day, women felt lucky to be able to *drive* somewhere. Long walks were something we *avoided* if we possibly could. Of course, we wore a different style of shoe back then—"

"Amanda's the EMT who helped unearth the remains, correct?"

"That's right . . . I'd had my hopes she and Tree would hit it off . . . They just looked so good together. Both tall, you know, and so, well, so vibrant and handsome—happy, too . . . Well, that's an old story. Water over the dam, as they say . . ." May returned to her perch on the sofa.

"Could we go back to John Stark for a moment . . . and the Bazinnes?"

May's shoulders hunched forward as she skirted part of the question. "John's the senior warden of Trinity Church. Has been for years. Anyone can tell you that . . . It was John who—" She pursed her lips.

Rosco looked at her. "It was John who what?"

"Well, let's just say that he and Milt are oil and water, salt and sugar . . . Milt's on the vestry at Trinity, too. Junior warden . . . It was John who kept making a lot of noise about stopping that construction up at Quigleys'. He was convinced it was doing structural damage to the church."

Rosco penned in a few notes although he realized that May Hoffmeyer had intended to say something quite different. "And the Bazinnes?"

She drew a breath and leaned back into the couch. "Never mind what I said about them. Frank Bazinne's seen hard times, that's all. The whole family has. Besides, we can't all be blessed with sunny dispositions."

Rosco didn't respond and May hurried ahead with a compelling: "Milt and I would do anything in the world to help Tree out. Anything . . . But like I said, that poor dead girl never came from around here—"

"Meaning that the murderer couldn't have been a local either . . . That's the police's theory, too."

"Which brings us right back to what Tree is so upset about: outsiders making Taneysville look bad. Like that man Gordon . . . an outsider, hiring outsiders . . . I probably shouldn't be saying this, but it does make you wonder." She frowned slightly. Rosco kept silent. "They say Mr. Gordon owns a company that makes magnets . . . I don't know why there's so much money in that. But there must be, or he wouldn't be so high-handed." She stood. "Now, are you sure I can't fix you some cake?"

CHAPTER

15

After all was said and done, Rosco had succumbed to May's offer. He'd not only eaten one but *two* pieces of pound food cake, then washed it all down with coffee that had been liberally laced with heavy cream. "Tree" Hoffmeyer was correct in his assessment: his grandmother didn't know from "fat content," "cholesterol count," or "dietary restrictions"—and the cake had tasted especially good because of this blithe disregard for modern health rules.

But when he was leaving her driveway, the dosage of sugar and cream-drenched coffee had made Rosco's stomach start to dance. He realized he'd need a meal before heading home, and what better way to pick up a few Taneysville tidbits? Food and information were often served right alongside one another in small-town America. However, he nixed the idea of stopping for a sandwich at Hoffmeyer's store. The elder Milt was unlikely to supply much more than May had, and since Milt Sr. had never laid eyes on him, Rosco felt it best to remain anonymous as far as the store was concerned. A lack of discernible connections or history was always handy in situations like this; it would give him a chance to invent an identity other than ex-cop turned PI. Because if outsiders, wealthy or not, were unpopular in Taneysville, private investigators were probably viewed as something the cat might drag in—on an off night.

A neon sign reading EDDIE'S ELBOW ROOM was approaching quickly—a hundred yards ahead of him on the left. Rosco had noticed Eddie's on his way into town a couple of hours earlier. From the outside it had appeared to be simply a roadside tavern, and he held little hope that the establishment served anything more than potato chips, beers, and shots. Hopefully a jar of hard-boiled eggs or a bowl of salted peanuts would be included in the standard bar fare. Almost anything without sugar would do.

Considering it was midday, Eddie's seem reasonably busy. Seven pickup trucks were spread across the gravel parking area, giving Rosco hope that there might be some form of food available after all.

He parked his Jeep in Eddie's lot and glanced down the line of vehicles. Despite the fact that the trucks were all somewhat late models, the New England winters and salted roads had left ugly marks on every one of them. Rusted-out fenders and peeling paint spots were the norm. Rosco and his Jeep fought the same losing battle against the elements each and every year. He dreaded the idea of parting with his cherished car, but guessed the time of reckoning was not far off. The Jeep, with its pitted red paint, fit right in with the pickup trucks. Rosco reached under his seat and retrieved a Boston Red Sox hat. He dropped it on his head, stepped from the Jeep, and ambled into Eddie's.

Seven pickup trucks in the lot translated to eight customers scattered around the room: all male, two at the bar, three at a table near what Rosco surmised was a kitchen door, and three more perched at a table closer to the bar. A large man behind the bar was handing two bottles of Budweiser to an attractive thirties-something waitress with dark hair. As Rosco entered, all conversation stopped and every pair of eyes wandered in his direction.

The glances didn't seem overtly hostile; they were more of a suspicious, *who's-this-guy* nature. Rosco took a seat at the bar, leaving an empty stool between himself and the two other patrons. As he did, a large man seated at one of the tables stood, exited, and returned less than fifteen seconds later.

"That Jeep yours?" he said to Rosco as he reentered.

"Yep."

Without saying another word the man rejoined his two friends at the table.

Rosco turned his attention to the bartender. "Can I get some lunch at the bar? Or should I sit at a table?"

"The bar's fine." He handed Rosco a menu. "Something to drink?"

Rosco immediately recognized a very slight Greek accent— not nearly as heavy as his own mother's, but enough to suggest the man hadn't been born in the States.

"Just a cup of black coffee," Rosco answered in Greek, "if that's okay. You're not Eddie, by any chance, are you?"

A broad smile crossed the bartender's face. "I am," he said, also in Greek. Then in English he added, "You have a good accent, but you weren't born in Greece."

Rosco returned the smile. "No. But my mother was."

"Mainland?"

"Náxos."

Eddie let out a boisterous laugh. "And how many times a day does your mother say she wishes she had never left the island of Náxos?"

Rosco laughed. "Ten? Twenty?"

"My wife, too." He tilted his head to indicate the woman

waiting tables, as she stepped into the kitchen.

"She's from Náxos?"

Eddie shook his head. "No. She's from Tínos. But these island women are all the same: 'Nothing . . . *nothing* is as good as the *island.*' "

"Sounds familiar."

"You ever been there?"

"Never."

"Well . . . you must go before you die. You'll begin to understand."

"Damn," the man to Rosco's left interrupted, "I needed a guy like you on my work site. I couldn't understand what my crew was talking about half the time."

Rosco turned. "Your crew is Greek?"

"Yeah . . . well, *was* . . . When I had one . . . Hell, I guess you get what you pay for, right?"

Both Rosco and Eddie gave him a pointed stare and he began to backtrack. "I mean they were good workers and all . . . It's just that . . . there was a language problem . . . you know? I don't speak Greek."

"But they spoke English?"

"Yeah . . . but only when they wanted to."

"So you were the foreman at the old Quigley place?" Rosco asked.

"Foreman . . . contractor . . . Wait a minute. How do you—?" He leaned back, his gaze resting on Rosco's face. "Hey, I know . . . you're a building inspector, aren't you? That's what you're doing up here . . ." His eyes narrowed. ". . . Newcastle ISD's sending out a new inspector? What's goin' on? What the hell happened to Parker?"

Without missing a beat, Rosco said, "Parker took a job up in Boston. Inspectional Services Department put me on the case. What's your name again?"

"Reilly. Sean Reilly."

Rosco pulled his pad from his jacket and flipped through a few pages until he found one chock a block with scribblings. "Right . . . Reilly . . . You're the guy I'm supposed to talk to."

"Ah, come on, Parker was up at that site a week and a half ago. Gave everything the go-ahead."

Rosco shrugged. "Hey, I'm playing catch-up here, what can I say? The guy left us with a real mess of paperwork. Nothing's in order . . . And you know ISD. Gotta have everything in order." Rosco looked at Eddie and said, in Greek, "Can I get a grilled cheese with that coffee?"

"You got it."

Eddie turned, filled a coffee mug, then placed it on the bar in front of Rosco.

He took a sip and focused on Sean. "I understand the cops have closed down your site? Someone was murdered—"

Sean raised his hands. "Whoa, hold on there. All that happened was . . . What'd you say your name was?"

Rosco took another sip of coffee. "Parker . . . Same as the last guy."

"Well, hell, that makes things easy."

"I thought it would."

"Wait—Parker? Didn't I overhear you telling Eddie you were Greek?"

"On my mother's side, sure . . . What can I say? The country's a melting pot."

Sean seemed to relax a little with this information. "Look, my guys just found a pile of bones when they were diggin' with the backhoe. That's all there was to it. Nobody was murdered."

"Did you get to see them? Before the cops got there? The bones, I mean."

"What cops? Just some local yokel . . . Yeah, I saw them."

"Parker" nodded in sympathy. "Rumor in Newcastle is someone dumped that body there. Maybe mob connected—"

"No way. The remains belonged to a woman. You didn't read that? The mob doesn't go after babes. But hell, I wouldn't care if it was Amelia Earhart. I just want to get back to work."

Rosco nodded again. "I'm sure you do . . . But as the new man on the job, Mr. Reilly, I'm going to have to take a look at what you've got going on there—"

"You guys can't just waltz onto a site unannounced. You gotta make an appointment."

Rosco took a sip of his coffee. "That's where you're wrong, Mr. Reilly. Your code book should provide all the necessary information as to the jurisdiction of the Inspectional Services Department. We can—and do—perform unscheduled spot checks . . . But that's besides the point. You see, Parker— that's my predecessor, the *other* Parker—didn't leave any con- tact numbers for you, or for the current property owner, for that matter . . . meaning that I was forced to drive out here and look for you. We can do this spot check tomorrow or the next day . . . whatever works for you . . ." Rosco took another sip of coffee. "Hey, look, Reilly, I'm on your side. I just need to get brought up to speed . . . Paperwork's a hassle, but it's gotta be done. I'm sure your Mr. Gordon will understand."

Sean only groaned.

"I'm going to have to talk with Gordon, too," Rosco added. "The sooner you can get finished up, the happier we'll all be, right? You want to get back on the job. ISD wants the same thing. Live and let live, and move on, right?"

"You're a hell of a lot friendlier than the *last* Parker." Sean pulled a business card from his wallet and jotted a phone number on the back. "That has my information on it: cell phone, the works. And that's Mr. Gordon's private line on the back. Don't tell him I gave it to you, okay?"

"You bet."

Sean finished his beer, tossed a five-dollar bill on the bar, looked at the man beside him, and said, "Come on, Rick, I want to get back to Boston before we hit rush hour."

After they departed, Rosco was left alone at the bar—but not for long. A burly man with a large mustache slid onto the stool next to him. He was the same person who'd stepped outside when Rosco had entered and queried him on his Jeep. He extended his hand toward "Parker" in what would normally appear to be a friendly gesture, but which Rosco gauged to be intrinsically hostile.

"The name's Gunston. Big Otto Gunston. I'm pretty much *it* when it comes to electrical contracting in Taneysville."

Rosco shook the proffered hand. Big Otto's grip was intended to cause pain and it did. Rosco ignored the ache in his fingers and said, "Bill Parker."

"Right. Excuse me for eavesdropping," Otto said, still keeping his grip tight, "but I hear that you're the new building inspector for these parts?"

"One of them."

"Well, I only care about the one that'll be handling Taneysville." He released Rosco's now-throbbing hand. "How come you're not driving a county car?"

Rosco let out a phony groan. "That was another thing my predecessor screwed up. Guess he liked to ride the brakes or something. Car's in the shop now. New shoes. Be ready next week sometime. In the meantime, I'm on my own . . . Not that that baby needs any added mileage."

Otto looked at Eddie as he placed Rosco's sandwich in front of him. "This man's meal's on me, Eddie."

Rosco wondered if the purchase of a two-dollar-and-sixty-five-cent grilled cheese sandwich constituted a large bribe in Otto's mind. He was tempted to ask him if his generous offer included the coffee, but instead simply said, "Thanks."

"Not a problem. That's how I work. You ask anyone in Taneysville about Big Otto. I take care of the building inspectors, and they look out for me . . . You like moose hunting?"

"Moose? Not my thing. Sorry."

"I take a few of the boys up north every fall. Keep it in mind. You missed this year's trip, but, hell, maybe next year. There's always room for another gun. They're good hunting— moose."

Rosco wondered if he should repeat *Not my thing,* but opted to leave it alone. "I didn't notice that you had anything on my checklist when I left Newcastle this morning. Do you have some work I need to be . . . inspecting?"

"Nah . . . Of course, *nobody* here . . ." Gunston swung his meaty arm to indicate the remaining five customers; "That is, *all* of us have been locked out of that job at the old Quigley place. Brought in a bunch of foreigners to do the work."

Eddie cleared his throat. "Just so you know, Mr. Parker: someone took the initiative to call immigration services—no one has any idea who that might have been." He gave Big Otto a disingenuous smile. "Agents went out, or should I say 'raided' the site. Everyone's paperwork was in order."

Rosco shrugged. "Not much you can do about a nonlocal crew. Contractors want to go out of town for their workers— that's their prerogative."

Gunston's face muscles began to tighten and his skin turned even ruddier. "Well, that's where you're wrong, *Parker.* We're Americans—you and me. I don't care who your mother was—or your pop, neither." He pointed at Eddie. "And you, too, Apollo. You've got your citizenship. You're one hundred percent, all-American prime beef." He spun his heavy frame back toward Rosco. "We've got people who need jobs right here in Taneysville, Parker. The way I see it, if you're from Maine, New Hampshire, Rhode Island—you're a foreigner. If we don't stop these Russkies, they'll drive us all out!"

Rosco set the remainder of his sandwich on the plate. "Wait a second. What 'Russkies'? I thought Reilly said his crew was Greek."

"Greeks, Vermonters, Russkies, they're all in it together. That Gordon? He's one of them."

"Gordon? The property owner?"

"Yeah, Gordon. You think that's his real name? Forget it. It's Peskov, or Pinchov, or something like that. I do my home-work. I suggest you do, too. They had a whole thing on Gor-don in the Boston paper a few years back . . ."

Rosco shrugged. "I must have missed it. But I guess people are allowed to change their names if they want."

Big Otto's face was now beet red. "Listen, Parker, you've got to understand something. There's no room for people like that Russkie in Taneysville. You ask around. Start with the people at the church if you want. If we can't get any support from people like you—our county employees—we're going to have to take things into our own hands. That site has to be shut down!"

"As far as I can see, it has been."

Otto stopped. He seemed to be considering the comment. Finally he said, "Yeah, right, but that's only temporary. They've got to get some locals working up there or they're going to be shut down for good."

Rosco took another bite of his grilled cheese. "Man, finding that skeleton must have been something else . . . I sure wish I'd seen it. Any idea who she coulda been?"

Gunston only shook his head.

"Just bones," Rosco continued. "No way to identify the remains . . . That's what the newspapers said . . ."

Otto tossed some money on the bar. "Gotta run, Eddie." He then turned to the two men he'd left at the table. "See you guys at my place tomorrow? The BU pregame starts at twelve-thirty."

"Thanks for the sandwich," Rosco said, but Big Otto walked out without acknowledging the remark.

CHAPTER

16

Surrounded by reference materials—foreign language dictionaries, a "red letter" edition of Shakespeare, and a quirky assortment of antiquated books on gardening, "home cookery," and barn building—Belle penciled in possible solutions to her newest crossword puzzle. To say that she constructed the cryptics that appeared in the *Evening Crier* "the old-fashioned way" would have been an understatement. Belle Graham took as much pleasure in linguistic conundrums as her many fans did.

In addition, she set strict rules for herself: No two-letter solutions, a perfectly symmetrical appearance, and always, *always* a theme that worked its way both across and down. Belle believed her puzzles should be both fun and educational. What was the point in filling in letters if you didn't feel you'd discovered something new?

"Arrrgh," she muttered to herself. "No go . . ." She erased letters from the grid she'd drawn, then counted on her fingers, shook her head, and said, "Darn . . . ten letters . . ." She needed an uneven amount of letters for the thematic solutions to a crossword dedicated to the six wives of Henry VIII. "Unless I could make Anne Boleyn 'Nan'—which was the name by which she was familiarly known . . ."

Kit's sudden barking and a heavy footfall on the front steps removed this query from immediate attention. Belle cast aside her work and walked through the house to open the door just as the mailman prepared to slide the day's deliveries through the slot.

"Hiya, Belle. Nice weather we're having. Cold, though . . ."

"It's only October, Artie. It'll get a heck of a lot colder before it gets any warmer."

"Almanac says we're in for a doozy of a winter."

"It wouldn't surprise me."

Kit danced around the legs of her mistress and the mail carrier while this familiar exchange took place. No matter the season, Artie enjoyed citing that well-known source for all atmospheric predictions, *The Old Farmer's Almanac*.

"Enjoy it while you can. That's what I always say." He bent down to give Kit a friendly pat. "Nicest dog on my beat . . . Some of them . . . you'd be surprised . . . growl, bare their teeth, fur all ruffled and mean looking . . . Don't know why people keep animals like that. I mean, pets should be something you can pet, right?"

"I guess folks think they need protection—"

Artie interrupted. He was a man who liked to talk, and he was trapped in an often uncommunicative job. "Well, if anyone needed protection I'd imagine it'd be you . . . especially after that kook targeted you and started sending those—"

"That was ages ago, Artie—"

"Only a year, by my reckoning . . . Besides, you never heard of copycat crimes? Happens all the time. I'm sure your hubby can tell you all about 'em."

Belle smiled and took the mail he handed her. "I'll keep your advice in mind."

"If I was you, I wouldn't be so quick and easy opening my door."

"But then we wouldn't be having this conversation."

Artie's face fell. "Gonna be a doozy of a winter," he finally repeated.

Belle turned toward the door. "Let's hope for the best."

"I'm betting snow before Thanksgiving—and we never see open ground till tax day."

She chuckled. "There's a cheery thought."

"April fifteenth. You mark my words."

"See you tomorrow, Artie."

"Don't you go flinging open the door, Belle. There's still plenty of loonies out there."

She smiled, but didn't reply.

Doozy, she thought as she idly sorted through the mail while returning to her office, *floozy, frowsy, blowsy . . . from the English dialect, a blowze, a wench with a coarse and ruddy complexion . . .* Belle's eye fell on her unfinished crossword. Anne Boleyn . . . ten letters . . . a woman who, by all accounts, was a plainish lady with a swarthy complexion, albeit extraordinarily vivid and expressive black eyes . . . Boleyn was the king's second wife; because of his passion for her, he divorced Catherine of Aragon—and severed his ties with the Roman Church . . . But Anne paid for Henry's obsessive ardor when, having produced only a female child—Elizabeth I— she fell from her sovereign's favor and was finally accused of adultery—even incest in the case of one of her lovers, her own brother, Lord Rochford . . .

"Divorced, beheaded, died"—Belle muttered the antique refrain under her breath—"divorced, beheaded, survived." With one hand she began counting letters in the names of Henry's queens: CATHERINE OF ARAGON, ANNE BOLEYN, JANE SEYMOUR, ANNE OF CLEVES, CATHE-

RINE HOWARD, and the only one to survive her willful and vindictive husband: CATHERINE PARR.

An envelope fell from between the pages of a catalog as Belle finished this exercise. The handwriting on the address was identical to that of the anonymous crossword she'd shared with Sara. Belle slit open the envelope and unfolded another meticulously crafted puzzle. *Swap meet.* She turned the page over. Like the previous offering there was no hint of authorship; therefore it would be impossible to include it in a collection of readers' contributions. She glanced at the Across clues, silently filling in answers: WHAT'S IN A NAME, TRADING PLACES . . . Then she shook her head, dropped the puzzle on her desk, and turned on the radio, hoping for some gentle background music to lull her back to work.

Divorced, beheaded, died, her brain recited, *divorced, beheaded, survived . . . There must be a clever lexical twist I can use with this one . . .*

But her thought process was interrupted by a political announcement that roared out of the radio at a decibel level that seemed twice that of the previous music selection:

". . . If he can't clean up crime in his own hometown, how can he promise he'll address the issue statewide? Nationwide? What we need are crime busters, not sob sisters like Milton Hoffmeyer the Third. And we don't need skeletons stuffed inside our neighbors' closets . . . Paid for by Concerned Citizens for a Better Bay State . . ."

Belle flicked off the radio in disgust. Honestly! she thought. For one thing those remains weren't found in a closet, they were unearthed in a field, in what had once been a vegetable garden. Then her facile mind spun into alliterative mode: *A Body Buried among Butter Beans; The Corpse in the Cowpeas; Skeletons and Scallions; Murder in the Maize.*

A rueful smile crept around the corners of her lips. She sighed, and with some effort returned to the precarious lives of King Henry's wives.

Across

1. Fr. holy woman
4. Tie results?
7. 5 & 10, e.g.
12. She
13. Passed on
15. Neutered
16. Poetically above
17. Stretcher?
18. "To be . . ." source
19. Juliet's rose comment
22. Hawaiian geese
23. Conflict
24. Latin love
27. Aykroyd/Murphy film
32. Even; abbr.
33. Tenth of twelve
34. Some gyms
35. 180
39. José or Buddy
40. Chinese export
41. Very in Vergara
42. Abba hit
46. Swedish river
47. Pub drink
48. Forces down
51. Classic deceiver
55. Hash mark
58. Dupes
59. Born
60. Flung over
61. Even better
62. Literary monogram
63. Feel
64. Fool
65. Isr. neighbor

Down

1. Exposed
2. Twitter
3. Backbone of some puzzles
4. Black Sea port
5. 20-Down torch
6. Exposed
7. Canned ham
8. Domesticated
9. Olive _____
10. Female ruff
11. NYC zone
14. Like Hollywood dreamers
15. Honed
20. Patio
21. Pester
24. Certain stolen items
25. Dense
26. CIA germ?
28. Badger
29. Chill
30. Soap stuff
31. An aardvark, e.g.
32. "Beat it!"
36. Cartoon denial
37. Admission
38. Sorceress
39. African antelope
43. Like a distant star
44. Patient's request; abbr.
45. Bikini blasts
49. Verse
50. Scowl
51. Tears
52. Rapier
53. On the briny
54. Rat's nest
55. 60's grp.
56. Tuscan three
57. Operated

SWAP MEET

CHAPTER

17

"Peskov or Pinchov?" Belle asked. She was seated at her desk, absentmindedly chewing on a licorice stick. Rosco was seated nearby, but instead of nibbling candy he was looking through his pocket notebook.

"Something like that . . . Of course, the information comes from Big Otto. And I wouldn't call him an overly reliable—or sympathetic—character."

Belle raised her eyebrows and smiled. "And it doesn't sound as if Sean Reilly is much of a sweetheart, either. In fact, from what you've been telling me, a good many of the folks in Taneysville are suffering from a fairly advanced case of xenophobia—"

"You can say that again. A welcome mat salesman would starve to death out there."

Belle released a small laugh, then grew serious. "Well, our supposedly enlightened city isn't always very welcoming or accepting, either. Like everywhere, we've got ethnic-related prejudices; people who get skittish when confronted with mental health patients or physical deformities. And then there are religious differences . . ."

Rosco put on a look of mock surprise. "Right here in River City! I don't believe it! . . . I'm Greek, remember?"

Belle smiled again. "As if your mom or sisters could ever let me forget that . . . the eldest son married to a 'white girl' . . ."

"Who's been made an honorary Greek. Don't ever tell me you're not the luckiest girl in the world. That title's not bestowed upon outsiders lightly by my clan. My brothers-in-law are still groveling for acceptance."

Belle grinned but didn't speak, and the two gazed at each other across the crossword-themed office. The look was filled with a desire to place everything on hold and slip upstairs— even just for a little while. They remained in that conflicted pose as the sun began to sink toward the horizon and the sky assumed a flame-red hue. Beyond the windows, the small garden was already drenched in shadow, causing the bare tree limbs and deciduous shrubs to appear even darker against this fiery backdrop. Then the sunset's rays momentarily filled the room, alighting on Rosco's and Belle's faces, making them seem as if they were glowing from within. Or perhaps it was inner happiness their expressions reflected.

"Well . . . ?" Rosco said; his mind was an open book.

"Wait a minute . . . I was just thinking of something . . ."

"I was afraid of that."

". . . Could the name Big Otto was hunting for be Peshkov?"

"I guess . . ." Unconsciously, Rosco mirrored his wife's pose, also leaning forward in his chair. "Although I was kind of hoping your brain was focusing on a different question—"

"Peshkov . . ." Belle repeated slowly, "Aleksei Maksimovich Peshkov . . . a.k.a. Maxim Gorki—"

"What on earth are you talking about?"

"The writer Gorki used a pseudonym—"

Rosco sat back and chuckled. "Stupid question, but how did you know that?"

"Huh?"

"How did you . . . ? No, never mind . . . I'll never be able to comprehend how much information your brain has packed away. We've got to get you on *Jeopardy*." Rosco chuckled again. It was the sound of a man who adored his wife. "Okay, Gorki a.k.a. Peshkov . . . What might this have to do with our Mr. Gordon?"

"*Alex* Gordon, right? Isn't that what you told me?"

"Right . . . ?"

"An English version of Aleksei, and Gordon instead of Gorki—"

"Where does Peshkov come in?"

"Well, *if* your Alex Gordon is indeed a Russian expatriate, and *if* his name is Peshkov—rather than Pinchov or Peskov, then his choice of alias shows a literary bent . . ."

"So?" Rosco smiled and shook his head. "I'm not sure this is getting us anywhere vis-à-vis the skeletal remains in Taneysville, unless you're suggesting we've finally found the long-lost Tsarina Anastasia . . . Besides, by assuming Gordon's real name is Peshkov you're utilizing a *very* circumstantial concept—as well as an unsound source . . . And in the long run, what difference does the name make?"

"Wait a minute!" Belle sat bolt upright in her chair. "Gordon, Alex . . ." She put her hands on her temples. ". . . Wife goes missing—"

"I'm going to have to ask you to back up here, Belle. I missed a segue."

She gazed at him, her gray eyes bright. Then she jumped to her feet and began switching on the room's lamps and overhead light. "It's coming back to me now . . . A businessman named Alex Gordon . . . He lived in Boston . . . had a very high-profile wife . . . She was always popping up in some society magazine . . . redecorating her bathroom, having the dining room *trompe l'oeil*ed . . ." Belle squinted, trying to remember. "It must have been twelve or thirteen years ago—"

"Thirteen years ago, I was NPD. I didn't worry myself with high-profile wives in Boston—or *trompe l'oeil*."

"And I wasn't even living in Massachusetts then," Belle countered as she paced the room. "This was national magazine stuff. She was young . . . very flashy . . . a real babe, if you go in for the bleach-blond, cosmetically altered, greedy, gold-digger type—"

"Which I gather you don't. I know *I* sure don't."

Belle cocked her head to one side. "You're so perceptive. It's one of the things I love about you."

"So, this Alex Gordon of yours had a trashy wife who was a publicity hound—?"

"Then one day, she upped and ran off with her husband's business partner—along with a sizable chunk of company cash."

Rosco winced. "Not a happy scenario . . . but not all that unusual. Infidelity isn't—"

"The partner was quite a looker, too, as I recall. A real Clark Gable type."

" 'Frankly, my dear—' "

"After that she plumb vanished from the scene." Belle sat on her desk, and again frowned in concentration. "Not a peep out of her. No more photo spreads of her at poolside or showing off her newest collection of handbags—"

"Maybe she finally found true love, and didn't need all the hoopla."

"Maybe . . . Actually, I remember thinking that the two of them had probably skipped the country and retired to a desert

isle." Belle shook her head in thought. "Mrs. Alex Gordon
. . . the wife of the 'magnet magnate.' "

"Huh?"

"I just remembered . . . that's what the press called the husband . . ." Then Belle almost shouted. "FYI! That was the
acronym for his company's name . . . I can't remember what
it stood for . . . Yes, I can! Far Yukon Industries."

"Sounds like it could be our boy," Rosco said, then remained silent a moment. "Wife disappears . . . business partner pulls a fast one . . . I have to start reading *Town and
Country* more often. Any other facts roaming around in that
fertile brain of yours . . . ? For instance: Was the partner accused of embezzlement?"

"He must have been . . . I guess . . . I'll tell you what: We
can do a Web search right now . . ." Belle spun toward her
computer, then sagged in dejection. "No, wait. I forgot . . .
We won't be able to retrieve information from that long
ago—at least not current newspaper articles and so forth. I'll
have to head down to the *Crier*'s morgue tomorrow morning
and use their microfiche. That way I can access the Boston
papers, too—"

"I wish you wouldn't call it that."

"Why? Microfiche is the official—"

"No, *morgue.*"

"The *Crier*'s reference room? Every paper has one. The nickname's been around since the early nineteenth century. Although"—she smiled briefly—"it might interest you to know
that the term doesn't come from the Latin word for death but
that it's French, and derives from *morgo,* or pride. A French
morgue was a place where the police examined newly captured
criminals—" Belle interrupted her own train of thought, and
jumped back to Alex Gordon and his wife. "Darn! I hate
conundrums like this."

"I thought patience was your middle name."

She made a face. "Well, buddy, you thought wrong."

Rosco stood and put his arms around her. "I've got to check my office for calls. Then what do you say we head out for dinner?"

"Sounds terrific."

Rosco walked to the phone on the desk, where he tapped in numbers and then jotted names and return numbers in his notebook while Belle pulled close.

"Mike Petri?" she murmured, peering over his shoulder. "What's that all about?"

"Never mind, Miss Nosy. Maybe it's confidential?"

"But who is he?"

Rosco laughed. "None of your beeswax . . . A guy who wants to talk to me. Didn't leave a number. Said he'll call back tomorrow . . . And, no, I don't know who Mike Petri is or what he wants . . . Now are you satisfied?" Then Rosco picked up the crossword Belle had been working on. "Your newest one?"

Belle sighed and nodded. "The wives of Henry VIII . . . The thematic clues are giving me a really rough time. Plus there are three Catherines and two Annes . . ."

"Any Russian tsarinas?"

"Ho, ho . . ."

CHAPTER

18

With Belle ensconced in the *Crier*'s morgue, Rosco drove north toward Boston and the offices of Far Yukon Industries. Gordon's secretary had been able to give him a twelve noon appointment, but had also made it abundantly clear that Saturdays weren't normally part of the boss's working schedule. If Rosco were detained—even by ten or fifteen minutes—he'd forfeit his chance for an interview.

That piece of peremptory business out of the way, the secretary had then provided detailed directions to FYI's headquarters, which were situated in a large industrial park in Dorchester on Boston's south side, not far from the Franklin Park Zoo.

Passing through the industrial campus, Rosco spotted what he identified as Far Yukon Industries at the rear of the park. The two-story cinderblock building appeared to house both office and manufacturing space, but unlike other tenants of the complex, FYI had no fleet of matching vehicles parked in its lot, and no trendy logos, signs, or awnings to indicate who occupied the space or what might take place within the walls. The sole marker was an unprepossessing 5245 ENTERPRISE WAY, painted in small gold leaf letters on a curbside signpost.

Rosco parked the Jeep in a spot marked GUESTS ONLY, and tried the door. It was secured, but before he had a chance to press the intercom button, an electric buzzer sounded, indicating the door was now unlocked. He glanced up at a video camera, gave it a slight wave, and entered the building.

It had been clear from the exterior that there were no windows in the building, but once inside Rosco found the effect claustrophobic in the extreme. The front reception area was no more than ten by ten feet. To the left was a desk. A tall and well-proportioned blond woman sat behind it. The only items on her desk were a telephone, a television monitor, and a nail file. On the right side of the small room were two office chairs with a table perched between them. Three back issues of *Cosmopolitan* sat on the table. Directly opposite the entrance was a gray door that appeared to be fashioned out of solid steel. It obviously led to the remainder of the building.

"You must be Mr. Polycrates," the blond said in a heavy Eastern European accent.

"Yes. I am." He motioned toward the TV monitor on her desk. "Is there some way you recognized me?"

"Ach, no. The sound of that door chime drives me coo-coo. I try to let people in before they can push that silly button . . . Besides, you are the only visitor we are expecting. At least the only one who might be wearing a sports jacket."

"If Mr. Gordon's secretary hadn't given me directions, this wouldn't be a very easy building to find," Rosco said by way of making conversation. "Far Yukon needs a sign or something out there."

"Mr. Gordon believes it is better that our neighbors do not know too much about the magnets."

She said this as if the word *magnets* was synonymous with the testing of nuclear weapons.

"The magnets?"

"We manufacture Muscle Man Magnets. Many people think we are creating force fields. A silly idea, but we've been forced to move our facility twice in the last five years . . . Other companies have suggested our magnets made a mess of their computers and video and recording tapes, phone service, ee tee cee. Not to mention the rearranging of the molecules in the blood systems."

"Are you serious?"

She raised her arms above her head and pushed her ample chest toward Rosco. "Do you see anything wrong with me?" She lowered her arms. "People are coo-coo. We make electromagnets. They're as harmless as . . . well, just look at me."

"Right."

"I will tell Mr. Gordon you are here. Please to have a seat."

Rosco turned, but before he could move anywhere near the chairs, Gordon stepped through the steel door and into the waiting area.

"Mr. Polycrates, I'm Alex Gordon." He extended his hand.

"Thank you for taking the time to meet with me."

"Not at all. I'm as anxious to get this mess in Taneysville cleared up as anyone. I was hoping to spend the holidays out there . . . Ah well, you know what they say about construction work . . . it takes twice as long as estimated and costs twice as much . . ."

Gordon was a good deal shorter than Rosco had expected— about five feet eight inches tall, round but solidly built, with a heavy dark brow, dark hair, an equally dark, neatly trimmed beard. The man Belle had recalled from memory hadn't had a beard, nor had he been so broad and bearlike. Rosco wondered whether Alex Gordon had once toyed with bodybuilding and then given up the practice—which could account for his muscled yet boxy appearance.

Rosco judged the CEO of Far Yukon to be in his early forties. His accent was middle American. If he'd been born in Russia, as Big Otto Gunston had implied, there was no hint of a previous speech pattern.

"Let's step into my office, shall we?"

He held the steel door for Rosco and they walked down a twenty-five-foot corridor lit solely by fluorescent ceiling lamps. They cast a sickly hue onto the brown walls; coupled with the gray/black commercial carpeting, the sensation was airless and close.

At the end of the corridor there were three doors. The sound of industrial machinery could be heard behind the center door. On the door to Rosco's right there was a sign reading MRS. TOLAND. Gordon turned the knob to his left and motioned for Rosco to enter. On this door there were two signs, one reading MR. ALEX GORDON—CEO, and another reading "ON A VACANT FACE A BRUISE BECOMES AN ADORNMENT." The quote was attributed to Maxim Gorki.

After reading the sign, Rosco smiled and said, "Gorki, huh?"

"Yes. My mother claimed we were related to him, but could never produce the documents to prove it . . . But then, things got a little out of hand during the Stalin era—to say the least. A good many official papers disappeared. So who knows for sure? Maybe it's only romantic family lore . . . but I like the idea . . . Have you read Gorki?" Gordon motioned for Rosco to take a seat as he spoke.

Rosco shook his head.

"No? You should. From the early stories like 'Twenty-six Men and a Girl' to the later novel *Decadence* . . . His was a real rags-to-riches story. Started out earning his own living at age nine . . . ended up living in Capri and Sorrento. Not bad for a poor kid from Nizhni-Novgorod . . ."

Rosco looked around the office as Gordon spoke, noting how spare it was: one large desk with a utilitarian office chair behind it and the chair Rosco was now sitting in. On the desk was the same type of video monitor that sat on the receptionist's desk. Again, there were no windows, and the only item on the walls was an eight-by-ten-inch black-and-white photograph of former President Bill Clinton.

"I thought Gorki's real name was . . . Peshkov or something?" Rosco said, trying to sound as if he were searching his mind for the assigned reading list of some lit class he'd taken in college.

Gordon smiled. "Very good. Not many people know that. Peshkov is my true name. I changed it to something less . . . well, less foreign sounding . . . This is America, right?"

"You have no real discernible accent."

"And I would guess that Polycrates is of Greek origin. Where's *your* accent?"

"Good point. Though I'm a couple of generations removed from the homeland."

Gordon only shrugged and spread his hands on the desk. The fingernails had been professionally manicured. They also had a decided sheen, as if clear polish had been applied.

"You're probably very busy, Mr. Gordon," Rosco continued, "so I'll get right to the point. As I told your secretary—"

"Before you get too far, let me tell you that I'm not a Hoffmeyer supporter. I'm backing the incumbent . . . as I have in the past, and intend to continue."

"Fair enough. But Milt Hoffmeyer asked . . . I should say, *hired* me to look into this Taneysville situation. Since you own the property I thought I'd start with you."

Gordon shifted in his seat. "I purchased that farm eight months ago . . . No, a little more than that now. Closer to a year . . . I probably know less about this mess than you do."

"I'm sure you've heard that the police have cold-cased the investigation until the experts can determine when the victim died . . . or, to be accurate, was murdered . . . and who she is."

No response came from Gordon, but the hands remained splayed on the desktop. At length he said, "I haven't been out to the site in well over a month. I'm not sure what you're getting at . . . ?"

"Do you have enemies, Mr. Gordon? . . . Assuming that the body was dumped on what is now your property, it's conceivable that you're the target of a hate crime . . . someone who wants to see your reputation damaged—"

Gordon interrupted. "I don't have any enemies. I make it a point to keep my employees happy . . ."

Rosco was about to bring up the subject of Gordon's former business partner, but something told him to hold back for a minute.

". . . In fact," the CEO continued, "one of the reasons Far Yukon's plant is built on this model is to enable management and labor to work in close proximity. I'm not viewed as a guy with a fancy car who drifts in once a week to peer down his nose at the peons. I can run every machine in this facility. *And* I put in time on alternate Saturdays—just like my crew."

Rosco wrote in his notebook, then asked another question. "Do you mind if we discuss your wife?"

"My wife?" Gordon leaned back in his chair, and tapped his fingers together in front of his burly chest. "Let me give you a tip, my friend . . . Never, and I mean *never,* let a woman get near a contractor. Remember what I said about a job taking twice as long and costing twice as much? Once the ladies are involved that estimate doubles. Even triples. 'I want the spa facing the window'; 'We need a Subzero in the master suite'; 'The ceiling in the foyer should have aged oak beams' . . ." Gordon laughed. "You get my drift? Women can't conceptualize . . . their brains are only programmed to rearrange . . ."

Rosco raised his eyebrows. "I was thinking of your former wife."

Gordon's eyes narrowed. His dark face turned darker, his brow almost menacing. "She's in California with my daughter. I haven't seen or spoken to either of them for eight years . . . Eight years. A long time to be legally separated from a child. A situation like mine could never exist in Russia. I would have my child." Beneath the black beard, the mouth was tight and unforgiving.

Rosco glanced at his notes. He made no attempt to hide his confusion. "Eight years . . . ? I must have been mistaken . . . I have information that predates that . . . when your wife was alleged to have disappeared—"

Gordon rose abruptly. "What is this? You come into my office and point fingers at me?"

Rosco also stood. He raised his hands in an effort to calm the situation. "I apologize, Mr. Gordon . . . I'm just trying to figure this out. I'm sorry if I'm opening a painful chapter—"

"Look, Polycrates, I don't care what's going on out in that hick burb. Or how any of this affects Milt Hoffmeyer. In fact, I hope he loses—big time. All I want is to get the contractor and his crew the hell out of my home so I can walk through the door and slam it behind me—"

"I apologize, Mr. Gordon, but is it possible that your former business partner—?"

"I don't want to discuss him! Not now. Not ever."

Rosco decided to press the issue. "But couldn't he be considered an enemy? A very serious one?"

Gordon's face grew nearly black with rage. "An enemy to *me?* I'd say you've got it the wrong way around, pal! I'd say the guy who's the mark should be the one bearing the grudge . . . the guy who was the complete *chump* . . . the boob . . . the simp . . . You know the term *cuckold,* Polycrates? Well, that's me. One of the suckers born each and every minute . . ."

With some effort, the CEO of Far Yukon began to control himself. "Look, Polycrates, ancient history is ancient history. Water under the bridge. Spilled milk, et cetera . . . You want to ask me questions about my property in Taneysville, fire away; but my personal life's off limits. Got it?"

Rosco nodded and made a mental note that Gordon, a.k.a. Peshkov, wasn't as sympathetic a character as he tried to appear. "I'm curious as to why you chose the area for a second home. I would have thought a man of your means would have purchased property in, say, one of the more established resort communities. Perhaps, in the Berkshires."

Gordon resumed his seat and his affable air. "The Berkshires are Boston with more snow. Who needs it? Chichi restaurants, overpriced art galleries . . . overpriced Italian markets. I don't go to the mountains to buy a Rolex. I can buy one here. Besides, I like forging my own way. Always have." He laughed. "You been up there? To Taneysville, I mean?"

"Briefly."

Alex Gordon leaned forward across his desk. "That's where you should be doing your snooping, Polycrates. Me? I'm just a weekend visitor with a home under construction . . . You want answers to why a body was dumped on the old Quigley site, I'd suggest you ask some of the locals . . . You met Frank Bazinne yet?"

Rosco shook his head no.

Gordon chuckled again. "Well, you've got a real treat in store for you. Bazinne and his buddies . . . they're, what do you call them . . . ? throwbacks . . . Neanderthals . . . misfits. And they're none too happy losing out on their slice of the pie . . . My advice to you, Polycrates, is to start with Bazinne . . .

I say that body was dumped there ages ago. By some local Tontos." The CEO pressed a button on his intercom. "I apologize, but I've got a meeting with the foreman at noon-thirty. My secretary will show you out."

Rosco placed a business card on the desk. "I can find my own way, Mr. Gordon—"

"You talk to Bazinne and his crowd if you want a true picture of Taneysville. And forget the enemy bit, Polycrates. I'm a good guy. A guy with friends. A lot of friends. Powerful friends."

As Rosco started his Jeep, Boston's all-news radio station chimed in with the weather report and traffic update. Interstate 93 was a logjam, so he decided to head south on Blue Hill Avenue. After a dozen blocks the radio announcer came on with the hour's top story:

". . . Boston police detectives have identified the body of this morning's presumed suicide. The man was apparently a local private detective by the name of Mike Petri. When asked if the police were still ruling it a suicide, Lieutenant Sid Tanner commented, 'We're still looking into it.' But speculation is, this latest development has given the police reason to re-examine their original assumption that Petri had jumped from the fifteen-story building . . ."

CHAPTER

19

Rosco was glad Belle hadn't been riding with him when he made the abrupt U-turn on Blue Hill Avenue and headed north, back toward Boston. He was certain he would never have heard the end of it—but he could easily imagine her response. "I can't believe you just pulled a stunt like that!" she would have gasped. "And you *never* get caught! That's what drives me nuts! If I did something like that, I'd be in jail right now."

He smiled at the picture but winced slightly, remembering her warning to drive carefully. He shrugged it off and returned to the business at hand: picking up the car phone in his right hand, dialing it with his left, and steering the Jeep with his thigh. His first call went out to Al Lever at NPD. As expected, Al had the number for Sid Tanner's direct line at the Boston Police Department. However, in typical Lever fashion, the number was only dispensed after two minutes of need-to-know, and what's-this-all-about questioning. Finally, Lever rang off with, "Keep me posted . . . and, dammit, I mean that, Poly—crates." The name was given Al's habitual three-syllable, mangled makeover—an old joke he never tired of.

"You'll be the first to know, Al."

A sigh, followed by a click ended the conversation.

Rosco then punched in the number to Tanner's private line. It was answered with a clipped, "Tanner."

"Lieutenant, my name is Rosco Polycrates, and—"

"Right, Polycrates," Tanner interrupted, "thanks for getting back to me so quickly."

"Huh?" was all Rosco could seem to come up with.

"You feel like taking a ride up to Boston? I work better face-to-face."

"Wait. You want to see me? You called me?"

"Yeah. Check your answering machine . . . Look, we had a suicide up here last night. A jumper. Did a swan dive off the fifteenth floor. Found by a jogger this morning. No note. All I got is a Newcastle Yellow Pages with the PI section dogeared. Your name's underlined in red. Ever hear of a guy named Mike Petri?"

"Yeah . . . Yeah, I have," was Rosco's startled answer. He didn't elaborate. "Where are you, Lieutenant?"

"Sixth District. South Boston. You know it?"

Rosco glanced at his watch. "Yes. I'm in town. I'll be there in fifteen minutes."

Rosco hadn't been in Boston's Sixth District Headquarters in nearly eight years, but it hadn't changed much. The same chaotic whirlwind of activity was omnipresent—so much so, that he almost suspected these were the exact same perpetrators, going through the exact same arguments with identical pushing and shoving matches, duplicate cries of "False arrest!" and "Police brutality!": all directed at the same roster of officers they'd wrangled with eight years before. Rosco was tempted to say, "Are you guys making a movie here, or what?"

but he didn't. Instead, he strolled up to the duty sergeant, presented his I.D., and said, "I've got an appointment with Lieutenant Tanner."

"PI, huh?" the sergeant said as he looked Rosco over with a fair amount of disdain. "How'd you get through the metal detector, wise guy?"

Rosco lifted his sports jacket above his waist, revealing his belt and shirt. "No piece," was all he said.

"Huh." The cop pointed. "Tanner's down the hallway. Third door on the right."

"Thanks." Rosco retrieved his I.D. and followed the hall until he reached Tanner's glass-paneled door. He could see the detective on the other side, sitting on his desk with his back to Rosco, telephone in hand, apparently leveling an angry tirade at the person on the other end. Rosco tapped lightly three times on the glass. Tanner turned, motioned for him to enter, and slammed the receiver back into its cradle.

"Problems?" Rosco said as he closed the door.

Tanner rolled his eyes, walked toward Rosco, and offered his hand. He was a big man; probably six feet eight inches tall, and built like a weight lifter who spent a good deal of time at the gym. His head was shaved, which made it impossible to determine his age. He could have been anywhere between thirty-five and fifty.

"Problems?" Tanner repeated, moving his head from side to side slowly. "You don't know from problems . . . Listen to this: The captain gives me two tickets to tomorrow's Pats game, right? I put them in my jacket for safekeeping. And then last night? After work? I take the jacket to the cleaners. Now, I *know* those tickets were in that jacket. I'd bet a month's salary on it. But do you think these clowns down at C.J.'s Laundry know anything about those tickets? . . . Hell, no." Tanner groaned and then put on a voice that was intended to sound like an insincere dry-cleaning employee as he moved back behind his desk and sat. " 'Oh, no, Mr. Tanner, we didn't find any tickets . . . For this Sunday's football game, you say? Maybe you left them in your car?' . . . In my car? My car? Why the hell would anyone in their right mind leave football tickets in their car?"

"Rhetorical question?"

Tanner smiled at Rosco. "Right. You must be Polycrates. Lever told me you were a smart-ass. Have a seat."

Rosco sat. "Al called you?"

"Don't worry, he put in a good word for you . . . said you and he were once partners . . . Actually, I was the first cop on the scene when your father-in-law croaked . . . ah, passed away, remember? That's when I got to know Lever. Anyway, he said you were on the level. Not like the rest of the sleazy PIs we have roaming around this town."

Rosco recalled the situation Tanner was referring to, but he also remembered that Boston had made an inaccurate assumption when Belle's father had died—misinformation that had cost time and energy and maybe another life, so Rosco balked when it came to bending over backward to thank him for his previous assistance. Instead Rosco returned to the case at hand. "Are we putting Mike Petri in the sleazy PI category?"

Tanner laughed. "The sleaziest. Never pegged him for suicide, though. Anyway, like I said, no note . . . unless we consider your phone number scratched on a pad by the phone a note. It was also underlined in the Yellow Pages. I checked with the phone company. He talked with you for less than a minute. But hey, you know that. More importantly, I'd like to know what he had to say to you."

Rosco shrugged. "He got my answering machine. Didn't even bother to leave his number. So I couldn't call him back."

"Do you still have the tape?"

"Nope. Someone recorded over it this morning."

"What did he say exactly?"

"It was short. Something like, 'My name's Mike Petri. I need to talk to you. It's important. I'll call back tomorrow.' And that was it."

" 'Important,' huh?"

"That's what he said." Tanner was quiet, so Rosco pushed on. "Although I have to tell you, it doesn't sound to me like a guy planning to kill himself would leave that kind of message . . . unless saying that he'd call back was some kind of a joke—or a decoy. But what's the point in that if no one knows what the game is?"

At the word "game," Tanner's face tightened. "Right," he said. "Game . . . Look, Polycrates, Mike Petri was a drunk, a flat-out, on-your-face-in-the-street boozer. We had more complaints on him than Tetley has tea leaves. As of yesterday he had three clients suing him for *theft of services*. He was this close"—Tanner raised his hand and held his thumb and index finger a quarter inch apart—"this close to having his license yanked, *along* with his pistol permit. The guy was a class-A loser. It was all over for him and he knew it." Tanner shrugged. "What more can I say? His blood-alcohol level was close to two-point-oh when we scraped him off the sidewalk."

"I don't know . . ." Rosco answered slowly, "but experience tells me that if a person has a handgun in the house, it's the weapon of choice when it comes to suicide . . . Have you placed a time of death?"

"Four-eighteen in the morning."

"Impressive accuracy."

"Ahhh, his watch was as smashed as his skull. MEs love it when things work out like that. The jogger didn't find him until around six, though."

"Was he wearing his piece? Fully clothed?"

"His gun was on the nightstand. In plain view. And he was dressed. Do you have any idea why he called you?"

"Can't tell you."

"Can't or won't? What are you working on?"

"Lieutenant, my current case is an open book. My client is Milt Hoffmeyer, and there's no major confidentiality involved. What he wants is to find out how the skeletal remains of an unidentified female ended up in his hometown of Taneysville. In fact, he'd love people to know he's looking for some answers . . . Crime busting in your backyard; the little guy fighting for a peaceful community—that kind of thing."

"Tell him he'd have my vote if he was in this district. Things need to be shaken up down in D.C." Tanner took a stick of gum from his desk drawer, unwrapped it, and shoved it into his mouth. None was offered to Rosco. "What brought you up to Boston today?"

"I was talking to a guy by the name of Gordon—the 'magnet magnate' . . . ?" Rosco paused for a beat, but the name seemed to mean nothing to Tanner. "He owns the property in Taneysville where they found the remains . . . But I'm not seeing any connection between Hoffmeyer and Petri—or Gordon." Rosco lowered his head and flicked a piece of lint off his trousers. "I'd love to know what Petri had in mind when he phoned me, too. Was there any sign of a struggle in his apartment?"

Tanner shook his head. "The place was a mess. But not from any struggle that I could see. Empty vodka bottles all over—the cheap stuff, too. Dirty laundry, pizza boxes; the junk in the kitchen sink looked like it'd been there for weeks. The bathroom was filthy, trash all over the place. And you know something? Just like you, this guy used to be a cop. It makes you sick, how low some guys can fall."

"As it were," Rosco interjected, but the comment seemed to go over Tanner's head. "So, Petri was a cop here in Boston?"

"Yeah. Before my time, though . . . I came here from LAPD ten years ago and Petri was already sliding . . . and fast . . .

Had a rep for being a sleazeball even then. People warned me about him, first day on the job."

"How old was he?"

"Sixty-three."

Rosco shifted in his chair. "I'd sure like to know why he contacted me . . . Where do you go from here, Lieutenant?"

Tanner raised a hand and then dropped it on his desk. The gesture was one of total indifference. "It's a suicide with no next of kin, and *you* obviously can't provide answers . . . Where do you *think* I go from here?"

"Obviously not the *Pats* game."

Tanner scowled at Rosco. "Very funny . . . I *will* get those tickets back, you can bet your sweet butt on that—even if I have to burn that damn cleaners to the ground."

"Can I get a look at Petri's police record? Going back to when he was on the force? And anything he might have been picked up for since? . . . I assume he had some kind of sheet . . . because I'll tell you, I'm not buying suicide . . . Sorry, but drunks like him are already killing themselves. They're just not in as much of a rush as some other people."

Tanner gave Rosco a don't-waste-my-time stare. "So? The guy got hammered and *fell* off the terrace. It's too bad he didn't get to blab his heart out to you, but he didn't. And from where I sit, the case has dropped to 'no priority.' You want a sheet on the guy? Here's how it ends: Cause of death: trauma resulting from a fifteen-story fall and a very abrupt stop—which sounds to me like a pretty obvious and natural consequence of a dumb-ass act."

Rosco resisted the temptation to say, " 'Natural causes' was your opinion when Belle's father died, too." Instead he opted for: "I still want to get a better idea of who Petri was."

Tanner groaned. "I gotta clear this with the captain. And you know what he's going to make me do? He's going to make me go through the whole damn file, piece by piece, before he lets you take a peek at it, just to make sure nobody's gonna get *embarrassed*. Or caught with their pants down."

"Nothing worse than a cop with his pants down, that's what I always say . . . How long's that going to take?"

"Don't call me, Polycrates. I'll call you."

CHAPTER

20

"You makin' up another one of them crossword puzzles?" The anxious eyes glanced up, then blinked, but no other response appeared. After a long, suspicious moment, the eyes looked away while a well-rubbed eraser began daubing at the paper's edge.

"Look, hon," the nurse's aide continued in a conciliatory tone, "I don't mean to be a wet blanket or nothin' but I sent those other two you asked me to . . . and, well, what I mean is: You haven't heard nothin' from that crossword gal . . ."

As the aide spoke, she fussed—a continual blur of pastel-hued uniform as she straightened the graying thermal blanket on the bed and its yellowed cotton spread. When she finally reached the armchair in which the room's resident sat, her beefy and active arms tugged at another blanket that had been draped over the narrow and brittle shoulders.

"I can take care of myself," was the sullen response to all this care.

"Sure you can . . . Sure you can . . ."

"Stop!" the old voice ordered with a coughing wheeze.

The nurse's aide drew back, her mouth suddenly irritable. "Have it your own way, then! You want to look a sight . . . sittin' there in that tatty robe, your shawl slippin' off . . . be my guest."

"There's no one here to see me . . ." The statement was quiet; it also contained a sad and unsparing assessment of the situation. "Not like before . . ."

The aide's heart immediately softened. "There's lots of folks who want to see you! Why, if you just let me bring you downstairs, everyone would—"

"No. I like being alone." The eyes returned to the crossword. The shoulders hunched.

"Ah, hon—"

"Don't you 'hon' me. You know I don't like it . . . Besides, I'm busy."

The aide drew a steadying breath. Dealing with the elderly sometimes required a superhuman amount of patience and forbearance. "But I don't think that gal at the newspaper is going to publish your—"

"I don't care. That's not the point."

"Hon . . ."

"I told you, I'm not your *honey.* Never will be, either—not if I have anything to say about it! And I don't care about the newspaper . . . Besides, maybe she hasn't received the puzzles yet. You know how irregular mail service can be."

The aide nodded. "Maybe . . . Still, if I was you I wouldn't want to waste my time—"

"It's my time . . . what there's left of it."

The aide wheeled her large body around to face her charge. "Look, you don't want to sit all alone up here . . . I know you don't . . . You're just being stubborn is all . . . A body's got to have a little pleasure. Any doctor'll tell you that . . . Fun . . . a laugh or two—"

"I—do—this—for—fun." The words were evenly spaced and almost fiercely emphatic. "F-U-N."

"Well, glory be!" the aide sang out. "Maybe we'll get a smile out of you yet." Then she bent down and studied her patient's creation. "I'll tell you what . . . My shift is nearly up. What if I drop that puzzle of yours off at Belle Graham's house on my way home. I know right where Captain's Walk is. That way you'll be certain it gets there . . ."

The old face looked up in surprise—to which was added the very faintest element of pleasure. "I already affixed a stamp, though."

"I'll get you a replacement stamp." She stifled an additional "hon," then gave her charge a kindly and encouraging pat. "That'll be my gift to the project." The aide stuffed the crossword into its envelope and dropped the missive in her pocket. "Nothin' to it . . . Now, I'm gonna bring in your lunch . . . alphabet soup, animal crackers for dessert. Gotta get them choppers workin'."

Across

1. Appeal
5. Sweet smells
10. School grp.
13. Rock's partner
14. Shrimps
15. Tennis shot
16. Child's rhyme, part 1
18. Shaker Lee
19. Emcee prop
20. Its capital is Bhubaneswar
21. Beer option
22. Belt position
23. Aroma
24. Child's rhyme, part 2
29. Hook's henchman
30. Church vault
31. Certain serpent
34. Gropes in the dark?
39. Over there
40. "_____Souls," Gogol work
41. Scan
42. Child's rhyme, part 3
46. Boy Scout site
49. Dental exams?
50. Go along with
51. King or general of 1776
53. Mayday
56. Child's rhyme, part 4
57. Child's rhyme, part 5
59. Light bedstead
60. Aft
61. Mr. Lugosi
62. Many, many mins.
63. Heyerdahl, et al.
64. Soon

Down

1. June event
2. Ms. Anderson
3. Power source; abbr.
4. Franklin's '36 foe
5. "Pause a while from learning to_____," Johnson
6. Soulé or Greeley dreamer
7. Meadows
8. Arizona city
9. JFK arrival
10. Tartan
11. Silverheels role
12. Dogpatch denizen
14. Danger
17. Slack off
21. Building site
22. Work unit
24. "Typee" follow-up
25. Bar light
26. New Deal project
27. Road-race turn
28. Stitch
29. Crafty
31. "Fit to_____"
32. Capone had one
33. Doctorate
35. Auto style; abbr.
36. Charge
37. Lout
38. Berlin et al.; familiarly
42. Go for
43. Goofs
44. "Fix one's_____"
45. Corrida cheers
46. Bag
47. Detest
48. Runs into
51. Emote
52. Outer; comb. form
53. Exposed
54. Norwegian capital
55. Ollie's partner
57. _____and mouse game
58. Celtics' org.

TWENTY-FOUR SKIDDOO

CHAPTER

21

Twenty-four Skiddoo. Belle's eyes glanced from the crossword's title to the clues as she passed through her living room and into her office. She was speaking to Rosco on the portable phone while she walked—and read. ". . . Okay, but you'll be home for supper? . . . Uh-huh . . . Uh-huh . . ." She nodded in assent, then cradled the phone against her shoulder while reexamining the envelope in which the puzzle had been sent. The stamp hadn't been canceled, meaning that the crossword had been hand-delivered and stuffed in with the letters Artie had left on his rounds—or, more probably, that the machinery in whatever station had sorted and redirected the mail had missed its mark. It wouldn't be the first time.

". . . And that's all you could find out about this guy Petri? . . . Okay, okay . . . I'll wait till then . . . Hey, no fair. You tell me what you've learned up in Beantown, I'll share what *I* found in the *Crier* morgue . . . Okay . . . Uh-huh . . . See you later . . ." Just before clicking off, she added a quick and loving, "Drive carefully," and grinned as he shot back his habitual:

"I'm so glad you reminded me. But, hey, you know me—Mr. Never-miss-an-opportunity-to-run-a-red-light."

"Smart alec."

Belle chuckled as she slid the receiver back into its cradle on the desk, then she turned her concentration to the puzzle in her hand. *Twenty-four Skiddoo* . . . a turn on the antiquated phrase *twenty-three skiddoo*. She closed her eyes, thinking: *Skiddoo* . . . an early-twentieth-century variation of the late-nineteenth-century *skedaddle*, meaning to hurry—or to flee . . . and *twenty-three*, which had been a slang expression used by telegraph operators to indicate dire news.

Belle opened her eyes, took up her red pen, and began filling in the crossword's blanks while muttering clues under her breath. "*Nursery rhyme, parts 1, 2, 3, 4, 5 . . . Mr. Lugosi . . . Heyerdahl, et al. . . . Franklin's '36 foe . . . Soulé or Greeley dreamer* . . . How old is the person who constructed this?"

For a moment, she was tempted to phone Sara and appease her fears by explaining that the fellow posting these anonymous puzzles was most probably a relic from a bygone era. But then Belle realized she'd need to justify her theory—which would mean getting into a potentially dicey conversation as to why choosing the clue *Ollie's partner* for 55-Down might be considered antediluvian. Better to leave sleeping dogs lie. Or in Sara's case, an octogenarian aristocrat giving orders to seditious shrubbery.

Belle cocked an eyebrow, shook her head, and returned to the crossword. Within a matter of minutes she'd polished it off.

ONE FLEW EAST, she'd penned for the answer to 16-Across: *Nursery rhyme, part 1. Nursery rhyme, part 2* at 24-Across was ONE FLEW WEST while the remainder of the rhyming clues at 42-, 56-, and 57-Across revealed the rest of the Mother Goose poem: ONE FLEW OVER THE CUCKOO'S NEST. Belle talked to herself as she reread the answers: "6-Down running the length of the puzzle: A WESTWARD LOOKER . . . 34-Across running the puzzle's width: LOOKS FOR A SWITCH . . . LOOK repeated . . . I wonder why . . ."

She glanced at the title again. *Twenty-four Skiddoo*. Twenty-four, not twenty-three . . . and *skiddoo* denoting trouble—even catastrophe. Then her thought process focused on the subject of the nursery rhyme. A cuckoo, she remembered, was a parasitic creature that slyly inserted its own eggs in other birds' nests while removing and then devouring several of the hosts' unborn offspring . . . Then, when the young cuckoo was hatched—usually in advance of its foster siblings—it repeated the same murderous pattern by burrowing under unhatched eggs, thrusting them from the nest, and then demanding so much food and care that the unsuspecting adoptive parents starved their natural babies in order to appease the hungry interloper.

Belle grimaced, cupped her chin in her hand. Cuckoo clock . . . crazy as a . . . She stood and walked to the window, where she idly watched what appeared to be a swarm of sparrows hopping and fluttering across her garden grass or swooping up into the trees. Something felt unsettling about this crossword. It wasn't the constructor's anonymity—the previous two had also failed to indicate the creator's name—no, it was the tenor of the puzzle. "Twenty-three," she muttered; "Danger . . . danger . . . danger—"

She gasped, then stared at the title again. Could the number indicate that she was supposed to pay attention to the answer to 24-Down? OMOO? Melville's classic novel, sure, but also the Polynesian word for a rover. And then, 24-Across? WEST . . . Go WEST, she thought, rove, hurry, skedaddle, SKIDDOO WESTWARD. And what's west of Newcastle? . . . Taneysville.

Belle yanked open a desk drawer and retrieved the two prior anonymous crosswords. *Swap Meet,* she read silently; *A Burning Question.* She glanced over the answers: SMOKE AND MIRRORS . . . SMOKE SCREEN . . . SMOKE 'EM OUT.

She looked at her watch. It was nearly three P.M. She'd have time to drive out to Taneysville, do some private sleuthing around, and be back by eight. Kit's evening walk and supper would be a little later than usual—but not by much.

Belle grabbed a pad of paper, wrote a quick note to Rosco, snatched up her purse, threw on a winter jacket, and bolted for the door.

It was the smell she noticed first; it invaded the car's interior even with the windows rolled up and the heater on. A smell of fire—of a large fire. Belle glanced at the woods to her right and left, but could see no smoke or distant flame. The road descending the hill was likewise clear, but as the pavement turned sharply to the right and began climbing another hill, she realized the acrid scent was increasing. Something big was burning, and it was in the vicinity of Taneysville.

Belle pushed ahead, but at a slower speed. Then, sure enough, there was the sudden wail of a fire engine, horn blaring, siren screaming. The sound grew closer to her; she expected the vehicle to race into view at any moment. Then, eerily, the noise ceased, leaving the landscape quieter than it had been before. She guessed the truck had reached its destination.

Belle's car climbed another hill—the official entry into the hamlet of Taneysville—and on the left was the cause for alarm. At the end of a tree-lined lane, a house was being engulfed in flames. Volunteer firemen darted to and fro;

neighbors gawked at a safer distance. The hiss of the water hoses, the shouts rising from those trying to save the building, the growling roar of the fire itself, was nearly deafening.

Belle pulled off the road and parked, then stepped from her car, transfixed by the primordial power of the ever-growing flame. Hot cinders sparked through air which seemed scalded. Orders, questions, barked-out answers competed with the crackle and crash erupting from the burning building.

An ambulance tore up the road, and jerked to a halt as a tall woman leapt out. "Amanda!" Belle heard someone shout, "Get back! You won't be doin' us no good if you get yourself burned!"

A knot of less intrepid townspeople huddled near Belle; others were hurrying up the hill, a stream of worry and fear and bewilderment. Belle could see a church spire in the hollow below, and past it, beyond yards and border trees now denuded and black, what she knew to be the town itself.

"Oh my," Belle heard a nearby woman sigh. She was middle-aged, plump, and her face was the picture of compassionate concern. "Oh, Curtis . . . It's just too . . ."

Curtis put his right arm around the woman, who stiffened ever so slightly. "What will people think?" she murmured, but his response was drowned by a sudden whoosh of flame exploding through the edifice's third-floor windows, sending a cascade of sparks into the night air.

"Ain't gonna save 'er now," a barrel-shaped man with an enormous mustache hollered to a younger companion, who nodded once, his eyes glued to the blaze.

Another man, slight with stiff white hair, was also trying to yell over the roar. ". . . Well, what do you expect, Gus? Empty place like that. 'Attractive nuisance,' like I've been sayin' all along . . . Probably been a bunch of kids playin'

around in there . . . Up to no good, as most of these kids are
nowadays—"

"I'll tell you, John, the place is beginning to seem like it's
got the devil's mark on it—"

"Don't say such things!" the plump woman argued forci-
bly, but Gus was not to be dissuaded.

"Maybe it's judgment day we're lookin' at here . . . Maybe
Lonnie and them police down in Newcastle is out-and-out
wrong about that girl's body bein' carted up here and dumped
in the garden. Maybe old Quigley—"

Curtis interrupted. "Rumors, Gus. Just rumors. And
there's no reason for any of us to revisit that." As he spoke,
he discreetly removed his right arm from the plump woman's
shoulders, pulling his left hand from his coat pocket. Belle
caught the glare of metal, and instinctively drew back, while
Curtis, aware of being observed, slid the prosthetic hook back
inside his coat. "Gossip only hurts the innocent. You should
know that as well as anyone, Gus."

"Alls I know is that old man Quigley . . ."

But the rest of Gus's theory disappeared in the fiery wind.

CHAPTER

22

It was a gloomy little band that sat in Trinity Church's undercroft following Sunday service the next morning: Warden John Stark at the imperious head of the table, Curtis Plano solidly beside him, Sylvia nestled close to Curtis, treasurer Gustavus Waterwick looking rattled and somber, a deflated Father Matthew, and, as far away as tact would allow, junior warden Milton Hoffmeyer, who kept nodding his head in the ponderous manner Stark had never been able to abide.

". . . So, Milt . . . you're suggesting we do *nothing?* Just like you did *last* week?" Stark's sharp eyes glittered with outrage. "We sit here on our hands and wait for another—"

"I'm not saying *nothing,* John. I'm simply advising caution. Don't jump in too fast—"

"Caution almost got the church burnt to smithereens last night—"

"Now John, you know that's not the case. For one thing, the wind wasn't coming out of—"

"I don't give a fig what direction the wind took—or didn't take! Why, if one of those embers had—"

"Well, one of those embers *didn't*! And I think your notion of attacking Alex Gordon is—"

"I'm not saying *attack*—!"

"You most certainly are, John," was Hoffmeyer's uncharacteristically stern reply. "You're suggesting an ultimatum that would—"

"Well, what's your idea then, Milt? Send a sympathy card up to Boston? 'Sorry your weekend house burned up . . . Hope you'll be rebuilding real soon. We miss all the hullabaloo. Signed, the Vestry—' "

"Gentlemen . . . gentlemen," was Father Matt's quiet remonstrance, "let us remember we are in God's house. Enmity has no place here."

Stark's white hair quivered as he choked back a response, while Hoffmeyer glanced at the priest and nodded agreement although his expression remained surprisingly severe.

In the ensuing silence, Sylvia Meigs leaned forward and rested her head in her chubby hands as if she were silently weeping. Curtis patted her arm, but made no bolder display of affection.

"It was so awful . . . !" she murmured, ". . . seeing that old place just . . . just *disappear* like that . . . All those generations who've lived there . . . marrying . . . having babies . . . growing old—"

"It's God's judgment," Gus Waterwick interjected in his sonorous accent.

Sylvia turned a grieving face toward him. "That's what you said yesterday . . . I don't like that kind of talk . . . And I don't believe that."

Gus leaned back in his chair. He took a long time before responding. "I'm not saying the Quigleys were good—or *not so good* people . . . Alls I'm saying . . . well, you remember the stories . . ."

All eyes except Father Matt's and Sylvia Meigs's dropped to the vestry table. "You're not going to repeat those rumors about old man Quigley, are you?" Sylvia demanded. "Because I for one . . ."

Gus Waterwick didn't reply, so the librarian continued in her brisk but kindly fashion. ". . . What I mean is, that's all they were . . . just rumors. The Quigleys were *reclusive,* sure, but not—"

"Where there's smoke, there's fire," Waterwick stated stubbornly.

"They were our neighbors," Sylvia protested with some warmth. "I don't remember them ever making a bit of trouble for anyone."

No one responded either pro or con to this statement, so Sylvia looked up and down the length of the table. "Surely you don't believe those tall tales? Do you, Milton? Or you, Curtis? Or John?"

"They were odd folks," Curtis said at length. "No doubt about it."

"They were old-fashioned," Sylvia countered. "They liked their farm, liked growing things, liked peace and quiet—"

"I don't know about peace," John interjected, "but they sure insisted on keeping quiet—"

"Well, you don't like noise either!" Sylvia asserted. "As I recall, you were up in arms when all the digging—"

"Different thing—"

"Is it?" Sylvia stood her ground, causing Trinity's senior warden to back down. He did so with an offhand jest:

"Watch out for her, Curtis. She's a genuine spitfire."

Gustavus Waterwick leaned forward again. "That fire up there . . . God's judgment. Maybe."

"But what did—?" Father Matt began, but the other males

clustered around the table regarded him with blank, you-don't-know-what-you're-talking-about stares.

"Well, I don't believe in idle gossip," Sylvia announced after another uncomfortable silence. "Whatever went on up at the Quigleys' was their lookout. None of us would relish folks making up stories about *us*."

"But that boy they hired—" Gus began.

It was Stark who interrupted. "Never mind all that now . . . Water over the dam . . . A hornets' nest after all the residents have buzzed off—and you know what they say about poking sticks into old hornets' nests . . . Besides, we've got our own situation right here and now . . . 'Attractive nuisance,' just like I been sayin'—just like Lonnie and every other law enforcement officer will tell you—"

"Then you're suggesting the fire was started by kids, John?" Sylvia asked the question; her voice was deceptively soft and still.

"Kids or tramps—hoboes, as they used to call them . . . That's why I'm *recommending*"—John turned to glare at Hoffmeyer—"that we write a letter warning this Alex Gordon that his property is a magnet for troublemakers, and—"

"I wouldn't do that, John," Sylvia said.

Stark stared at her. "You goin' over into Milt's camp now?"

Sylvia shook her head, then finally mumbled a nearly inaudible, "I don't think it was kids that started the fire. Or vagrants, either."

Both Stark and Hoffmeyer sat erect in their chairs. "How do you know that?" they asked almost in unison.

Again, Sylvia's voice was whisper soft. She kept her eyes glued to the table. "Well, I don't . . . I mean, I don't know for certain who . . . Well, you see, late yesterday afternoon I went up there . . . I was out for my usual walk . . . I didn't mean to trespass, but you know where the property's gone all wild . . . there's this whole tangle of bittersweet vines, and I thought I'd cut some to make a wreath for the door. You know those twisty vines look so pretty all tied up with ribbon . . ."

Stark tapped his fingers on the table. Curtis Plano hushed him with a swift: "Let the lady finish, John."

". . . Anyway, while I was climbing around . . . down below where the old kitchen garden used to be, a car swung up the drive, with no headlights on; it was getting kind of dark by then . . . And I admit I did a stupid thing . . . I sort of hunkered down out of sight. I thought it might have been the contractor—or maybe a watchman the owner had hired on account of all the machinery being left exposed . . . And I didn't want to . . . what I mean is, I wasn't supposed to be there—"

"What did you see, Sylvia?" Stark demanded.

Sylvia drew in a long breath. When she spoke again, her voice was quieter yet. "Well, it wasn't the contractor or a watchman who drove up there. It was Frank Bazinne and his wife."

Silence covered the table. No one stirred; no one cleared a throat; even the old wall clock seemed to cease its noisy ticking.

Finally Milton Hoffmeyer spoke. "They were probably up there collecting wood for the winter. I know that's technically stealing, but, heck, everyone does it now and then."

"She was crying, Milt," was Sylvia's toneless answer. "Hard."

"Frank's not an easy husband. Never has been," Hoffmeyer observed, while Stark and Curtis Plano and Gus Waterwick kept their counsel. As did Father Matt, although his behavior was motivated by pastoral concern and theirs by civic worries. Bazinne was a misfit, a man who could bear a grudge for a long time; and it was a known fact that Frank—and his sib-

lings—was more than indignant over the hiring of "foreigners" to work the Quigley site.

"Did Frank see you?" Stark finally asked.

Sylvia shook her head.

"Or his wife?"

"No. I was hiding . . . well, not really *hiding,* but I—"

"And you didn't come forward?"

Again, Sylvia shook her head, then looked at Curtis in
appeal. "What was I going to say? 'Hi' . . . 'Nice evening' . . .
'What brings you folks out tonight?' . . . You know, things
aren't any easier for me when it comes to Frank. And with
his wife wailing away . . . well, I didn't think it was my place
to interfere . . ." Sylvia's voice trailed off, then she shook her
round shoulders, as if hoping to return the incident to the
past where it belonged. "Then they walked around to the
other side of the house . . . and I just . . . well, I hurried down
here."

Again, the room fell silent.

Again, it was Stark who took charge. "Are you all thinking
what I'm thinking?"

"Torched." Gus nodded slowly as he spoke. "Pure and simple. And it would be just like a Bazinne to take matters into
his own hands."

"That's my guess," Stark replied.

"And mine, too," said Curtis Plano.

Milt Hoffmeyer shook his shaggy head. "I can't believe
Frank would do a thing like that."

"Can't you?" was Stark's astringent response. Then he returned to Sylvia. "You haven't told anyone else about what
you saw, have you?"

"Not even Curtis—till now."

"Good girl. We'll keep it that way."

The table echoed with murmured assent until Father Matt's

CORPUS DE CROSSWORD • 161

boyish lilt rose above the rest. "But arson . . . well, it's our duty to inform—"

"Father," Stark's voice commanded, "it's time you learned how things are done here in Taneysville. Past time, I'm thinking . . . Now, Frank and his brother may be bad apples, and none of us may cotton to them, but they're part and parcel of this community; and folks around here don't turn against one another. We never have; we never will—"

"But you're talking about possible criminal—"

"Sylvia didn't see Frank start any fire, did she?"

"No, but—"

"And you didn't tell us that Frank was carrying anything to indicate he *intended* to commit arson, did you, Sylvia?" Stark's eyes leveled on the librarian's soft face.

She hesitated for a second only. "I just saw Frank and Mrs. Frank."

"And were they carting anything that looked suspicious? A bucket or a gallon can?"

"They weren't carting anything at all."

Stark moved his gaze back to Father Matt. "There you go, then. There's no point stirring up the suspicions of the Newcastle law enforcement establishment when there's nothing to it. It's a rumor at this point, and we have no call to spread it."

"But—"

"No buts about it, Father."

"We can't obstruct justice—"

"No one's obstructing anything, Father."

"But I—"

"You've been serving our church very well, Father. We like you, and we admire you." Stark looked into the eyes of the other vestry members. "I know I speak for us all when I say that you would be missed if you left."

Aware of this threat or not, the priest persisted in his argument. "But Lonnie Tucker's a long-standing member of the community. Surely he should be informed—"

"If I were you, Father," was Stark's decisive reply, "I'd let the residents of Taneysville work things out for themselves. For instance, your notion about telling Lonnie? The first thing he'd do is run off to the Newcastle police; and that could hurt Frank . . . it could hurt him real bad—"

"The Bazinnes haven't had an easy time of it, Father," Sylvia added. "We don't need to make things tougher than they already are."

CHAPTER

23

"You three mouseketeers find out whose body was dumped out Taneysville way yet?" Martha's laconic New England accent turned *mouseketeers* into *mouseketee-uhs* and *body* into *baahdy*. As she spoke, she tossed three laminated menus on the Formica tabletop of the corner booth at Lawson's coffee shop. Top dog at this Newcastle institution, the vivid pink of Martha's uniform matched the color of the banquette, the counter, the stools, and even the walls of the establishment. None of Lawson's many regulars knew which had come first: the coffee shop's unique color scheme or the head waitress's choice in clothing shade.

"Would it be impossible for you to bring us some coffee first and ask questions later, Martha?" was Al Lever's gruff response. "Besides it's musketeers, not mouse—"

"Hey, Al. You're the one who's hired to smell *rats*, not me." Martha laughed at her own joke, creating the rustle and creak of extra-strength undergarments not commonly heard in the twenty-first century. "I thought I brought you guys your coffees." She made a point of looking into Rosco's cup and then Belle's. "Nope, I guess not . . . Back in a jif."

Al groaned—albeit softly.

"A might touchy for a late Sunday morning, aren't we?" Martha observed. "You know what they say about caffeine, Al . . . it's an addiction. That's what they say."

"Spare me, Martha. I hear that kind of talk enough at home. That's why I come here."

"Well, maybe you should start listening to your little missus." With that she bustled off while Lever uttered another soft, coffee-deprived groan, then turned his attention on Belle.

"Okay . . . what else can you tell me about what happened in Taneysville last night?"

"I just saw the fire, Al—"

But Belle's recitation was interrupted by the waitress's return, in one hand a coffeepot, in the other an order pad she rarely used. Martha took pride in knowing not only her regulars' eating habits but most of their life stories as well. "What'll it be? The usual for the lovebirds?" Her beehive hairdo nodded briefly in Rosco and Belle's direction: "Grilled cheese for my man; French toast for his lady . . . ? You, Al?"

"BLT—extra mayo." Al took a long and satisfied swig of coffee while Martha stared, her blond hair fairly bristling in surprise.

"You never have a BLT on Sunday morning. You always have flapjacks. BLTs are for Wednesdays—"

"Well, my, my . . ." Lever crossed his arms over his expansive chest. "The world is full of surprises, isn't it?"

Martha arched a disbelieving—almost disapproving—eyebrow. "Have it your own way . . . but don't you blame me when your entire week's thrown way off kilter. Not to mention your . . . well, you know. Hope you've got plenty of them purple pills." Then she softened, as she always did. "You want extra pickles like usual, right, Al?"

"You're an angel."

But before leaving, Martha couldn't resist a parting shot. "Keep an eye on him, will ya, Rosco? I think the lieutenant may be coming down with something. *Angel,* indeed." Then she sloshed more coffee into Al's cup and left, striding in quintessential Martha style across the restaurant while barking out orders to Kenny, the fry cook.

"Tell me again, Belle," Al said after a moment's pause. He pulled a small pad and pen from his jacket. "Who was there at the scene?"

"I don't know that I can describe them very well . . . It was getting dark by the time I reached Taneysville . . . and the fire had a way of lighting up faces in peculiar ways—as if they were all telling ghost stories around a campfire." She thought. "Besides, what does it matter who I saw?"

It was Rosco who answered. "People who commit arson generally return to the scene of the crime to witness their handiwork . . . Sometimes they're even the most obvious volunteer rescue workers or firefighters."

"That doesn't make sense," Belle replied slowly.

"It does if you're a firebug," was Al's terse reply. "So, let's see . . . You remember a couple of old guys . . . How old?"

"Seventies, maybe. One had white hair, but he was in good shape physically, very wiry. Smallish stature. He could have been younger than seventy—"

"And his buddy?"

"Al. They were two senior citizens! People like that don't burn down buildings."

Lever sipped his coffee. "Lonnie Tucker told me folks were pretty upset about the new construction at the Quigley site—"

This time it was Rosco who interrupted. "So the fire marshal believes the arson was an amateur job?"

Lever nodded. "He's still out at the location, but that was

his initial read. Amateurs usually make fairly typical and easily recognizable mistakes. In this situation, apparently there was a clear burn pattern commencing at an electrical outlet . . ." Al turned to include Belle in his explanation. "That's the direction in which a fire burns; it's also called a V pattern . . . Your pro will try to make the job look as if it were an accident—faulty wiring, that kind of thing—that's why they'll start it all off at a fuse box or attic light. The nonpro might try to copy that approach, but they won't get it right—"

"But the house wasn't occupied," Belle interrupted. "Wouldn't the electricity have been shut off?"

"Not if the contractor thought he could sneak in some interior work while no one was looking," Rosco answered.

"But the site was shut down," Belle countered.

"What can I say? There are honest guys, and there are dishonest guys. The ISD boys—building inspectors, that is—can't be expected to hang over these guys' shoulders on a daily basis. Speaking of building inspectors, Al . . ."

"Parker said he could stay away from Taneysville; give you a week to play Parker Number Two," Lever said. "He's only doing it as a favor to me. Don't make me regret this, Poly—crates."

Martha returned balancing three large platters in her hands. "Extra syrup for Belle . . . pickles for Mr. Diet-conscious . . . salty grease for the new hubby . . . I don't know how you keep your waistline, cute stuff." Martha beamed at Rosco, who remained one of her favorites, while Lever scowled.

"Age is all he has going for him, Martha."

"And exercise, Al." Rosco chuckled. "Don't forget I run almost every morning."

"Oh, please don't remind me, Mr. Universe. Mr. Perfect." Lever lifted his eyes to the ceiling and bowed to Rosco in mock reverence. "You know that stuff's murder on your heart. I'd be careful if I were you."

"What? Grilled cheese sandwiches and fries?"

"No. Exercise," Al growled.

"Enough, you two." Belle laughed, then turned to Lever; "I'm still a little confused by this fire. You've got a burn pattern starting at an electrical outlet—why *couldn't* it have been simply a short?"

"For one thing, the fuse box had already been upgraded— replaced with an all-new circuit breaker board. So a circuit breaker would have been tripped if the situation was merely an internal malfunction. For another, you've got traces of combustible material at the fire's point of origin. A can of lighter fluid is all it would take in an old structure like that."

"At the risk of playing devil's advocate," Belle continued, "don't a lot of construction sites have flammable material: gas for generators, paint thinner that could accidentally—"

"Sure, but in the case of an incendiary fire—which is how this one has been officially listed—the flame will burn a heck of a lot longer at the point of origin before spreading to the remainder of the building where those items were located; i.e., you douse part of a wall with gasoline, that area's going to see more meltdown than any other area . . . At the Quigley site, we're seeing extensive damage to the electric wiring in a *new* section, a small side mudroom. That's where the fire began, not the old house. And there's sleeving, which means the insulation has come loose, and a lot of beading up or melting of the actual metal. And the fire marshal is positive when tests are done on the ashes, he's going to find traces of something."

"I see . . ." Belle finally said. "And you think someone standing on the hill near me may have been the culprit."

"I do."

"That's the profile, the one that usually pans out," Rosco

added. "Unless you're dealing with a professional . . . which this situation doesn't have the earmarks of."

Belle shuddered slightly. "But all the voices I heard sounded so upset. Horrified, really. And why not? It was a scary and tragic sight."

Lever crunched down on a pickle. "So, aside from the two old guys . . . ?"

Belle went into a description of the bodies and faces surrounding her, describing, without realizing it, the vestry of Trinity Church; John Stark's wife; May Hoffmeyer (whom Rosco recognized and named); the electrician Big Otto Gunston (whose name Rosco also supplied); Stu Farmer, Otto's sometime assistant; the mason Gary Leach; Clarice the postmistress; Amanda Mott; and Frank Bazinne and his wife.

"Sounds like quite a party," Lever observed.

Belle's expression grew pensive. "Well, you'd have to expect the whole town to show up, but it wasn't any party, Al. In fact, it was really, really sad. I got the feeling everyone was sick at what was happening."

At that moment, Martha returned with checks, more coffee, and a mound of hot fries, which she set squarely in the center of the table. "I been watching you, Al. I seen you drooling over Rosco's food . . . So have yourself a ball. No one's looking."

"Except you three and my cholesterol count."

"And who are we gonna tell?"

"My wife? I don't trust any of you farther than I can throw you."

Martha winked at Belle, who looked at Rosco, who answered for them all. "Mum's the word, Al."

Lever drew the plate of fries closer. "Wipe that smug smile off your face, Poly—crates."

"I will if you'll do me a favor."

Lever effected his stagiest groan. "What is this? Blackmail by committee?"

"No committee. Just me . . . You remember Sid Tanner up in Boston?"

"Why do I break bread with you, Poly—crates? If you can remind me, I'd be real grateful. Because from where I'm sitting, you've been bringing me nothing but trouble. I should learn to keep you at arm's length."

"It's Tanner's arm I'm thinking about, Al . . . It needs a little twisting."

CHAPTER

24

"Sid Tanner . . . of course I remember . . . he's the Boston cop who first contacted Al when my father died . . . I knew the name sounded familiar." Belle and Rosco were walking Kit on the near-deserted premises of what had once been the lawns, gardens, and croquet court of the Dew Drop Inn, a seaside resort hotel built in the boom days of the early 1920s. The building itself was now boarded up, the turrets, dormer windows, cupolas, and porches slightly atilt and sagging, giving it a mournful stare as if it were pining over its lost youth: the "boys" of summer with their white flannel tennis whites, the "girls" in their party dresses of printed silk and linen. Despite the former inn's sorry state, Belle loved walking its perimeter, loved the proximity to clifftop and sea, loved, in fact, its sense of bygone enchantments. And that same affection had been kindled in Rosco and Kit—although the dog probably didn't dwell on the finer points of historical context. "I don't remember Al being particularly happy about dealing with Tanner," Belle added. "For that matter, I don't recall you taking much of a shine to him, either."

"Your memory has not let you down." Rosco smiled as he tossed a stick for Kit, who bounded after it, a flying fur ball of puppy enthusiasm and energy. "Of course, I never met Tanner back then, not face-to-face, but he was certainly a guy who liked to get things cleaned up and off his desk quickly— and that character trait doesn't seemed to have changed much. I don't think he's a particularly bad cop, just not as thorough as I like."

"Do you really think it's going to do any good to have Al contact Tanner?"

Kit raced back—with the stick, naturally; and Rosco had to pause, first to wrestle it from her mouth and then to throw it again. "I'm still not buying the fact that Mike Petri took his own life. Al seems to have a relationship with Tanner. Maybe a nudge from Al will get him to look into Petri's death a little closer."

Belle thought and, as she did, dug her hands deeper into her jeans' pockets, hunching her shoulders against the cooling Sunday afternoon air. "I know I may be stepping on your turf here . . . but wouldn't it be better to concentrate on Taneysville first? Petri can wait until after the election, right? One step at a time . . ."

Rosco paused before answering. "Something tells me there's a connection—"

"Between Petri's death and Gordon's skeleton?"

"It's a wild hunch, I know."

"I don't really see it."

"I don't understand it myself, Belle . . . But Petri did leave that phone message for me just before he *supposedly* jumped."

"He could have been trying to contact you regarding another situation."

"You're right. Sure. But either way, you don't leave a message for someone saying you'll call back, then take a wild leap from fifteen floors up. Unless . . ."

"Unless?"

"That's just it. I don't know. That's why I need Al to prod Tanner. Expedite delivery of the case file if nothing else. Get me some hard facts: priors, possible criminal associates, absolutely *anything* at this point." Rosco turned to Belle. "Petri was a sleazeball. No doubt about it. Dirty cop turned equally shady PI. Someone you'd never want to invite over for a meal—unless you locked up the valuables first . . . But he leaves a message . . . then jumps . . . ? Come on! It stinks. Something tells me Petri was being muzzled. In a permanent fashion. I'd also like to see Tanner send a forensics team into Petri's apartment. I want to know if he was alone Friday night."

"Someone got to him before you did." Belle nodded slowly. ". . . I follow that hypothesis, but I'm still in the dark about *who* your supposed murderer might be."

"Tree Hoffmeyer hired me to solve the cold case in his hometown, right?"

"Right . . ."

"And he alluded to the fact that his opponent might use the issue of an unsolved down-home crime against him."

Again, Belle nodded thoughtfully. "Right . . ." Then her head jerked upward, sending her fine blond hair jittering in the breeze. "Are you thinking . . . are you *suggesting* that the incumbent is somehow responsible for the skeletal remains being dumped on Gordon's property? And Petri knew something?"

"I don't know *what* I'm thinking yet. But you know me and my feeling about coincidences—"

"Where there's smoke, there's fire."

"That about sums it up. Seems to bring it all full circle, too."

"You mean, about the arson—?"

Rosco looked at Belle. "You tell me . . . Of course Petri died *before* the Quigley house burned."

They walked on while Belle began murmuring almost to herself. "SMOKE SCREEN . . . SMOKE 'EM OUT . . ."

"Huh?"

She kept plodding forward as she spoke, her gaze fixed on the leaf-strewn grass. "Those were answers to an anonymous puzzle I received the other day."

"Refresh my memory—did you tell me about this? Because if you did, I must have missed it." Rosco's tone had taken on a worried, protective air.

"Mmmm-hmmm," was the nonanswer. "SMOKING—"

"Hey, Belle! Hello? Wake up."

She lifted her eyes from the ground. "What?"

"You didn't tell me you'd gotten an anonymous puzzle."

"I told Sara."

"Oh, great. Fine. She's my secretary now? And what was *her* reaction?" But before Belle could answer, Rosco continued in an equally concerned tone: "Look, you know how weird and spooky things got the last time an anonymous puzzle-guy appeared on the scene—"

"That was Sara's response, too," was Belle's airy reply.

"Belle!"

She turned to face him, her face suddenly flushing and her shoulders squaring off. "Rosco. I'm not a baby, and I don't need my hand held—" Then she saw the change in his own expression: hurt mingling with something that fleetingly resembled humiliation. "I know I'm being blunt, but—"

"It's time for me to back off."

"I didn't say that . . ."

"You didn't need to."

He smiled then—a little crookedly—while she smiled

gently back, and after a second's pause held out her hand. "I'm being cautious, Rosco. I am! I promise."

"I don't know about *cautious,*" he said as he squeezed her fingers.

"Okay . . . *sensible—*"

"Still not an adjective I'd use to describe you . . . *Obstinate* would be more like it—"

"That's what Sara said, too."

Rosco raised his eyebrows. "It takes one to know one."

"And *that's* precisely what I told her myself."

Rosco shook his head and stifled a chuckle. "So, you received a mystery crossword, and decided to hide it—"

"I didn't hide it! Don't be so dramatic! It simply wasn't relevant—"

"And now it is?"

Belle looked at her hand in her husband's, their fingers so effortlessly entwined that she almost couldn't feel where her skin began and Rosco's ended. "*A Burning Question* . . . that was the puzzle's title—the theme being answers containing the word *smoke:* SMOKE AND MIRRORS . . . SMOKE SIGNAL . . . and now we have a case of arson in Taneysville . . ."

Kit barked and dropped her stick on Rosco's feet, but the puppy, for a moment, was ignored. "And you're guessing that coincidence has nothing to do with it . . ."

Belle nodded. "To quote someone I'm quite fond of: 'That about sums it up.' "

The couple resumed their walk while Kit, now bored with these decidedly dull, slow, two-footed creatures, raced on ahead, bounding after rabbits or even leaves that whisked squirrel-like across the rolling landscape.

Finally Rosco spoke again. "Maybe it comes back to the simple fact that Alex Gordon has an enemy . . . Maybe we need to be looking for possible motives out in Taneysville: a construction worker who wasn't hired—"

"And that person would be angry enough to bury a skeleton on Gordon's property and then set fire to the house . . . ? I don't know, Rosco. That's behavior that not only indicates a high degree of rage, it's premeditated—and pretty sophisticated . . . Besides, where did this frustrated local find the skeletal remains in the first place?"

"That's it. That's the ten-dollar question."

"Sixty-four thousand."

"Huh?"

"The expression you're looking for is: 'the sixty-four-thousand-dollar question.' "

"Eh, what's a few bucks here and there?" Rosco put his arm around Belle and drew her close. "So, what's your theory, Miss Mathematics?"

She nestled close, but her sigh remained one of frustration. "You got me . . . My research into Gordon's former wife's disappearance did nothing but point out what a swell guy he was . . . No charges pressed against the business partner who absconded with the dough, a lot of 'no comments' as to his wife's motives. In print, he never lashed out at her, or her new fella—just took it on the chin . . . a good guy done a dirty deed . . . Reading the microfiche—brief as the articles were—made you admire his sense of decency and fair play. And, although the authorities alluded to an impending inquiry into the missing funds, it clearly didn't become breaking news since Far Yukon isn't a publicly held entity. Apparently, it was up to Gordon to pressure the Boston DA's office if he expected an investigation of his fraudulent partner and wife."

Rosco let out a frustrated groan. "That's who we need to talk to, Gordon's ex-wife. But she's in California with his daughter. Sounds like she's keeping her distance, too—hasn't seen him in eight years."

"Eight years? She ran off over fifteen years ago. That's what the articles indicated. Meaning he's had contact with her since she left him . . . Darn, that scratches my other theory."

"Is this a theory you'd like to share with me?"

"Well, his wife was a 'trophy' type. You know, a real babe—and very young; eighteen when they married, and barely twenty when she took off with the partner."

"What are you getting at?"

"It's nothing. The numbers don't work."

"Well, let me hear it."

"Okay. It was kind of far-fetched, but I just thought if his wife was twenty when she disappeared—the body might have been hers. But it doesn't work if Gordon saw her eight years ago. She would have been twenty-seven."

Rosco pondered this information for a few minutes, then finally said, "Do you feel like doing some entertaining tonight?"

Belle shrugged. "I guess. Who were you thinking of asking over?"

"Abe Jones."

CHAPTER

25

"No. No, really, Belle, it was really good. Great, in fact. Really great." Abe Jones gave the statement more enthusiasm than was called for, then covered his rather disingenuous expression by lifting a mug of steaming coffee up to his lips.

It was all too much for Rosco. He exploded with a raucous laugh. "Nice try, Abe, but I've always been of the school that says if someone uses the word *really* three times in one sentence, it lacks a certain amount of sincerity. I thought you had more charm than that, or at least were a better actor."

"You stay out of this, you jerk," Abe shot back with a smile. "Besides, it was two sentences, not one." He then returned to Belle. "No, really . . . it was great. It's just that my mom's tuna casseroles are . . . I don't know . . . more tuna-ey, I guess. Hey, she's always prone to overdo things. Maybe she puts more tuna fish in hers. Who knows? But I thought yours was great, too. Really, I mean that . . . The spinach was an interesting addition . . ."

"Thanks, Abe. It did taste a little bland to me, but I followed the recipe exactly. The chopped spinach included. Maybe I should have put more cayenne pepper in it."

Rosco raised his hands. "Whoa, whoa . . . Let's not go back to overdoing the cayenne again."

Having just finished dinner, the three were sitting on stools around the work island in Belle and Rosco's kitchen. And although Abe Jones was well aware of what they wanted to talk about, the subject had yet to come up. Rosco and Abe had been such close friends, for so long, that conversation until this point had focused mainly on handball, Abe's long list of lady friends, when was he ever going to settle down and get married, the Patriots' chances of getting into the Super Bowl again, the dismal finish of the Sox's season, the best places to pick up inexpensive second-hand furniture, et cetera.

Abe set his coffee mug down on the butcher block work island and picked up a large unopened can of tuna fish that sat on the counter next to the refrigerator. "Maybe this is the reason," he said. "You're using Chicken of the Sea. I think my mom might use a fishier-tasting brand than this."

Belle took the can from him and gave Rosco an odd look. "Did you buy two cans of tuna?"

Rosco shook his head, fearing the worst. Belle opened the cabinet under the sink and pulled out the recycling bin. She began pawing through the empty soup and dog food cans.

"Forget it," Rosco said. "That's the only can I bought."

"I can't believe this. I can't believe I forgot to put in the tuna. I can't believe it."

"Well, it did lack a certain amount of . . . chewiness," Abe said—as politely as he could. "The noodle and cream part and the mushrooms were all great, though . . . if you think about it."

The three of them erupted in laughter; after they settled

down, Abe said, "Great coffee," and they began laughing again.

"Look at the bright side," Rosco said, "we still have something for lunch tomorrow." He took a long swallow of his coffee. "I do want to yak a little bit about this skeleton, before you hit the road, Abe. Have your tests yielded anything more specific?"

"I have definite DNA samples, but that doesn't do me a heck of a lot of good at this point."

"Why not?" Belle asked.

"Unless I can match my samples to a family member, I can't make an I.D. And I have no idea where to start looking for matches. We're not about to start taking DNA samples from everyone in Taneysville to see if they might be related to our mystery woman. Which, to be honest, I don't see happening."

"Right. I think consensus—at this point—is that her body was dumped there. The odds of the woman coming from Taneysville seem to be nonexistent," Rosco muttered.

"I'm having trouble with the 'dumped there' theory, though."

Belle cocked her head slightly and said, "Why's that, Abe?"

"Where'd the remains come from in the first place?"

"Grave robber?" Belle said, somewhat unsure of her answer.

"No, that doesn't work for me. I've got major organic decomposition samples from inside the rib cage, skull, and pelvic area—basically, the worms had a field day with her; and clothing samples were next to nothing. Meaning she was never buried in a casket—ever. Ergo, her body wasn't stolen from any cemetery . . . And it would also mean that someone would have had to remember where this homicide victim's body was hidden, then gone and dug it up and transported it to the Gordon property. Why? If you think about it, there's only one person on earth who knew of the whereabouts of this lady's skeleton—the person, or persons, who murdered her. And by moving the body from *another* location, and then reinterring it on the Quigley site, that person only brings a forgotten murder to the light of day. What criminal's going to risk that? . . . Unless we're looking at the psychology of the killer who wants to get caught—like an arsonist camping out at the scene of the fire . . ."

"Whew," Belle groaned. "I had this theory that it might have been Gordon's first wife. I guess there's no way the body could have belonged to a twenty-seven-year-old?"

"No. This woman was in her late teens . . . Possibly twenty or twenty-one, but that's it."

Rosco opened the freezer. "Didn't we used to have some ice cream in here?"

"I put it on my cereal this morning."

Abe gave Belle a strange look, and she uttered a blithe: "It was vanilla. That's the same as milk and sugar, right?"

"Ooohh-kaaay . . . I guess that makes sense. Anyway, all I'm saying is that I don't believe the body was put there *recently.*"

"And you have no read as to when our young woman might have died?" Rosco asked.

Jones shook his head. "No. The problem I'm having is this: If she was buried a number of years ago, the decomposition rate is completely up in the air, because the plot was used as a garden. Normally, textile samples can be a fairly reliable indicator, but with a vegetable garden, you have to factor in how often the ground was watered—you can't just analyze average rainfalls; and then, what type of fertilizers were used, and with what regularity. All of that information died with the Quigleys. She could have been down there for fifteen, twenty, *forty* years."

Belle spoke up again. "But the coincidence of these two situations occurring on what is now Gordon's property seems extreme, Abe—despite everything you're telling us about the remains and the risk of reinterring them. After all, somebody torched Gordon's house last night."

"Most probably, the two situations are unrelated . . ." Jones mused. "Or at least perpetrated by different people—"

"On the other hand," Rosco said, "they might be very closely related. What if the house contained some scrap of evidence, something hidden within the walls, so to speak, that would have shed a light on our mystery woman? Maybe even identified her murderer?"

"There's no question the Quigley place held a lot of secrets," Belle added. "And now they're all gone . . ."

"Any other theories you two would like to run past me before I pack it in?"

"Mike Petri?" Rosco said.

"Who?"

"Just another piece to the puzzle. I only wondered if you'd heard of him?"

"The jumper up in Boston, right?"

Rosco nodded.

"There is something familiar about his name. I felt it when I read about him in the paper this morning. Can't put my finger on it, though. How's he involved?"

"Can't put my finger on it either."

CHAPTER
26

"I'd call that a fairly inflammatory allegation, Congressman Spader," the late-night TV newscaster responded, her smile incapable of disguising her steely tone. It was becoming obvious that she was hoping to push the legislator into increasingly contentious statements. "Some voters might even suggest your words were provoked by the fact that you, the incumbent, are now trailing Mr. Hoffmeyer by nearly ten percentage points in the latest poll. Certainly not an enviable position to be in—with the election only nine days away."

Refusing to take the bait, the congressman leaned back in his chair while his face assumed a smug and placid smile. "All I'm saying, my dear, is that no unclothed bodies of eighteen-year-old girls have been dug up in *my* backyard."

"Arrrgh," Belle nearly screamed as she reached across Rosco to the nightstand on his side of the bed, grabbed the remote, and shut off the TV. "I can't stand that guy! 'My dear'—hah! *My dear,* you make me want to puke . . . And 'unclothed'? How can he say that? Come on, everyone knows that the woman's clothing decomposed long ago. And where does he get off with this 'backyard' business? Whose backyard?"

Rosco watched his wife, an amused smile slowly lighting up his face. "I gather this means we're not watching the news anymore? At least, not long enough to catch the sports report and find out who won today's all-important football games? Or maybe even see the highlights?"

"It'll all be in the newspaper tomorrow."

"Somehow highlights aren't quite as exciting in black-and-white still photographs as they are on a color TV. I don't know why that is . . ."

Still caught up in her state of righteous indignation, Belle failed to detect the tongue-in-cheek humor in Rosco's voice. "That self-satisfied smirk of Spader's? It makes you want to throw something at the TV. Don't tell me you could bear to look at him for another second?"

Rosco shifted his position in the bed slightly, so that he could face Belle. "You're right. I'd much rather be looking at you."

She leaned into him. "More than football highlights? Or basketball or whatever it is?"

Rosco didn't answer quickly enough, so she sat up a little straighter.

"I'm thinking, I'm thinking," he said. "Yeah, you're even better than watching the highlights. Although . . ." He placed his arm around her, and they fell into a long and loving kiss.

"You know what I was thinking?" she said after their lips parted.

"I hope it was the same thing I was thinking, but I suspect it might not be."

"Your brain only revolves around one subject, Rosco."

"You're right; I've never been much of a multitasker."

Belle flopped onto her back. "What I was thinking was

that *I* should go out to Taneysville tomorrow and do some snooping around. The newscaster's correct. With the election only nine days away, things can only get nastier. And until this mystery body's identified and the case put to bed—"

"No pun intended, I take it?"

Belle narrowed her eyes. "This is definitely a two-man job."

"And who would the other *man* be?"

"Okay, *person* . . . A two-*person* job. Don't split hairs. We've got to get to the bottom of this, Rosco. I couldn't stand it if I had to look at Spader's mug for another term. And if we don't learn who the dead woman is, and who killed her, Hoffmeyer's lead will evaporate. Mark my words. Spader's going to bring it up in *every* ad and *every* interview; just like he did tonight. No dead bodies in *my* backyard, my *dear*."

"Okay . . ." Rosco agreed, although he sounded unconvinced, "what did you have in mind?"

"Well, one place I should investigate is the library. A lot of these smaller towns devote major space to local information: homegrown publications, self-published volumes by neighborhood history buffs, collections of community newsletters, clippings from Boston and Newcastle papers that deal with the area, something like that."

"And this is a task you think I'm incapable of doing—walking into a library?"

"No, but you're supposed to be the building inspector, this Bill Parker person, whereas I . . . well, I could walk in and no one would pay any attention. I'd be anonymous. And if anyone questioned me, I could invent a phony name and say I'm thinking of buying a house in Taneysville and want to get to know the area a little better."

Rosco shook his head slowly. "Aren't you forgetting the fact that you've had national exposure in the way of magazine and newspaper photos . . . ? Besides, even if the entire town of Taneysville doesn't have a single crossword addict or gossip

188 ■ NERO BLANC

column devotee, a number of people saw you at the fire last
night. They're bound to remember. It's a small town, Belle."

"I didn't speak to anyone . . . And even if I was noticed, no
one has any idea who I am . . . Also, it was pretty dark . . ."

"But saying you're looking to buy property puts you into
Alex Gordon's category. We all know what they think of him.
No one'll give you the time of day."

"Not if I say I'm looking for a *tiny* house. I can pretend
I'm a nurse or something, tired of living in the city."

"Hmmm. Florence Nightingale, no doubt."

"I'm serious, Rosco, no one will recognize me. I can stroll
into the post office, Hoffmeyer's General Store, anywhere. I
may be able to pick up something. Where's the harm? Besides, you once referred to me as a subcontractor of the Polycrates Agency, remember?"

"I know . . . and I realized it was a huge mistake the moment it came out of my mouth." Rosco slid down in the bed
a little and kissed Belle's neck. "Okay," he finally said. "Why
not? But I want you to stay in public places. Don't get into
any cars with strangers, and don't go snooping around anywhere all alone, okay?"

Belle laughed. "What do you think I am? Ten years old?
Besides, what can happen?"

Rosco seemed to think this over for a moment before answering. "Nothing . . . I suppose. I was hoping to go out there
myself tomorrow. I'd like to talk with the two construction
workers who found the skeleton, but I have to contact Sean
Reilly first. Ideally I'd like to meet them at the Quigley site,
although from what I understand, he and his crew are based
up in the Boston area. Even if I can arrange to meet them,
they wouldn't get to Taneysville before noon." Rosco
thought. "Why don't we take separate cars—and remain completely unconnected to one another."

"Well, that settles it," Belle said as she snuggled up to Rosco, "I guess we'd better get some sleep."

"Ahhh, as bad as I am at multitasking, I haven't forgotten the first thing I had on my mind . . ."

She rolled on top of him, turned out the light, and said, "Neither have I."

CHAPTER

27

"I know who you are." The person who uttered this definitive statement was attired in oil-streaked, brown canvas coveralls; a navy blue knit ski hat was pulled low on a brow also dabbed with oil and grime. Belle believed the speaker was a woman but didn't have anything to go on except instinct. And her instincts, as she well knew, could be less than reliable.

"You're that big-time crossword editor over Newcastle way. Your picture was in a magazine . . . gettin' married, maybe . . . There wasn't no photo of your hubby." The speaker scowled, although Belle couldn't tell whether the expression indicated a general mistrust of people whose photos appeared in national publications or disapproval over a bride appearing without her groom. Whatever the cause of the sour expression, the fact was that Belle's many planned disguises were a total bust. If the first resident of Taneysville she spoke with recognized her, everyone was sure to learn of her identity—and arrival in town—within the hour.

Involuntarily, Belle's chin sank a little lower and her spine curved a little tighter. Rosco was going to have a field day when he heard about this exchange. Her very first conversation as the celebrated Polycrates Agency subcontractor, and she'd blown it. Not only blown it, but paid extra for her gas. The idea behind having the attendant fill the tank rather than doing it herself was to start up a seemingly innocent conversation, thereby gathering information on the town and its denizens while pretending to merely shoot the breeze.

The man (Belle had changed her mind) finished squeegeeing the windshield, then returned to the rear of the car and replaced the gas nozzle on the pump. "Want me to check the oil?" he bellowed while Belle answered a faint but polite "No, thanks."

As the change from her twenty-dollar bill was passed through the open window, Belle again rethought the person's sex. The hands were muscular, the knuckles creased with black, but they definitely belonged to a woman.

"Receipt?"

Belle murmured a dejected "Sure."

"You out here cruisin' around 'cause of that skeleton Lonnie took out of Quigleys'? A lot of gawkers been——"

"No," Belle interrupted while simultaneously cursing herself—again. What was she here for if *not* to talk about the mystery woman? "That is . . . well, of course I've *heard* about the situation, but . . . umm . . . this being Monday—the day I usually take a break from work—I thought I'd drive around and see some of the more interesting parts of the county——"

"And that's Taneysville?" The woman snorted. (Belle was now almost one hundred percent certain the gas station attendant was female.) "I've lived here all my life . . . my folks before me . . . and I ain't never heard nobody accuse this town of bein' interestin'."

Belle tried for a companionable smile. "Pretty, then."

The woman raised her heavy eyebrows. "In the eye of the beholder—like they say. I guess you and that guy Gordon—"

"That's the gentleman on whose property the woman's remains were discovered?"

The attendant's mouth twitched. She ripped off a makeshift receipt.

"I suppose you know Mr. Gordon?" Belle continued. "He must buy his gas here—"

The receipt came barreling through the window. "You want to be like all those others . . . come out here to gawk at the rubes—go ahead. But don't waste a busy person's time—"

"Actually . . ." Belle began, smiling as hard as she could while feverishly trying to figure out how to get this problematic conversation on track. "Actually, I was hoping to do something similar . . . find a quiet little town, a small house—"

"And make one unholy mess of it—"

"Oh, no, I don't intend—"

"Keep the locals off the work site. Hire a bunch of no-account foreigners—"

"But that's not—"

"I got me a brother who couldn't get work up there. No way, no how. A brother with a wife and little kids. Kids who need food, new clothes . . . How's it supposed to make him feel if he can't provide for his own family? How's it supposed to make *me* feel scrapin' together every spare nickel to give him and his missus? These are tough times—"

"I'm sorry, I didn't mean to—"

"Us Bazinnes have worked hard all our lives. What do they want? You can't get no blood from no stone!" With that, the woman turned and stormed back into the garage, leaving the gas pump and grease-speckled pavement deserted and silent.

Belle waited a moment before starting her car. Special subcontractor to the Polycrates Agency strikes out big time. She turned the steering wheel in the library's direction, not even attempting a hopeful smile.

"Oh, that would be Jeanne Bazinne. She works for Lonnie," the librarian answered while an expression Belle could only categorize as apprehension raced across her face. "She's a good person despite first impressions. Like they say, after a little soap and water we're all alike."

Belle wasn't so sure about this assumption, but decided not to voice another opinion. "Jeanne said her brother's out of work—that he wasn't able to find employment at the Gordon renovations?"

By way of response, the librarian (Sylvia Meigs, according to the nameplate on the desk) burbled a cheerful, "I'm really so *very* happy you stopped in, Miss Graham. Happy and honored. You know, we have a number of crossword aficionados in Taneysville, and I can tell you they'll be tickled to—"

"Please call me Belle."

"Belle, of course . . . And you're considering purchasing property out here?"

"I'm just in the initial stages . . . but I thought I'd take a look around, see what the village feels like, how the residents interact. The library seemed a logical first stop."

"A *lexical* first stop," Sylvia added. She beamed.

Belle smiled in response.

"Well, I can assure you that you have some very stalwart fans in the neighborhood, if that makes any difference: May Hoffmeyer, John Stark, Father Matt—"

"He's the priest at the church I passed?"

Belle watched another brief cloud flit across Sylvia's face—covered swiftly with a bright: "Yes, he is. And a nicer young man, we couldn't wish for. Plus, he believes wholeheartedly in reading! He even started a special story hour for the children. Even if they don't go to Sunday school, they get a good dose of Father Matt's graceful good humor. Although, he doesn't like *Cheeky Chimpanzee* series. Says the monkey encourages kids to act crazy, that they're liable to hurt themselves if they follow the antics in the books. You know, I never looked at the books that way. But I guess he has a point . . ."

Belle only nodded. "Do the Bazinne children come to story hour?"

"Frank's and Luke's little ones?" Sylvia laughed. "Oh, my, no!" Then her eyes opened wide and her mouth snapped shut around the final "o." Belle could see she was thinking. Hard. "Let me show you around our cozy space, Miss . . . Belle. You may not know it, but this used to be Taneysville's school back in the old days . . . a one-room affair with a second chamber at the rear to house a teacher, who was responsible for educating the students as well as maintaining the building, keeping the woodfire burning, and all . . ." Sylvia babbled away as she led Belle through the stacks.

". . . And this is where we keep pictures of our past and present . . . That's Tree Hoffmeyer, you see there. He's from Taneysville, if you didn't already know . . . May, who I just told you about? She's Tree's grandmother. Her husband, Milt, owns the general store. The apple doesn't fall far from the tree out here . . . Oh, my, I didn't mean to force that awful pun on you." Sylvia laughed, giggled actually, her round face breaking into childlike dimples. "Anyway, the town's awfully proud of young Milt. Our favorite son, I guess you might say . . . May lent me those boyhood snaps . . . wanted to inspire the local kids . . . That's Amanda Mott in that picture with him . . ." She hesitated. "Well, no matter . . . As I was saying, we're all mighty pleased for young Milt's success . . ."

Belle let the chatter continue, but her mind kept returning

to the Bazinnes. What was Sylvia Meigs avoiding? What was she purposely omitting? What was troubling her so much she needed to change the subject every time the family was mentioned? As Belle pondered these questions, her eyes traveled over the shelf of photographs: the library as a school; a waifish-looking, black-clad young woman standing rigidly among what obviously were less-than-enthusiastic pupils; an evening lecture captured in 1940s black and white, the glare of the flashbulb bouncing off darkened windows, the men sporting coats and ties, the women in dresses with dirndl skirts; then sixties Kodachrome and sixties fashions, although the adults were caught in poses almost identical to the previous generation's. Then snapshots of kids sprawled on the floor doing craftwork and drawings, a man Belle assumed was Father Matt reading from a large picture book, and finally several newspaper clippings yellowed with age. It was here that Belle's casual glance stopped.

"Who's this? Katie Vanovski?"

Sylvia Meigs did a little gasp and jump. "You'd know her as Paula Flynn."

Belle stared blankly, so Sylvia continued:

"An actress. In Hollywood. She started life as ordinary Katie Vanovski of Taneysville. A long time ago—"

"I'm sorry, I've never heard of her, but she must be a favorite *daughter* of the town if Tree Hoffmeyer's the favorite son." Belle smiled as she spoke, but Sylvia's expression grew suddenly taut and wary.

"Not Katie. She just walked out, walked away from the community, straight to Hollywood, and never looked back . . . Never kept up with her family, never shared even the smallest part of her good fortune . . . and I would imagine it was considerable. Not that she was a major star, but she was successful . . . had any number of roles. That was way before my time, though." As if she couldn't help herself, Sylvia continued with a quiet "Katie—or Paula, as she decided to restyle herself—is . . . well, she's Jeanne Bazinne's aunt. Frank and Luke's aunt, too, of course. Though I don't think they ever really knew her . . ."

Belle took all this in. No wonder the woman pumping gas was bitter. How would it feel to be barely scraping by when your blood relative was living in the lap of luxury?

While Belle pondered these issues, Artie, the mailman, casually slipped his day's offerings into her postbox in New-castle. The assorted junk mail, catalogs, and bills were dropped atop an envelope that had been placed in the box a scant half an hour earlier: an envelope that contained a black-and-white grid. Someone else seemed to have money on their mind.

Across

1. 35-Across, e.g.
4. Block up
7. Doc's org.
10. _____the ante
13. _____Maria
14. One of the Peróns
15. Winner
16. La La lead-in
17. Dudley Moore movie
18. Theater where there's no talking?
21. Oppose
23. Mr. Capote to friends
24. "Mother_____"
26. Lyric poem
28. Whacks
32. Dad's dad
35. Expert
38. Wrath
39. Word with steak or sauce
40. Reminder
41. By way of
42. Mint a locution
45. Turkish title
47. Hirschfeld girl
48. Acting awards
51. The good earth
52. Mr. Williams
53. Cap
54. Flower base
56. Desire
59. Vitamin doses; abbr.
60. Grill
63. Won out
66. Eleven leader
70. Certain acct.
73. Falter
74. Whichever
75. Also
76. Annoyed
77. The last mo.
78. Shad delight
79. Extra periods; abbr.
80. Summer in France

Down

1. Mr. O'Brien
2. "_____Got a Secret"
3. Amusement hall
4. Disavow
5. Rara_____
6. Portuguese territory
7. Iron or Gilded
8. Tuna _____
9. Cupid
10. Shoshonean
11. For
12. Diego or Marcos
19. Dramatist Thomas
20. Burns & Allen, e.g.
22. Try
24. MBA's goal
25. Mr. Parseghian
27. Apiece
29. F. W. Woolworth, e.g.
30. Just before Sat.
31. Ocean
33. Grease_____
34. Palmer with an army
36. St. John's bread
37. Remove
40. Retreat
43. Mr. Williams
44. Startle
45. Fool
46. Retrieved
49. Inlet
50. Court time?; abbr.
55. Scratch
57. Decline
58. "Cool"

"CHANGE" OF HEART

61. Headliner
62. Vegas game
64. Tax
65. Knocks silly; abbr.
66. Oft-used Latin letters

67. "Look Back in Anger" star, Mary
68. Bow
69. Bread choice
71. Sell out
72. Summer drink

CHAPTER
28

B elle recognized the car a full block away. Rosco's ancient
red Jeep, parked smack dab in front of Hoffmeyer's General Store. What was he doing down here instead of prowling
around the Quigley/Gordon work site as they'd discussed?
And the second question—the really big question—was:
How was she supposed to walk into Hoffmeyer's, order up a
sandwich to go, and avoid broadcasting to all and sundry that
the guy who was supposed to be building inspector Bill Parker was really her husband, i.e., private eye Rosco Polycrates?

"Darn," Belle muttered under her breath. Her top-notch
gumshoe scheme was obviously over before it began.

She pulled herself from her car and trudged disconsolately
toward Hoffmeyer's. She didn't even *look* like a potential
home buyer, nor did she resemble a city dweller out for a
drive through the countryside.

The picture that first arrested her when she entered Hoffmeyer's—aside from the timeless appearance of the place: the
floors with their oiled-wood planking, the antique cash reg-

ister, the wall placards advertising products long-since de-
funct—was her health-conscious husband removing a large
bag of extra-thick, spicy, fried pork rinds from the snack shelf.

Belle gaped. "Pork rinds?" she said as she pulled abreast of
him. "You're eating pork rinds? What about cholesterol?
What about fat content? Don't tell me you're actually planning to *ingest* that stuff!"

Startled by his wife's voice, Rosco looked up. He proved a
good deal better at concealing their relationship, however.
But then, he'd had a head start in the training department.
"What's it to you, lady?" He smiled when he said this, and
assumed a jocular ease: the look of a guy on the make. Belle,
though, turned scarlet at his words. Even her blond hair
looked pink.

Near Rosco stood a thin young man sporting a carefully
combed ponytail. He'd also been reaching for a bag of pork
rinds when Belle appeared. Instead of continuing with his
purchase, he now dropped his hands to his sides, angling his
face so that he covertly watched Belle while seeming to gaze
at other products on other shelves.

"I . . . well, I . . . I just . . ." Belle struggled for words as
Rosco held on to the cherished snacks. "I thought . . . well,
you're right . . . It isn't any of my business." She moved to
the rear of the shop and the sandwich counter while Rosco's
silent companion nudged him hard in the ribs.

"You don't do that, man . . . A foxy chick like that comes
up to you, comes *on* to you, you *smile,* dude . . . You *smile.*
You don't give her no *lip* . . . See, a chick walks over to a guy,
and *instigates* the conversation—meaning, she starts it—well,
you got it made in the shade . . . know what I mean . . . ?
Like, you're *gold,* dude . . . !" He put out his hand. "Name's
Stu, by the way."

Rosco shook it. "Bill Parker."

"Parker . . . right . . . Bill Parker . . ." Stu nodded as the light slowly dawned. *"Right* . . . You met my partner, Big Otto? Up to Eddie's Elbow Room? Otto told me ISD put on a new guy . . ." His concentration returned to Belle, who was busy ordering her lunch. "Dude, you *really* blew it with that babe. And she's a real looker, too. I wouldn't mind makin' a little time with her myself. What can I say, bud? You gotta take some lessons on handlin' the ladies . . ." Stu began moving away from Rosco, then immediately returned.

"Hey, you're gonna put them dang foreigners up to Quigleys' out of work, ain't you? Permanent-like?"

"Well, I—"

Stu raised his hand in a conspiratorial gesture, leaning forward as he whispered, "That's okay, bud. You don't have to say nothin' in no public place . . . Otto told me you was a good guy, though." He then walked to the rear of the store, hitching up his trousers and proudly flipping his ponytail.

Rosco followed close behind. His "subcontractor" for the Polycrates Agency was about to experience an interesting exchange.

Belle's incipient conversation with her would-be suitor was forestalled by the arrival of another customer—this one in a clerical collar; out of breath and making a beeline for the crossword queen. "Sylvia told me you were here, Miss Graham, and that you're considering purchasing property, too . . . Well, this is certainly Taneysville's lucky day!"

Stu stopped in his tracks. To say that his eyes were nearly jumping out of his head would be an understatement. First the schmo of a building inspector got the pretty chick's nod, then the nebbishy priest started trailing after her. "Huh . . . ? You know this lady, Padre?"

"Ahh, Stuart. And how are you? I didn't see you standing there . . ." Father Matt smiled warmly.

"Just fine." Stu seemed to have run out of conversational gambits.

The priest nodded and smiled at Big Otto's "partner" again. "In answer to your question, Stuart, I know Miss Graham only by reputation. I'm one of her biggest fans . . ." He turned slightly and extended his hand to Belle. "I'm Matt . . . Father Matt from Trinity Church."

Stu stared at Belle. "I *thought* you looked like somebody special. You been on TV, right?"

"Oh, no, Stuart, Miss Graham's a wordsmith . . . She creates crossword puzzles for the newspaper. Very clever puzzles, too—"

"Huh?"

Father Matt gave Belle his full concentration. "It's a shame your husband couldn't join you, but Sylvia said you—"

"Husband?" Stu interjected, then glanced at Rosco as if to say: *You and me both got burned, dude. Big time.*

"Miss Graham's husband is a private investigator."

Stu took this in while his feet began doing a slow backward shuffle. He moved close to Rosco and winked in stagy sympathy, while Belle stared from Father Matt to the long-haired electrician to the "building inspector." Rosco noticed she was at a total loss for words—unbelievable as that seemed.

"Oh, yeah, I read about him," Rosco said. "The PI who used to be a cop . . . Supposed to be a pretty tough customer."

A response finally found its way into Belle's still-wide-open mouth. "Maybe that's because he doesn't eat pork rinds . . . just so he can stay *pretty*."

"Dude!" whispered Stu. "Let's get out of here."

But Rosco put out his hand and shook Belle's. "Nice to meet you, Miss Graham. I guess it must be difficult being so famous that everyone knows you wherever you go. If you're thinking of purchasing property, like Father Matt here says, I'd be happy to do an inspection on it. On my own time—if you get my drift."

"Dude . . ." Stu muttered again while Belle considered giving her husband a swift kick in the shins.

"Thank you, Mr. *Parker.* I don't think that will be necessary."

"Well, you know what they say: It's a nasty job, but someone's got to do it."

Rosco tipped his Red Sox hat and followed Stu out the door.

"   Oh, Katie Vanovski . . ." Father Matt dragged out the name as he and Belle strolled up the road toward Trinity Church. As he spoke, his boyish face turned immeasurably sad. "That was way before my time . . ."

Belle waited for the priest to continue, but instead he retreated to pensive silence.

"Well, it seems to be quite a story, Father," Belle said, "a Hollywood actress and the family she left behind. I went to the library hoping to learn a little of the town's history, and instead—"

"Matt."

"What?"

"Matt. Please call me Matt. I haven't really gotten used to the 'Father' part yet—especially coming from people old enough to be my parents."

Belle arched an eyebrow, but didn't otherwise respond.

"I don't mean you, of course, Miss Graham. I assume we're more or less the same . . . well, the same *generation*—"

"Belle."

"Belle . . . Sure . . . okay . . ." Belle could tell from his hesitation that he was trying—but not succeeding—to put her into the category of peer. "Well, I'm glad to show you Trinity's archival materials, if that would be of help in learning more about the town's past. We have a scrapbook, too. A number of them, actually."

Out of the corner of her eye, Belle watched Rosco drive past, heading to the former Quigley place. He waved cheerily as he popped a large pork rind into his mouth. She didn't return the greeting.

"I guess you're subjected to a lot of inappropriate male behavior," Matt observed.

"Some days, it's more difficult to cope with than others."

As promised, the priest produced a plethora of documents for Belle's perusal. She munched her sandwich, making certain to keep one hand mayo-and-egg-salad free as she sifted through Trinity's archives. There were lists of marriage banns, wedding and funeral announcements, old service leaflets, newsletters, decades' worth of minutes from vestry meetings— as well as the promised scrapbooks detailing innumerable church suppers, Sunday school classes, and special liturgical gatherings. Belle noted that most of the family names were repeated through multiple generations: some existing from the church's founding, some, like Quigley, appearing and then vanishing, others, such as Hoffmeyer and Stark, remaining in the forefront. Nowhere was there mention of Bazinne or Vanovski.

"Why is that, Father?" Belle asked as she sifted through the piles of paper.

"Matt."

"Matt." Belle smiled as she looked up. Her question had been merely curious, but as she looked at the priest's unhappy face, she wondered what unpleasant truth she might have stumbled upon.

"I guess none of them have ever been churchgoers . . ." His words were quiet and halting.

"Not even for a wedding? Or a funeral?"

The priest frowned. "I try to reach out to Jeanne and her brothers, but they're not comfortable around strangers." His frown deepened.

Belle nodded. "It must be tough knowing a relative has so much when you have so little."

No response greeted this remark.

"I guess I find it curious that Katie—or Paula Flynn, as Sylvia said she was later known—never made any real contact with her relatives. Even if just to show off her success."

The priest sighed. "I'm not sure . . ." he began. "I'm not sure she could have done that."

"But wouldn't the town have been thrilled to see her?" Belle prompted. "Look at Tree Hoffmeyer. The library's devoted an entire—"

"The Bazinnes aren't the Hoffmeyers." Again, a distressed intake of breath. "Miss . . . Belle . . . I know the Bazinne family doesn't attend church—never did, in fact—but that doesn't stop me from worrying about them pastorally . . . And, well . . . I guess you could learn what I'm going to share with you from anyone else in Taneysville . . ." He paused, staring at the table, staring at his hands. Not once did he glance at Belle.

". . . It's common knowledge that the older Mr. Bazinne—Jeanne's father—was a rough man, even a cruel one. When he married, his wife's younger sister, Katie, came to live with the newlyweds. This was in the late 1940s . . . No one seems clear on what necessitated that situation—only that the sisters arrived in Taneysville together. The older of the two was Rachel; I believe they'd been raised in upstate Vermont. Katie wasn't even in her teens when they came here.

"At any rate, these are second-hand reports—although they're pretty consistent. The common theme is that Bazinne made life hell for young Katie. Sexual abuse has been hinted at; definitely there was emotional abuse, threats, beatings that were never admitted to . . . It's more than the human heart can conceive, and sometimes even imagine . . ."

Belle opened her mouth to speak, but didn't. In her mind's eye she kept seeing Jeanne Bazinne accoutered in her sexless garb, a perpetual frown creased into the lines on her weathered face.

". . . At any rate," Father Matt continued, "as soon as Katie turned sixteen, she left her sister—and Bazinne—and rented a room over Hoffmeyer's store, then went to Boston, where she won some kind of beauty contest. The prize was a trip to Hollywood and a walk-on in a movie . . . and that was the beginning of Paula Flynn."

Belle didn't respond for a long moment. She wasn't sure what information pertaining to the skeletal remains she'd been hoping to retrieve, but this wasn't it. "And so Katie just left? Left her sister, Rachel, with this monster?"

Matt released a long and heavy breath. "My understanding of these situations is that they don't generally foster collaboration between the abused; that, in fact, the opposite can hold true. Katie may have blamed Rachel for permitting the problem to exist, while Rachel blamed Katie for being . . . well, a temptation, a lightning rod, if you will . . . or just plain younger and prettier. Maybe Rachel was glad for Katie's sake that she'd escaped. Or maybe she was simply trying to save her own hide.

"Codependency is a weird thing. Victims protect their persecutors; families are divided by twisted allegiances. Who knows? Rachel's thought process could have been so subverted that she viewed her sister as 'wrong' or 'bad,' and her husband as 'right' and thereby justified in his actions."

Belle stared at the tabletop and the scrapbooks with their depictions of healthy family life: the beaming babies on their christening days, the engaged couples holding hands, the marriage portraits, the Christmas parties and Easter egg hunts—even the funerals seemed times of love and celebration. "What happened to Rachel after Katie moved to Hollywood?"

"Jeanne was born the year after Katie left. Then came Luke . . . then Frank seven years after Luke. Rachel died soon after he was born."

"So Jeanne grew up without another woman around." Belle's words were more reflection than question.

"It definitely wasn't a healthy situation," was all the priest replied. "But Jeanne won't talk about it. Not to anyone. She never has. As I said, all this is pieced together from stories I've heard around the parish."

"Is the father still living?"

"No. He passed away a good while back. Well before I got here."

Belle shook her head. "No wonder Sylvia Meigs was so unwilling to discuss the Bazinnes."

At that Matt's head jerked up, his lips pinched into a tight line. "Is that what she told you? That she was unwilling?"

"She didn't 'tell' me anything, but I knew she was hiding something."

Father Matt let out a painful sigh, then bent his head so low it nearly touched the table. "It's not Jeanne she's unwilling to talk about. It's Frank."

CHAPTER

29

Rosco was sitting on the left front fender of his Jeep along-side the burnt-out shell of the former Quigley house a little after one o'clock. A stainless steel box-clipboard rested on his lap. He'd already made an extensive tour of the entire area. The ground was still damp from the thousands of gallons of water that had been pumped onto the blaze by Taneysville's volunteer fire department. Smoke no longer rose from the blackened rubble but the sickening smell of the home's charred remains hung in the air like a malevolent cloud. He found himself wondering how many memories of holidays and anniversaries, happy times—and sad times—had gone up in smoke on Saturday night. *How many secrets did this old house hold?* he wondered. *How many births? How many deaths? What's been lost forever?* However he was soon jarred out of his private thoughts by the sound of Sean Reilly's pickup truck roaring up the now muddy entry lane.

Sean parked about twenty yards from Rosco's Jeep and turned off the engine. Sitting in the cab were two other men.

All three stepped out, and with Sean in the lead, they approached the Jeep. Rosco was surprised to see how relaxed the contractor appeared. When Rosco had phoned him earlier in the morning, Sean had seemed none too pleased to drop what he was doing, pick up Nikos and Taki, and make the hour-and-a-half trip down to Taneysville from Boston.

"Good to see you again, Parker," Sean said as he approached. He shook Rosco's hand and cocked his thumb over his shoulder in the direction of the other two men. "This is Nikos and Taki. They're my backhoe boys."

The two men gave Sean a look that clearly said "backhoe boys" was not one of their favorite expressions. Rosco greeted them in Greek and offered his hand. They smiled broadly and introduced themselves in Greek.

"Whoa, hold on there, boys," Sean interrupted. "Let's everybody speak in English here, okay. It's America, right? I gotta know what's goin' on."

Nikos shrugged and said, "Sure, boss."

"Well, Sean," Rosco started, "like I told you on the phone, I want to get a definite fix on this property. I want to know exactly what Gordon has in mind, so that when the police and fire marshal are done here I can cut your permits without any further delays. To be honest with you I'm getting tired of driving all the way out here in my own vehicle. There's something wrong with the heater and I'm freezing my rump off."

"Ya need to get yourself one of these king cabs, my friend—rides like a Caddy on the inside."

"I need the city to give me a raise first; that's what I need."

"You're just in the wrong business. Hey, you want some work on this job? I can use a guy like you who speaks Greek. I'm makin' out like a fat cat here." Sean smiled broadly. "I spoke with Mr. Gordon a little while ago, and believe it or not, he didn't seem all that upset about this fire. Apparently it was his wife who liked the old section of the house. Gordon's kinda pleased he's gettin' a brand *new* home out of the deal . . .'Course that's with a little help from State Farm Ins—" Sean stopped short and took a breath. "Huh. Maybe I wasn't supposed to say that . . . Well, hell, it doesn't take a genius to figure out he's due some insurance money, right?"

Rosco laughed. Then joked, "Yeah, what the heck, as long as he has an alibi for Saturday night, he's in the pink."

Sean laughed as well, but it faded quickly.

"Anyway," Rosco continued, "that's why I wanted your heavy equipment operators to come with you; just so we can be real specific as to where and how you'll need to dig once you get the green light from me."

"Hey, I'm with you, Parker," Sean said as he gave Rosco a semicongenial pat on the back that seemed totally devoid of sincerity. "I liked the old residence—from a historical point of view, that is. But Mr. G's ready to throw some big bucks at this now. He's already talking about doubling the size of the swimming pool and going with a six-car garage instead of four."

"So you're talking about new foundation designs, I take it? Deviating from the original plans?"

"Possibly."

"Okay . . . Let's have a look at the main house first," Rosco said.

The four men walked over to the site. The few remaining blackened and shattered timbers had collapsed through the main flooring and now rested in the basement, looking like a giant, and very dead, black widow spider.

"Are you planning to keep this original foundation?" Rosco asked. "I'll need to do a structural examination if you are."

"Nah, everything goes. All new construction, according to Mr. G. No damp basements for the missus."

Rosco turned toward the area where the new addition was

to be placed: the spot where Nikos and Taki had found the skeleton. "And the six-car garage? That's going to connect to the new construction?"

"You got it."

"So this revised foundation's going to be a lot bigger."

"Not necessarily. The garage still will sit on a concrete slab—just like before, only larger than what was shown on the original plans."

"You're going to need to do some additional digging. Have you roughed out those plans?"

"Yeah, I got them in the truck."

"I'd like to see them."

"Now?"

"Uh-huh."

Sean groaned slightly and moved off toward his truck. When he was out of earshot, Rosco addressed Nikos and Taki, in Greek:

"Don't get upset, but I'm not the building inspector. I'm a police officer from the Newcastle homicide division. I won't pull my badge out because my real identity isn't information Sean needs to know. Not yet."

The two men nodded in unison. It was obvious they appreciated being taken into the confidence of "the police."

Still in Greek, Rosco said, "The bones you discovered here last week were those of a murder victim."

The two men shared a glance, then Nikos answered, "We suspected as much . . . before we read it in the newspaper."

"So you've given this some thought?"

Both nodded but said nothing.

"I'd like to hear what your ideas are. There's been speculation that the skeleton might have been brought here from another location. Possibly only the night before. Is that consistent with the way you uncovered it?"

Again it was Nikos who spoke. "If that was the case, the

person who did it would need to be very clever, and even then . . ." He shrugged. "No, I don't think so. Even though the earth *around* the skeleton was loose, the dirt *within* the bones had been there for many years. The entire section of ground must have weighed eight or nine hundred pounds. A person would need to use heavy equipment to move it and place it here."

"And where exactly was that?"

Nikos pointed into the newly dug pit that was to be the basement of the new addition. "There is no sign of where we found the bones. It rained shortly after the constable removed the body. And the fire department has made a bigger mess." He shook his head slowly and placed his hands into the pockets of his worn blue jeans. "I learned to operate equipment like this when I was digging graves and repatriating remains on the Macedonian border . . . This is not an unusual experience for me. My thought is that the body was originally buried here . . . a long time ago. And had never been moved."

"I don't suppose you'd like to guess how long that might have been?"

"I believe it must have been over ten years, at least. Beyond that? Who can tell?"

A cold wind blew up from behind them, making the smell from the fire all the more pungent. All three grimaced.

"This fire was set intentionally," Rosco continued. "In your opinions, do you think this is the type of thing Sean, or Mr. Gordon, might have set up? For insurance money, maybe?"

Neither man spoke for a moment. Taki glanced back toward Sean's truck. He was just emerging from the cab with a roll of papers. Nikos said, "I have never met this Gordon, but I have worked with Sean for a long time. He doesn't need to do this sort of thing. He's an honest businessman . . . But then there is a lot of money to be had here . . . Who can say?"

"Hey, hey, hey," Sean shouted as he approached, "what's

going on here. English, boys, English. What the hell are you guys talking about?"

"Restaurants," was Rosco's immediate answer. "You like Greek food?"

"Me? Nah, I'm a meat and potatoes kind of guy."

"Believe it or not, you can get potatoes . . . and meat, for that matter, in a Greek restaurant."

Sean handed his roughed-out plans to Rosco. "Nah, you can keep your foreign restaurants as far as I'm concerned. French, Chinese, Italian . . . Forget it. Give me a steak anytime."

Rosco took the plans from Sean, returned to his Jeep, and spread them across the hood. The other three men followed him in silence.

"Hmmm-hmmm," Rosco said, inspecting the blueprints, "you're just adjusting the original drawings?" He handed Sean a pen. "Just initial the changes and I'll run it by the zoning board. There shouldn't be any problems with this."

Sean took the pen and initialed the plans.

"Apparently the fire marshal is labeling this blaze arson," Rosco said as he rolled up the blueprints.

Sean laughed. "Didn't take a genius to figure that one out. This hick town's been throwing up roadblocks at every turn."

"Any ideas who it might have been?"

"Hell, anyone. I've been harassed by every local yokel there is. Electricians, painters, masons, carpenters . . ." Sean pointed to his truck. "See that big ding on the rear fender near the gas tank? That witchy babe down at the filling station did that with the nozzle. Said it was an accident, but I know better."

"So what makes you think a fire won't happen again? After you've framed the place out? Or worse yet, after you've done all the finish work?"

Sean's face took on a disgusted look. "Nah, not gonna happen. Mr. Gordon's knuckling under; told me so this morning. I'm going to have to work with these clowns, put a few of them on. Mr. G says hire the locals, I hire the locals. Like buying insurance, he said. That's why I offered you a job; you seem to have a lot more on the ball than these other bozos."

Behind Sean's back, Nikos and Taki laughed silently until everyone's attention was distracted by the sound of another pickup truck working its way up the Quigley lane. Sean groaned loudly and spit onto the wet ground.

"Problems?" Rosco said.

"Mr. Lonnie Tucker. Taneysville's answer to law and order. What the hell does he want?"

CHAPTER

30

"I got a call from a concerned citizen," Lonnie Tucker said, stepping from his pickup truck and giving the word "concerned" more emphasis than necessary. "This work site has been shut down until further notice. I thought I had made that clear to you, Mr. Reilly? I'm going to have to insist that you all vacate this property immediately. You're setting yourself up for some serious fines otherwise."

Sean raised his hands in mock innocence. "Hey, nothing would suit me better, Constable. I was called down here by the building inspector." He cocked his head toward Rosco. "I'm only following orders from one of your own civil servants."

Rosco stepped forward and extended his hand to Lonnie. "Bill Parker," he said. "Sean's right. I asked him to meet me here. Lieutenant Lever didn't inform me that this site was still off limits."

"You know Lever?" Lonnie asked.

"Well, I can't say that I *know* him," was Rosco's quick

reply. "Personally that is, but I consulted with him before I came out here."

"And he said it was okay?"

"Look," Sean interrupted, "me and my boys gotta be getting back up to Boston. I got work to do. I can't be diddling around here all day."

"So leave," Lonnie said coolly. "We all have work to do."

"Right." Sean walked toward his truck with Nikos and Taki following. He started the engine, pulled alongside Rosco and Lonnie, and lowered the window. "Listen, Parker, you let me know when those changes to the plans are approved, and 'John Law' here decides I can bring a crew back onto the site." He raised the window and drove off without waiting for a response.

"Sorry about that," Rosco said after he was gone. "I wouldn't have bothered getting Reilly down here if Lever had mentioned—"

"Forget it, Parker." Lonnie shrugged. "I don't mind officials from Newcastle poking around; to be honest, I can use all the help I can get. I just don't want Reilly pulling any fast ones until we find some answers. He—or Gordon—isn't above suspicion for arson as far as I'm concerned. Folks can collect big time on insurance—sometimes a heck of a lot more than the original structure's worth."

"Sean seemed to think it was a local who set the blaze."

"Why doesn't that surprise me? What I'd love to know is what Gordon's insurance agent thinks."

Rosco shrugged. Depending on who Gordon's insurer was, it could very well be the Polycrates Agency who would be hired to investigate the fire. "At any rate, you'll be happy to learn that Sean plans to hire local craftsmen when he gets the go-ahead to return."

Lonnie laughed. "If he can get 'em. They're a funny lot around here. At this point they're all as mad as wet hens;

most of them wouldn't work for Sean if their lives depended on it. Of course, that could flip-flop come spring. Anger has a way of dying out when the rent's due."

"Any leads as to who that skeleton might have belonged to?" Rosco asked in an offhanded manner as he tossed the architectural drawings into his Jeep.

"Nope. That one's got us all stumped. No way she was a local, though."

"I understand the Quigleys had a teenager working for them back in the sixties . . . a blond kid."

Lonnie stiffened noticeably. "Where'd you hear about that?"

"Someone mentioned it down at Hoffmeyer's store when I was picking up lunch earlier. You know, come to think of it, you would have been a teenager in the sixties. Did you know him at all?"

Lonnie considered his answer. ". . . Yeah, sort of . . . Our paths crossed every now and then."

"Every now and then? I would have thought that in a town this small—"

"What's it to you, Parker? The Quigleys are long gone. Who cares who they had working up here?"

Rosco laughed. "Ahh, yeah . . . you're right. It's just that these kinds of stories fascinate me. You know, mystery body and all. Sure is a shocker. The way folks described this kid . . . well, hell, it seemed to me like it could have been a boy *or* a girl."

Tucker didn't respond.

"You don't remember his name, do you?"

Lonnie stared at the ground. ". . . Terry . . . I think."

"See, there you go. Name like that—coulda been a boy or a girl, like I said. Probably has some interesting ideas on the situation . . . if he's still around."

Lonnie glanced at his watch, but made no move to leave.

He then leaned against his truck, looked over at the charred remains of the house, and shook his head. An expression of sorrow crossed his face. "That old house sure held some memories, I can tell you that. Kinda tough seeing it like this."

Rosco leaned against the truck next to Lonnie. They were quiet for almost two minutes. Finally he said, "Terry was a girl, wasn't she?"

Lonnie let out a long breath; his eyes were half closed. "I figure I was the only person in Taneysville she let in on her little secret . . . Man, we had ourselves some fun that summer. Nothing like a city girl to teach a country boy which end is up."

"But she fooled everyone else, huh?"

"Yeah, Terry was really into weird clothes. I mean, it wasn't the kind of stuff other girls wore; and she cut her hair real short, too . . . See, her dad had been a marine—took most of the islands in the South Pacific during World War Two, then re-upped when Korea broke out . . . Must have been a real scrapper. He died trying to stop a convenience store robbery, back in the mid-fifties, Terry told me. She was four years old at the time . . . Anyway, she was really attached to her dad's old clothes. Wouldn't take 'em off for anything . . ." Lonnie smiled again, and looked at Rosco. "Well, obviously she took 'em off *some* times . . . But that's why everyone mistook her for a boy—she wore khakis and guys' shirts long before they were trendy like they are now."

"And you don't think Mr. and Mrs. Quigley knew she was a girl? I mean, wouldn't the agency who sent her out here have told them?"

Lonnie laughed. "Sure . . . if the agency had *known*. But summer programs like that—the kinds that relocated what they called 'troubled' inner-city kids—weren't open to girls back then. Terry was desperate to get away from her mother. Her mom was what they called a 'loose' woman—a different man in the house every night. The only way Terry could get out of there was to lie and say she was a boy . . . Everyone bought it, including the Quigleys."

"But not you?"

"Well . . . I had been befriended, so to speak."

Rosco brought his gaze to the spot where the skeleton had been found. "Don't you think you should have told Lever about all this? It sounds to me like your Terry fits the description of the body that was found—she's certainly the right age."

Lonnie shook his head. "I didn't put two and two together until I found out the bones belonged to a woman, but Terry was a little taller than me. And that skeleton . . . well, it looked to be about my height."

"How old were you that summer?"

"Sixteen. Why?"

"You haven't grown any since then?"

Lonnie folded his arms across his chest and gave Rosco's comment some thought. "I see your point."

"Have you spoken with Terry since then?"

He shook his head. "Nah . . . summer romance; you know how that is."

"Do you remember her last name?"

Lonnie looked at Rosco with more than a touch of suspicion. "What do you care?"

"Nothing really." Rosco cleared his throat; he sensed that any confidence he'd gained with Lonnie Tucker was rapidly evaporating. "It's just that I've got an appointment to see Lever this afternoon . . . He's supposed to give me an estimate as to when Sean can start up again. Anyway, I just thought I could pass Terry's name on for you . . . If you want."

". . . I'll think about it. Anyway, I've got NPD's number. If anyone fills 'em in, it'll be me. Got it?"

"Sure . . . Whatever." Rosco walked over to his Jeep.

"Guess I'll be heading back to Newcastle." He sat in the driver's seat. "Say . . . You've never heard of a guy named Mike Petri, have you?"

"Mike Petri . . . Mike Petri," Lonnie repeated. "Nope, can't say that I have. Has he done some work around here?"

"That's what I'm trying to find out."

C H A P T E R

31

"But Rosco, that's not what Father Matt believes happened." As she spoke, Belle was simultaneously opening her mail and a series of kitchen cabinets and peering distractedly inside. "He said Trinity's vestry is convinced that Frank Bazinne started the blaze, but they're also equally determined to sit on the information. 'Protecting one of their own' is how Matt put it . . . Apparently, Sylvia Meigs spotted Frank immediately prior to the supposed mishap. Frank *and* his wife—who was crying, by the way."

"Well, an insurance company isn't going to let this sit; and if they hired me to investigate it, I wouldn't let it sit either."

"The Bazinne family has had a really tough time of it, Rosco. I don't know . . ."

"It sure doesn't give them the right to break the law."

"I realize that . . ." Belle plunked the mail and a pot onto the countertop, bent her head, and made a sound that came close to being a groan. "What an awful story . . . Who can blame Katie—or Paula Flynn—for not coming back home?

And who can blame her niece and nephews for feeling deserted and betrayed? And *angry* . . . It really makes you hate the kind of world that lets people like old man Bazinne walk around loose. Look at all the misery he created."

Rosco put his arms around his wife and held her tight. "How about we go out for a bite instead of you trying to cope with dinner?"

Belle looked up, wiped her eyes, released a long and weary breath, then attempted a chipper smile. "Since when have you known me to *cope* with anything culinary? You're the chef, remember? I'm the one who believes that if you throw enough butter or mayo at it, the recipe works . . . Speaking of which—"

Rosco winced. Dramatically. "Don't say it. I know what's coming."

"Pork rinds?"

"I happen to like them . . . On occasion."

"Well, you sure kept me in the dark, Mr. *Parker*. Unless, of course, that was part of your 'good ole boy' disguise: munching on snack foods, ogling the girls, and making suggestive comments." She squeezed his hand, and smiled again. This time, the expression was in earnest. "Speaking of which: if Father Matt hadn't arrived on the scene, was it your intention to let the guy with the ponytail—?"

"Stu . . . He's Big Otto's 'partner.' Or so he likes to suggest. Seemed like a good person for one of us to get to know."

Belle cocked her head. "Don't try to change the subject, wiseass. I believe the subject here is a certain Rosco Polycrates—" But even as she was preparing to critique her husband's chivalry in regards to protecting innocent maidens, her fingers slit open one of the envelopes. "Well, look at this . . . Another crossword from my mystery admirer." She turned over the envelope. "And hand-delivered, just like the last one."

Before either Belle or Rosco could comment on the puzzle, however, the phone rang; while simultaneously an ear-splitting crash of crunching metal and breaking glass echoed from the street. The noise was immediately followed by a screech of automobile tires.

"*That* doesn't sound good," Rosco said as he reached for the receiver. "Al said he'd call to debrief on Taneys—" The words stopped in his throat. "Who is this?" he demanded after a few seconds. The gravelly voice on the other end of the line ignored him.

". . . you *and* your damn wife . . ."

Even at a distance, Belle could hear rage reverberating in the speaker's voice.

"Who *is* this?" Rosco repeated.

". . . I'm warning you, Polycrates—back off . . . Take a peek outside if you don't believe me. I doubt you want your pretty little lady ending up looking like that piece of junk you *used to* drive."

The line went dead. Rosco punched in the caller retrieval code, jotted down the number, then looked at Belle again. "Seems somebody doesn't want us asking questions in Taneysville."

He walked toward the front door, pulling his pistol from the holster hanging in the coat closet. Belle was right behind him.

"I don't want you outside," he said as he opened the door. "Whoever called is probably—"

Parked beside the curb where he'd left it was what remained of his beloved red Jeep. The windshield was a sea of shattered glass that now rested on the front seats. The canvas top had been slashed, and the shredded remains left to flap angrily in the night breeze. The headlights and taillights had been smashed; the hood, fenders, and door panels battered almost beyond recognition.

"Scratch one Jeep," Rosco muttered.

*   *   *

Al Lever eased himself onto a kitchen stool while Rosco finished detailing the Jeep's damages to the patrolman who'd been dispatched to the crime scene. Belle was perched on a stool nearby. She'd made coffee, but it sat untouched in four now-cooling mugs. "I can't believe none of the neighbors saw anything," she muttered into her cup. "The noise was so . . . so . . . Of course, we didn't get outside in time to I.D. the vehicle either . . ."

Lever glanced at her huddled form as he let out a heavy wheeze. "It's not something people really want to get involved in—even if it sounds like a hit and run, which you originally thought you heard . . ." He shook his head. "But this was a violent act, Belle. If I were one of your neighbors out for an evening stroll, I wouldn't want to mess with those guys either."

"Guys?" Belle asked. "You think there was more than one person?"

Al nodded. "With that kind of damage? Absolutely. It'd take one person too much time to pull off a stunt like that. Besides, the bozos who do these things aren't brave enough to go it alone; they're like dogs, they travel in packs." He glanced down at Kit and shrugged. "No offense, buddy."

"I'm sure there was none taken."

"Okay, let's go over this threatening call again, Poly—crates . . . By the way, the number traces to a phone booth. We're dusting it for prints. You're sure you don't have any vocal recognition? No speech pattern you could identify?"

Rosco shook his head. "Southern accent is all I can say, possibly from Texas? Who knows? He wasn't New England."

Belle sat straighter. "The attack on the Jeep came almost at the same second the phone rang," she said. "As if someone was doing the synchronized watch routine. If Rosco hadn't figured it was you calling and answered, we probably would have raced outside to see what the commotion was—"

"And gotten yourselves in worse trouble than you are already. These guys are serious about wanting you off the Taneysville situation." Lever sighed again, and leaned his bulky body forward. "So . . . let's talk about your last trip out there." He looked at Rosco. "You're telling me the townsfolk know who Belle is—both by reputation and by sight recognition—"

"*Some* of them," Belle interjected.

"Trust me, Al," Rosco added, "when Belle says 'some,' it's 'all.' News travels fast out there . . . And, yep, that about covers it: Belle's effort at undercover work didn't last two seconds—if that . . . The infamous 'Miss Graham.' " He gave his wife a smile, but the loving effort failed. At the moment, neither Rosco nor Belle was up to giddy expressions of joy.

"So, you've been more successful; i.e., the folks in Taneysville don't know what the famous '*Mr.* Belle Graham' looks like—only that he's a Newcastle PI . . . since they *assume* you're Parker, part two, from ISD." Lever ran a hand across a chin that needed a shave.

"Yup . . . that's me. Bill Parker with the red Jeep . . . the *former* red Jeep."

"Get over it, bucko, you were due for a new set of wheels years ago." Lever tried to give this statement a happy-go-lucky tone, but it fell to the kitchen floor like a ladleful of raw pancake batter.

"Okay . . ." he continued, "this is what's bothering me: The person threatening you is aware of your real identity . . . I mean, think about it, he knows you're married, knows where you live, what kind of car you own—*used to* own, that is . . . and he knows you and Belle have both been visiting Taneysville—"

It was Belle who interrupted. "But the only residents privy to this information are Milt Hoffmeyer Senior and his wife, and they're sworn to secrecy. After all, it's their grandson—"

"And I'll bet you a thousand dollars that none of the Hoffmeyers know exactly where you live. Which brings me back to what young Hoffmeyer hired Rosco to do. Simply get the goods on an ancient body unearthed on Alex Gordon's property . . . Sorry, I'm just thinking out loud. Sometimes it works better than drumming my fingers."

"And smoking cigarettes?"

"Nothing works better than smoking cigarettes." Lever paused, and rubbed his chin again. "Get the goods . . . Get the goods. But on who, really? On a murder that may be threatening to end his political career? Or are we looking at two different problems here? If so, that would mean the murderer is still alive, right? Because somebody has an awful lot to hide." He glanced from Belle to Rosco. "I don't like this. I don't like it at all. This Jeep business isn't just the work of some slippery politician manipulating the press. This has hired gun written all over it, and I'd venture to say that the hired gun section of the Taneysville Yellow Pages doesn't have many listings."

CHAPTER

32

Lack of sleep, anger mingled with fear, and the constant presence of Rosco's ruined Jeep didn't make for a great start to Tuesday morning. Belle wandered around the kitchen, making coffee, shaking granola into bowls, and cutting oranges into wedges while Rosco and Kit went on an abbreviated run—for the puppy's sake, not her master's.

Before embarking on these activities, conversation between the two humans had been minimal; even Kit, watching Rosco don sweats and track shoes, had been surprisingly quiet and sedate. It hadn't helped that the front door had been carefully locked when dog and man stepped onto the porch or that Rosco's last words to Belle had been: "Don't open the door for anyone. I'll be twenty minutes, max." Kit had recognized the tone: Serious. No fun. No frolic. No tennis balls to chase.

Alone in the locked house, Belle perfunctorily performed her household tasks. As she worked, her eyes were slowly drawn to the crossword she'd received the evening before. There it was, lying on the counter where she'd dropped it when the threatening phone call had arrived. Idly, she picked up the puzzle, but a sense of distaste immediately swept over her. It was as if all her feelings of frustration and anxiety were leveled on this single sheet of paper.

Why doesn't this person leave me alone? she wanted to shout, although her brain simultaneously produced an even more compelling culprit in this sorry state of affairs: herself. *A few mystery word games, and I go tearing out to Taneysville . . . What am I thinking? That the puzzles are going to reveal our murder victim—or who started the fire . . . ? I bet these clues are no more than a bunch of silly coincidences. I bet I invented connections that never even existed. Typical! Jumping to conclusions. Going off half-baked. What a total dodo!*

Belle half-sighed, half-moaned. She felt mighty irritated at herself. She stared at the puzzle, willing it to prove what a dupe she'd been.

" *'Change' of Heart,*" she muttered. "That's a lesson right there. I should get a change of intellect!" But, involuntarily, her brain and fingers began filling in answers. "PENNY . . . NICKEL . . . DIME . . . QUARTER . . . Terrific . . . just terrific . . . 'A' for effort on a themed word game! But there ain't no murderers hiding in these clues or teenaged girls dumped in a vegetable plot!" Belle sloshed coffee in a mug, and stared moodily out the window. What she could see of the street looked weirdly empty.

When the phone rang two seconds later, she jumped so high, coffee leapt into the air and spattered her shirt. "Oh, for pete's sake. What now?" Belle stood stock still. *What if it's the caller from last night? What if there are more threats? What if Rosco and Kit have been—?* Then logic fought back. *Al's on top of the situation; a squad car's cruising nearby. The caller's probably the insurance company—or Al himself.*

"Belle Graham."

The voice at the other end was familiar; ordinarily, it would have been very welcome. At the moment, however, Belle wasn't feeling chatty, or brave, or even particularly polite. Her response was a dull: "Hi, Sara . . ."

"Oh, my dear, I was so upset when I got the news! Rosco's darling little red car. What a despicable and heinous act . . ." It didn't occur to Belle to ask how Sara had heard the story. Despite being a good-sized city, Newcastle had an information/gossip network worthy of any small town.

"Well, the culprits will have to be found, that's all. Found and brought to justice . . ."

Rosco and Kit walked in. Belle smiled in relief, cupped the receiver, and mouthed, "Sara"; Rosco executed a brief wave indicating *hello from me,* then scooped food into the puppy's bowl and headed toward the stairs to change into work clothes. He snagged a mug of coffee on his way while Belle pointed to the full cereal bowls and raised her shoulders in query.

"Start without me if you want," was the whispered reply while Sara's disembodied voice rattled on with a blithe:

". . . of course, it was *your* Mr. Gordon's wife I was seated beside, of all the peculiar coincidences—"

"Who?" Belle interrupted. She realized she'd missed a significant portion of this conversation.

"It *is* Alex Gordon, isn't it? The man who owns property in Taneysville?"

"That's right." Belle drew out the words. "And where did you—"

"Oh, my dear, you *are* distracted today . . . Of course, I don't blame you in the least; not with everything that's happened . . . But, as I was saying, I was seated beside Mrs. Gordon at the fashion show fund-raiser for the animal shelter . . . Although, as I mentioned a moment ago, I'd hardly call what the models wore *couture*—unless you believe patched blue jeans—"

"Patched—?"

"I admit I can be old-fashioned, Belle dear, but in my day dress design was . . . well, no matter. Raising money for the shelter is such an important cause; and I shouldn't quibble about modern style . . ."

Belle felt her head was spinning. *Maybe I should have eaten earlier,* she thought. She eyed the granola, but it suddenly looked less than appealing.

". . . Of course, remarks at ladies' functions like these can be extraordinarily catty—no pun intended—so it came as no surprise that a number of *sotto voce* comments had to do with speculation as to when this Gordon fellow will tire of wife number three—"

"Number two."

"Oh, no, dear . . . The woman I sat beside is his third wife. She made quite a point of mentioning the fact. Goodness knows why . . . But her statement did engender several unpleasant jests about when he'll be commencing his quest for number four. Fortunately, she wasn't present to hear them, although I don't imagine the speakers stopped to consider—"

But—"

"Exactly, dear. I also found it unusual that the *current* Mrs. Gordon would take an interest in Newcastle when she obviously resides in the Boston area—Back Bay, I would imagine . . . However, it seems her mother is a long-time resident of our fair city . . . The poor dear is in failing health, unfortunately, and now resides at a nearby facility for the elderly—'managed care,' I believe one calls it nowadays . . . Oh, my goodness! Look at the time. I must run, dear child. I have a tennis date . . . you know my Tuesday morning regular . . . Give that dear husband of yours a kiss from me." With that, the phone went dead.

Less than a second later, Rosco reappeared, shaved, showered, and ready for the day.

"We're missing one of Gordon's wives," was all Belle said.
"Come again?"

"He's on his *third* wife, not his second. One of them's still unaccounted for . . . which *could* mean . . ." Belle paused, frowned, then shook her head in perplexity. ". . . which *could* mean that the body your Greeks unearthed . . . What I mean is, maybe she didn't run off with the business partner . . . Maybe she—?"

"You're not going to suggest Nikos and Taki dug up an *ex*-Mrs. Gordon?" Rosco also frowned. He looked utterly bewildered. "That's not possible. Gordon only bought the Quigley property a short while ago, and the remains were—"

The phone interrupted the discussion. Like Belle, Rosco started at the sound, then lunged for the receiver. "That better be the insurance company . . . although they're probably going to tell me the Jeep wasn't even worth three hundred bucks . . . This is Rosco Polycrates."

The voice at the other end boomed into the room. "Got some news from Tanner up in Boston, Poly—crates. Don't say I've never done anything for you."

"I'm all ears, Al."

"It seems Tanner accidentally discovered a little connection to your buddy Alex Gordon. Through our jumper, Petri . . . who apparently was once on Gordon's payroll—that would be *unofficially,* of course."

CHAPTER

33

Belle's gray eyes had turned into slits; her brow was creased in concentration. "Go over that again," she said as she paced the kitchen. "Tanner told Al—"

"That Petri did 'unofficial' work for Gordon."

"What does that mean, Rosco? 'Unofficial'?"

"He wasn't on Gordon's company books, meaning the work was of a personal nature—"

"But you told me Petri was a dirty cop before he—"

"What can I say? Maybe Gordon was owed money . . . maybe he needed someone who could do a little 'persuading.'" Rosco paused. "Gordon made a point of discussing his Russian roots . . . his real name, the Gorki thing . . . He also took pains to let me know he was very connected to 'powerful' people. Maybe he's in with the Russian mob. Maybe he double-crossed the wrong people, and needed Petri to perform a little dirty work of his own. Who knows?"

Belle whistled. "That's a dangerous game."

Rosco shrugged his shoulders. "None of those thugs would be *my* first choice for soul mates."

"So you're thinking Petri could have been some kind of bodyguard?"

Rosco studied his notes and shook his head. "No . . . the dates are too erratic . . . My guess is that Petri was brought on board for special projects—"

"Like breaking kneecaps—"

"I don't think Russian mobsters are quite that *easy* on their victims."

Belle looked over Rosco's shoulder. "Wait a minute . . . Petri and Gordon first connected fifteen years ago—"

"According to Tanner's info . . ."

"And what happened fifteen years ago?" The look Belle gave Rosco was one that stated an astonished: *How come we didn't figure this one out earlier?*

"Gordon's wife and business partner disappeared."

"Bingo. It matches perfectly."

"You're not going back to the body buried on the Quigley site, are you? Because if that's what you're thinking, the ages don't jibe. Remember, Abe Jones said he believed the victim was . . ." Rosco scratched his head as he pondered the situation. "Or do they . . . ?"

Belle waved a hand requesting silence as she reached for the phone. "It's time to call in the big guns."

Rosco raised an eyebrow. "Big guns?"

"Bartholomew Kerr."

"The *Crier*'s gossip columnist? What does he know about all this?"

"Are you kidding? Snoop *extraordinaire* and repository of all high society scuttlebutt—whether seemly or not. Preferably not. I don't know why I didn't think to contact 'Mr. Bizzy Buzz' before. If anyone has the lowdown on Alex Gordon and his happy homelife, or -*lives* in this case, it's Bar-

tholomew. And now that Sara detailed Missus Number
Three's local linkage—" Belle's explanation ceased as she
punched in numbers, tapped a foot, cradled the phone against
her shoulder, and snagged a pencil and pad of paper from a
nearby drawer.

Amazingly, Kerr answered his office phone on the first
ring—amazing because his adaptable hours often included
late-night deadlines that resulted in a late start to his
workday. And amazing because mornings weren't Bizzy
Buzz's sunniest times. Every one of his callers was well ac-
quainted with his voice mail's curt outgoing message.

Belle expressed surprise and gratitude at finding Bartholomew not only in but answering the line; his response
whooshed through the phone line. For a man who appeared
so diminutive and frail, he possessed a commanding voice.
"But I haven't been *home* yet, dear lady. I'm still operating on
Monday's long-distant and, I must confess, somewhat *tedious*
hours. Theater people and their Monday night shenanigans
are just—"

Belle interrupted what she knew from experience was
bound to be a lengthy reply. "What can you tell me about
Mrs. Alex Gordon?"

"You mean Number One, Number Two, or Number
Three . . . ? Forgive me, Annabella. I realize I'm sounding like
a shopworn game show host . . . but I fear I'm a little punchy
after last night's festivities at—"

"Which wife was romantically involved with Gordon's
business partner?"

"Ah . . . you want 'dirt,' I take it."

"An apter choice of word than you may know."

A breathy snort greeted this remark. "Oh goody! Do tell
Bartholomew all."

Belle opened her mouth to respond, but Kerr beat her to
the punch. "Never mind, Annabella . . . My lips are sealed. I
detect a hush-hush situation in your inquiry. Early morning

phone calls involving missing mates of magnet magnates are rife with possibilities . . .

"So, you want all the sordid details on the perfidious pair . . . Well, it was Wife Number *One* who absconded with the partner . . . a sordid little piece of baggage, she was. She'd appeared quite suddenly on the periphery of the Boston social scene—a 'party girl' would be a kind description. You may ascribe something naughtier if you wish . . . At any rate, after snagging said husband and propelling him into the gilded limelight of the very rich, she then proceeded to wheedle her ostentatious way into every society magazine, every layout involving home and garden design, every prominent function—"

"How old was she?"

"When she first came to my attention or when she decided to ditch Gordon?"

"Either."

"Let me think . . . She wasn't married to Gordon very long before she jilted him . . . Three years, perhaps; if memory serves—which it may not. Fifteen years is a long time when one's gray matter is so overcrammed with the age's most capricious trivia . . ." Bartholomew paused and sighed. Belle could picture him: his outsized glasses magnifying his myopic, colorless eyes, his narrow shoulders, his pinched physique, his tiny, restive hands. There was no doubt that Bizzy Buzz, the *Evening Crier*'s gossip columnist, was an odd duck, but beneath the posturing and mannerisms, he was immensely loyal. Once a friendship had been formed, it was there for life.

". . . But you asked about age, Annabella . . . In her mid to late twenties, I should imagine. Although it's conceivable she could have been quite a bit older. Expensive spas and pricey cosmetics can take years off a face. Decades, sometimes."

"Could she have been younger?"

Bartholomew paused again. "Well, it's *interesting* you ask that question, Annabella. Obviously I assumed . . . we *all* assumed she was well into her twenties when she blew onto the scene . . . and then with all the media attention focused on the doings of *Mrs.* Alex Gordon . . . However, now that I think back on it . . . well, there was a sort of pouty adolescence about her. Nothing remotely innocent, mind you. If anything, Madame Gordon was quite the opposite, a street-toughened—"

"In your estimation, Bartholomew, could she possibly have been in her teens when you first met her?"

"She could have been *anything,* Annabella. The woman invented herself. As far as everyone in the press was concerned, she'd never existed before appearing in Boston . . . So she could have been a runaway from the Midwest or a thirteen-year-old prostitute from Ukraine who'd latched onto Gordon during a business trip. *Or,* she could have been a late-thirties gold digger afraid of growing old. Names, as you know, are not reliable sources when they can be acquired and discarded as readily as one changes the tint of one's hair."

Belle was taking feverish notes. *Age?* she'd written. *Nationality? Appearance . . . history . . . hair color . . . ? Get height, weight, etc. for Abe . . .* "What about the man Wife Number One took off with?"

"There, I'm afraid I can be of less help. He only blipped onto my radar screen when the two of them absconded with Gordon's filthy lucre. Prior to the unfortunate love triangle, *she* was the person the media was fixated upon. Afterward, it was all Gordon's show. The wounded husband whose only desire was to await his beloved wife's return, et cetera, et cetera. Gordon's public persona was Mr. Forgiveness himself—"

"I'm gathering from your tone of voice you didn't exactly believe him."

"Let us simply say that, to date, the dual worlds of commerce and philanthropy have not lauded Mr. Alex Gordon for his altruism—nor for his upstanding professional practices . . . The word among my cohorts is that Monsieur Alex is most probably involved with money laundering—as well as what a good many other Russian, Ukrainian, and Albanian mobsters have links to, i.e.: the 'dirty diamond' trade—"

" 'Dirty diamonds'! That sounds dicey—"

"To borrow a phrase: 'You don't want to know' . . . 'Dirty diamonds' . . . 'blood diamonds' . . . at issue, are precious stones that are traded for weapons that promulgate wars in African republics. The losers are quite naturally the general populace. The winners? Well, you can bet your boots it's not your common villager . . . The Russian mob is heavily involved in the trade, as are the Israelis . . . I take it you've been apprised that Gordon is an assumed name, Annabella?"

Belle answered a preoccupied, "Hmmm-hmmm . . ." before continuing with another query. "And Wife Number Two?"

"A rebounder . . . now relocated to sunny California with their kid. A daughter. I believe that a restraining order was issued . . ."

Belle again scribbled several pertinent notes.

". . . He's not a very nice man, Annabella . . . A diamond in the rough—if you'll pardon the reference—and I imagine at heart, quite a nasty character."

"Sara Briephs told me that Wife Number Three—"

"Ah, the darling daughter putting in her appearance at a local fund-raiser . . . No black eyes—yet, I noticed. No broken arms and so forth, but give it time, Annabella. Give it time. Tigers don't change their stripes—or in this instance, a bear."

"One final question, Bartholomew, and then I'll let you get back to work——"

"Don't remind me, Annabella! In truth I'd much rather shoot the breeze with our illustrious young puzzler——"

"What finally became of Wife Number One and her lover?"

"I'm afraid I have no answer to that. The lady chose to vanish without a trace. No more photo ops or titillating tales. No topless sunbathing on remote Pacific isles——"

"But you intimated she was a media hound——"

"Of major proportions."

"Well, wouldn't she have attempted to remain in the lime-light with Mate Number Two? Wouldn't her bad-girl status have afforded her *additional* press coverage rather than less? What I mean is: Why would she decide to give up her celebrity status when she'd worked so hard to attain it?"

"A good question, Annabella. Alack and alas, I have no ready response, unless of course there was a chance of a criminal investigation——all that missing money, don't you know? But the lady simply 'went to earth,' as they're fond of saying in fox-hunting circles. She and her paramour . . . And now, I'm afraid duty calls . . . Give my regards to your handsome husband. And, Annabella . . . let me know if you discover any new 'dirt' with regards to Mr.——or Mrs.——*Alexei* Gordon."

Belle hung up the phone and turned back to Rosco. Her eyes sparkled with feverish thought. Rosco could almost see theories, hypotheses, and deductions pinwheeling around in her brain. "Well, there you have it!"

"I take it from your gloating tone that you think you've discovered our murder victim."

"Could anything be more obvious?"

"Well, yes, as a matter of fact . . ."

"Rosco! Come on . . . This is as plain as the nose on your face. Gordon had Wife Number One killed. Can't you see that? Along with the larcenous business partner——"

"You don't know they're dead."

"Not for *certain* . . . You're right . . ."

"So?"

"Okay . . . okay . . ." Belle's face crinkled in concentration. "But I know I'm right, Rosco. I *feel* it . . . Wait! Wait, I have it! It was Petri. Everything points to it. He was the hired assassin—"

"Presuming Wife Number One is—"

"Stop, Rosco. Let me finish. Petri bumps off both the lady and her paramour . . . plunks the bodies into the trunk of his car, and drives them out into the wilds—"

"That would be Taneysville—?"

Belle gave him an aggravated look. "Then he secretly buries the evidence of his crime, and hightails it back to Boston."

"Your theory has a major flaw. Two, in fact."

"What's that?"

"Gordon didn't own the property fifteen years ago—meaning the discovery of his ex-wife's remains beside his future weekend home would be an extraordinary coincidence. And two: Where's the partner's body?"

Belle's mouth opened and shut and opened again. "I'm thinking . . . I'm thinking."

Rosco's expression also grew serious. He scratched his chin, then rubbed at his forehead. "You know, during my initial interview with Gordon, I asked him why he'd chosen Taneysville for a weekend retreat. His response seemed fairly prerehearsed and glib, i.e.: It didn't have a ring of truth about it . . ." Rosco shook his head. "However, your theory discounts the fact that the Quigleys were then occupying—"

"But they were old, maybe hard of hearing—whatever. Meaning that Petri could sneak in during the dark of night, and do the dirty deed—"

"And keep Gordon in the dark as to the location he'd chosen?"

"He'd have to, Rosco—if he wanted to save his hide . . . Maybe . . . maybe Petri was blackmailing his former boss, threatening to tell all, et cetera . . . Finally, Gordon learns the truth—"

"How?"

"I don't know how, but he does . . . then he races out to Taneysville and buys the land—"

"Only to have his construction crew unearth his wife's remains . . . ? I don't know, Belle. This concept of yours is sounding sketchier and sketchier."

But Belle was on a roll. "Not if Petri never disclosed the precise placement of the burial sites . . . meaning that your Greek backhoe operator accidentally digs up the lady's skeleton—putting Petri in *bigger* trouble, and forcing Gordon to kill him to keep him quiet . . . Remember how close in time those two events were? The discovery of the body and Petri's death?"

Rosco was silent for a long minute. "I have to admit your notion is plausible—albeit far-fetched."

Belle folded her arms across her chest. "You're just jealous."

"What?"

"You're jealous you didn't dream up this scenario first."

"Well, for one thing, investigative work doesn't entail *dreaming up* scenarios—"

"You always tell me you play your hunches, don't you?"

"Right . . ."

"Well, this is *my* hunch. And failing uncovering a better one at the moment, I vote we try it. I say we smoke Gordon out."

"What's this *we* bit?"

"Subcontractor to the Polycrates Agency."

"Right . . . I keep forgetting . . . my stalwart employee . . ." Rosco picked up the phone.

"Who are you calling?"

"I thought that was your suggestion—that I have another conversation with *Alexei Peshkov.*"

Belle drew in a quick, nervous breath while Rosco chatted with Far Yukon's executive secretary, then hung up the phone. "It seems the new homeowner has a meeting at the work site . . . Apparently, he's on his way there now." Rosco headed toward the closet and pulled out his jacket while Belle reached for her purse.

"Ah-ah, where are you going?" Rosco said as he held up his hands. "I'm drawing the line on the *we* part. This guy has the potential for being very dangerous."

She stood silently for a few moments, then said, "So, you'll need to take my car." She brandished her keys, then lowered them as her shoulders simultaneously sank into a worried slouch. "Be careful, Rosco. If I'm right, this guy's more than dangerous . . . He's a killer."

"Killer? You think I don't know that? If you're right, he's the guy who killed my Jeep."

"I'm talking about *people,* Rosco."

"So am I . . . sort of." Then he stopped and looked at her. "Promise me you'll keep the doors locked. Because if it's not Gordon . . . or if the goons who—"

"I promise I'll be careful."

They exchanged a lengthy kiss.

"Take your gun," Belle said after they pulled apart.

CHAPTER

34

"I only want to *talk* to him," Rosco kept mumbling as he made the trip to Taneysville and the Gordon property. "Be cool, be relaxed . . . just chat with the guy . . . nice and easy . . . A little information gathering . . . A little *talk* . . ."

The muttered phrases were intended to have a calming effect, but the fact that Belle had been threatened, that Rosco had lost his trusted Jeep, and that he was now driving his wife's *sedan* only served as a reminder that this particular conversation was bound to be anything but easy—or normal, or relaxed. *Keep your eye on the prize,* he kept reminding himself, *there's no actual evidence that Gordon had anything to do with what happened Monday night—or with a body, or even multiple bodies, unearthed on his premises. Belle's theory is only conjecture.*

But the longer Rosco drove, the more plausible his wife's idea seemed. He reached for his phone, called home, and breathed a huge sigh of relief when her cheerful voice answered. "Keep the doors locked till I get home, okay? Kit'll be fine without her midday stroll . . . And if there's anything even remotely suspicious—" Then the connection broke off, and he found himself on the outskirts of Taneysville.

He eased Belle's sedan up the old Quigley lane. There was no sign of Gordon, only Sean Reilly's pickup truck with the contractor sitting peacefully on the opened tailgate. Rosco parked a few feet away and stepped from the car. Slowly. He took in a long and steadying breath, but his shoulders were tight with anger. *Was Sean in on all this?* he wondered. *How much does he know?*

"Heya, Parker," Sean said with a smile, "What happened to that *classy* ride you used to have?"

Rosco took a long time to answer. He studied Sean's face the entire time, looking for a crack, a little twitch or tick that might indicate how much he knew about the Jeep's destruction. "It met with an accident."

"Not too serious, I hope," Sean continued in an affable tone. "Those older models are starting to become real collector's items."

"Yeah, that's what they tell me."

"So, what brings you back here?"

"I might ask you that same thing."

Sean let out a short groan. "Man, Parker, I hate to tell *you* this, of all people, but Mr. G's supposed to meet me here. He wants to change the plans for this addition—again." Sean pointed to the area where the body had been found. "No more building on *this* side of the house. That's change number one. The idea's been totally scrapped—by the little missus, natch. I told ya these ladies love to bust a builder's chops . . . Apparently, now we're gonna have to backfill *all* the foundation area my guys already dug, and relocate to the north side. It seems it's 'better light' for the little lady's paintings. Go figure, huh? Man, I sure wish I had that kind of dough to throw around. Though I wouldn't be wasting it in this hicksville, I'll tell you that right now . . . Anyway, Mr. G's gonna lay it all out for me when he gets here." Sean looked at his watch. "He shoulda been here twenty minutes ago."

"Don't count on any backfilling just yet. I have a feeling before anything gets filled, there's going to be a lot more digging done right here."

"Not according to—"

Sean was interrupted by the sound of Alex Gordon's Mercedes working its way up the lane. It pulled up to the far side of Sean's pickup and stopped with a jolt. Gordon switched off the motor and stepped rapidly from the car. He wore a dark gray overcoat with the collar turned up against the cold air, and his expression looked equally steely and grim. Watching him approach, Rosco knew for certain Belle had been right. If Gordon hadn't actually killed his wife, he knew who the murderer was.

"What the hell are you doing here, Polycrates?" The question was a snarl. "This is private property."

"Polycrates . . . ?" Sean asked. He looked from his boss to the man he knew as Parker. He made no attempt to hide his confusion.

Gordon's glance took in Belle's sedan. "What happened to your Jeep? Meet with a mishap?"

Rosco smiled coolly. "Interesting question. How did you know I owned a Jeep?"

"I guess a little birdie told me." Gordon turned to Sean. "Get this lowlife out of here, Reilly. This is private property and we've got work to do."

"Polycrates?" Sean said once again. "I thought your name was Parker."

"Parker?" Gordon growled. "You mean the stooge who's the Newcastle buildings inspector? Is that who this bum told you he was?"

"Ahhh . . ."

"I don't know what bill of goods you've been sold, Sean,

but he's a private investigator by the name of Rosco Poly-crates, and he's been hired by those rubes down the hill to shut this work site down—and I mean permanently. So get him out of here . . . Now!"

Sean took a step toward Rosco, who held up a placating hand. "Hold on there, Sean," he said. "What your boss is telling you, that's basically true—except for the 'closing down the site' part—"

Gordon moved closer. "Then what the hell are you doing here?"

"There were a couple of issues we left unresolved." Rosco looked from Gordon to Sean, the smile on his face determined and aggressive. "Sean tells me you've decided to move the addition to the north side—"

"You want to keep your job, Reilly? Get this bozo out of here."

But Sean's large body didn't move. Rosco could see he was trying to play catch-up with the situation, although the outcome was anyone's guess at this point. *Two to one,* Rosco told himself, assessing the odds, *and one of the two a probable killer.* "You know, Alexei, when we first met, I didn't compliment you sufficiently on losing your Russian accent; it must have taken a lot of work . . . I guess it shouldn't surprise me that you'd have no trouble sounding like a Texan on the tele-phone—"

"What the hell are you talking about?"

"You don't think I recognized your voice? What do you take me for?"

"You're living in a dream world."

Rosco tried a bluff. "Maybe, but the prints the police lifted off a certain phone booth matched the ones left in Petri's apartment." He studied the reaction on Gordon's face as the Russian absorbed Petri's name. "It's only a matter of time before those prints are I.D.'d, but it's beginning to seem fairly obvious who they belong to."

"Mr. Gordon . . ." Sean said, looking for a few explanations . . . or instructions . . . or anything.

"Get this creep off my property, dammit!" Gordon shouted. In a Pavlovian reaction, Sean moved toward Rosco.

"Just a minute. Just a minute . . ." Rosco interjected.

Gordon glared at him. "I don't have anything to say to you, Polycrates."

"Well, I think you're wrong about that. Because it's my opinion—as well as that of the homicide detectives who happen to be working this case—that you may know very well whose body turned up here two weeks ago."

Gordon made another angry step toward Rosco, and Rosco turned his attention to Sean.

"Man, it's got to really gall you to have to dig a new foundation and backfill this one . . . and all because some dumb bimbo, some rich—"

"Leave my wife out of this, Polycrates . . ."

"Let's see, would that be Wife Number Three, Alexei? Or Wife Number One? The hot little lady who dumped you and then disappeared with her new stud . . . ?"

Sean's big face swung slowly toward Gordon.

". . . 'Cause this is how Homicide in both Boston and Newcastle are piecing this thing together, Alexei . . . and all because of a down-and-out PI named Mike Petri who happened to wind up dead; a PI who you just happened to have hired fifteen years ago—"

"Are you charging me with murder? I'm a little confused here, Polycrates. Because if you are, I think you just overlooked my rights—"

"I'm not charging you with anything. I'm just discussing a guy named Petri—who happens to have contacted me the day before his death. But then, you must know all about that from one of your little birdies . . . But Petri's not the real issue. I'm more concerned about one of your exes and a certain one-time business partner; both of whom *happen* to be on the missing persons list." Rosco looked at Sean. "As the man in charge of this work site, Sean, let me ask you a question: Did 'Mr. G' here give you specific instructions to follow if you happened to come across any 'Indian' graves?"

"Don't answer that, Sean. I've got lawyers who'll handle this guy—"

"Mike Petri was murdered on Saturday morning. Murdered, Sean." Rosco paused to let this soak in. "Do you hear what I'm saying? Someone threw him off the balcony of his high-rise. You can check that with Boston PD if you want. They have fingerprints of—"

"You've got nothing on me, Polycrates."

"No? Well, let me mention another fact to Sean here . . . We've got positive proof that fifteen years ago the same Mike Petri murdered the first 'Mrs. G' and her friend, then drove the bodies out here—"

Sean's perplexed stare swept from Rosco to Gordon. "But the property belonged to—"

"Come on, Sean, use your head; why do you think Gordon bought into this hick burg?" Rosco was almost shouting now. "Because Petri dumped the remains here, that's why. But, instead of revealing the exact locale of the bodies, he blackmailed his old boss until your backhoe operator . . ." He stopped and took in a deep breath in an attempt to slow down. "That's who Nikos dug up, Sean. Gordon's first wife! And that's why 'Mr. G' doesn't want you digging here anymore. His old business partner's probably right under our feet—"

Rosco's speech was stopped short as Gordon's shoulder slammed into his chest, propelling him backwards into the door of Sean's pickup. The force of the blow was so severe that it caused the window to pop out and fall across the driver's seat. Rosco was left hunched over and gasping hard for breath. Then Gordon turned sideways, chopping his elbow into Rosco's side. The sound of ribs cracking reverberated across the landscape as Rosco slumped over the front fender of the truck.

While he struggled to right himself, Gordon began walking toward his Mercedes. Rosco reached for his pistol, but before he could locate it, Sean moved forward, his posture perplexed and troubled as he grasped Rosco's arms from behind. "Okay, fella, let's calm down here . . . I'm sure Mr. G's got an explanation for this whole mis—"

Before Sean could finish, Gordon spun back on the two men, stepping toward them and swiftly bringing his knee into Rosco's groin. At the same time Gordon's right fist drove into Rosco's jaw, snapping his head backwards and sending a spray of blood splattering across Sean's work shirt. The contractor jumped and released his grip as Rosco collapsed on the ground.

"Good work, Reilly."

Sean looked down at the unconscious body. ". . . I wasn't trying . . . All I wanted to do was—"

"Get that backhoe rolling. We're filling up this hole right here and now . . . You've got an opportunity to make a lot of money, Sean. Big money. All you have to do is keep your mouth shut."

Gordon spun on his heel and walked toward his Mercedes. When he returned a moment later, Sean was nowhere in sight. Gordon looked toward the backhoe, smiled once, then raised his right hand. In it was a 9mm semiautomatic pistol; attached to the gun was a silencer. He brought the barrel down to meet the back of Rosco's head, then reached across with his left hand and chambered a round. "Tsk, tsk, tsk . . . Creatures That Once Were Men—"

"I wouldn't get too carried away if I were you, Mr. G."

Gordon jerked up his head to see Sean staring down at him. A 30.06 hunting rifle pressed into his shoulder, the scope pointing directly at his boss's face.

"Sean, what the hell are you doing? I'm offering you big money. More than you've ever seen. Don't be stupid."

Sean shook his head. "What I'm thinking is this: you're just lookin' for another patsy . . . another fall guy. And I'm afraid that ain't gonna be me."

Gordon slowly began to raise his pistol.

"Don't even consider it, fella . . . Unless you'd like to see your head hanging in my den next to an eight-point elk."

CHAPTER

35

The phone call had been a wife's direst fear.

"... hospital ..." Belle had heard, "... fractures of the ... a contusion where the ... will need to continue to assess ..." Clenching the receiver, her fingers had turned cold, as had her face and finally her body. The man's voice on the other end of the line had wavered in and out of her conscious hearing, but finally Belle had understood the salient fact: Rosco was going to be okay. He'd been hurt, but he would mend. And Belle could bring him home—as long as the patient had a local physician to follow through on treatment. "Naturally, he's experiencing some discomfort," the voice had concluded. Belle translated from doctor speak into ordinary English: Rosco was in terrible pain.

As she'd returned the receiver to its cradle, she'd pulled her shoulders back and taken several deep breaths. Then she'd lifted her chin and reached for the phone again. Her eyes had glittered with a combination of relief and rage. Alex Gordon was going to pay big time for hurting her husband. *Kill your own spouse if you want, bucko,* she'd silently ranted, *but leave mine alone.* It hadn't been one of Belle's most rational moments.

Then she'd picked up the receiver and called Sara, whose antique Cadillac would make ideal transport for a "patient" experiencing "discomfort."

Insisting that Belle was too shaken to concentrate on the road, Sara drove them both toward St. Mary's Hospital near Taneysville. Her back was ramrod straight; her silk-lined kid gloves clutched the wheel. She was outfitted in a fur-collared coat with a matching hat and color-coordinated shoes and handbag, as if she'd anticipated the necessity of impressing her status and might on the emergency room personnel.

Beside her, Belle felt like a complete loser and fashion fiasco. Her hair was unbrushed, her cable-knit sweater tatty, her cotton turtleneck losing its elasticity such that the neck sagged like a wet scarf. She was carrying a *brown* purse; her feet were shod in *black* boots (scuffed); her *blue* jeans were faded. Sara didn't even wear such outfits to garden in. Belle slouched in the seat; concern over Rosco heightened her criticism of herself.

After another few minutes of self-reproach, she reached into her jeans pocket and fished out the crossword she'd received on Monday—the one she'd been doodling with just before Rosco had left to confront Alex Gordon. " 'Change' of Heart," she announced bitterly. "I can't believe I didn't notice how obvious the connection was before!"

"What's that, dear?" Sara's driving technique was as old-fashioned as her automobile. She believed in total focus at all times: no distractions from cell phones, car phones, radios, CDs, or books on tape. No eating with one hand, opening or slurping beverages, reaching into a purse for sunglasses, or squinting sideways at a map. "What did you say?"

"That I should have recognized how this money and metal theme related to Gordon . . . I mean, it's evident what we're looking at: NICKEL, DIME, PENNY . . . The words are right in front of me—"

"I see, dear." It was clear, though, that Sara didn't *see* at all.

Belle grumbled at her own stupidity. "After all, what does Far Yukon Industries produce? Magnets! Which are obviously made from metal. Clearly, he must use copper and nickel in his business. And what did Bartholomew insinuate that Gordon was clandestinely involved in? Money laundering, illicit diamonds, the Russian mob—people who don't fool around when it comes to vendettas or revenge or silencing informers . . . ! If I'd only made these basic deductions earlier, then maybe Al or Tanner could have arrested Gordon, and Rosco wouldn't have—"

"I'm afraid I'm not following your rationale, dear."

Belle's shoulders slumped. "It's nothing."

"Nothing? But my dear, you were making a point. About the latest crossword you received . . ." Sara flicked on her turn signal—she liked supplying other drivers with *plenty* of advance warning—then cautiously eased into the fast lane, pulled around the car in front, and carefully returned to the slow lane. "Another anonymous word game? That brings the total to four, doesn't it?"

Belle mumbled a response. She was still deep into personal blame mode.

"And your mystery puzzler hasn't attempted to contact you?"

"No."

"I wonder who it could be?"

"I imagine someone who lives in the vicinity, because one had no stamp and another had an uncanceled stamp—meaning the envelopes had been hand-delivered."

"Unless that's a clever ruse, and only a liaison-type person lives in Newcastle."

Belle considered the suggestion. "A possibility, I guess . . . But the crucial point is this: Whoever constructed the crosswords knows all about Alex Gordon, knows that he killed both his wife and his former business partner, as well as the whole sordid situation involving Mike Petri . . . Our puzzler predicted the fire, tried to reveal Gordon's change of name, even urged me to go 'west' to Taneysville in the first place— and I didn't see any of it! Even though it's been sitting right in front of my nose—"

"Belle, dear, it's not your fault that Rosco—"

"But that's just it, Sara! If I'd made these connections earlier—"

"But you didn't, dear. At the risk of oversimplification: There's no point in crying over spilled milk. Guilt is an unhealthy emotional state, and it won't help either you or your husband if you're castigating yourself over circumstances that have passed. And that may well have been unavoidable—prior hypotheses or no."

Belle had no response to those words of wisdom. Sara had no additional advice to dispense. The two continued in pensive silence for some minutes. "Anonymous . . ." Sara finally murmured. "A strange choice when so much was at stake . . ."

"Given what happened to Rosco—and what befell Petri before him—I would imagine possessing incriminating information on Alex Gordon would require anonymity."

" 'Befell'? An interesting word choice, dear girl . . . Well, I suppose you're right . . ." Sara mused, "but it still seems odd, doesn't it? A discreet phone call to the police would have served the same purpose if the desired result were to put Gordon behind bars . . . And then there's the matter of waiting for fifteen years before coming forward—"

"But the body wasn't discovered until two weeks ago."

"The *first* Mrs. Gordon," Sara added quietly.

Belle smiled wearily. "Bartholomew's going to have a field day with this."

"He'll need to be careful if he doesn't want to jeopardize any legal proceedings." Sara again flicked on her turn signal and changed lanes. Nothing was said until she'd safely guided her aged auto back to the relative serenity of the slow lane. "What other deductions have you made, dear? Do the clues or solutions suggest personality traits? Or whether the constructor is male or female?"

Belle hesitated before speaking. "My only theory is that the person is old. At first I assumed it was a man, but I realize I have nothing to base that on."

Sara laughed. "And what, may I ask, are you basing 'old' upon?"

"The clues don't strike me as ones a younger generation would be familiar with. Plus"—Belle glanced at Sara sideways, not sure how she would take her next statement—"the hand's a little too precise . . . a little fearful of betraying unsteadiness."

Sara sniffed; her proud jaw jutted higher. "And the crossword you hold in your hand, does it also contain antediluvian references—as well as what you perceive as overcompensation for wobbly, old fingers?"

Belle decided not to take the bait. Instead, she began reading clues and answers. "1-Down: *Mr. O'Brien* . . . Solution: PAT. Not the hippest use for PAT . . . 2-Down: I'VE *Got a Secret* . . . a former game show . . . When did that go off the air? 3-Down: *Amusement hall,* which is PENNY ARCADE." She spread the paper across her knees. "18-Across: *Theater where there's no talking?* . . . NICKELODEON . . . A modern parlance would use *Cable TV Network* . . . 29-Down: *F. W. Woolworth, e.g.* . . . FIVE AND DIME . . . *Mr. Williams* at both 43-Down and 52-Across, the solutions being ANDY and TED respectively rather than the more contemporary Garcia and Danson . . . *Burns & Allen, e.g.* at 20-Down . . . Answer: DUO—"

"I see what you mean," was Sara's gentle reply. "So, what's your theory?" Then she interrupted her own query. "FIVE AND DIME . . . NICKELODEON . . . PENNY ARCADE . . . I agree with your financial references, but also . . . also . . ." She paused. "Read me the other puzzle solutions involved with money."

"QUARTERBACK . . . COIN A PHRASE."

"Curious . . ." Sara mused, "very curious . . . Something's piquing my memory, but I'm not certain what it is—"

"Then I'm right in my assessment that the crossword constructor is—?"

"A person of a 'certain age,' I believe is the expression you're searching for, dear child." With that Sara wheeled her grand old car into the parking lot opposite the hospital's emergency entrance. "If that darling husband of yours hasn't been receiving the very best of care . . . ! Well, I hope I don't lose my temper, that's all."

Grunting in pain, his rib cage encircled with tape, his head bandaged, his chin swathed in gauze, Rosco had been gently eased into the backseat of the Cadillac. The pain medication made his voice sound muffled and distant, and his concentration drifted in and out.

The basic components of the story had been supplied by the discharge nurse. They'd involved Constable Lonnie Tucker, an ambulance, a witness, and a man taken into police custody. "Folks are saying it's the new owner up to Quigleys' they've arrested," the nurse had added before dispensing information Belle felt to be more immediately significant: Rosco's two broken ribs were "gonna make him feel like one sore puppy for a couple of days." But after all was said and done, that he'd be "right as rain." Belle had liked the assessment far better than the prior "experiencing some discomfort."

O n the way home, with Rosco dozing in the rear seat, Belle let out a little yelp of impatience. "My car . . . It's still at the Quigley—"

"Tomorrow's another day, Belle . . . Unless you want me to turn around and—"

"No, you're right. The only thing that matters right now is to get Rosco home and into bed."

"He's lucky he didn't sustain other—"

"He's lucky to be alive, Sara."

Neither woman spoke for a long while. Finally Sara broke the silence. "It's a shame you can't actually thank your mystery puzzler, and explain that Gordon's going to pay for his crimes—that it's safe to come forward."

"I'm sure TV cameras have been covering the situation, Sara . . . in depth."

"Still—"

"You're right. It would be nice to say thanks in person."

"Precisely." Sara fell silent again. "An old person," she murmured, "an old person . . . What were those solutions again, Belle?"

Belle reached for the crossword. "PENNY ARCADE, NICKELODEON, FIVE AND DIME—"

"Hmmm, I don't know. There's a little bug in the back of my brain that tells me those phrases have another connection entirely."

"Uh-oh," Rosco said dreamily from his pillowed nest in the rear seat, "sounds like Sara has a bee in her bonnet."

CHAPTER

36

"I t's not her," the raspy voice on the other end of the phone stated. The tone was halfway between brusqueness and exasperation.

Rosco sucked in his breath in order to respond but winced as a new pain shot through his chest. When the torture subsided he squeaked out, "What do you mean, Al? Who else could it be? It's got to be Gordon's first wife."

"No way, buddy. Your theory was close—so close, even the Russian thought it was numero uno—but the thing didn't go down the way you figured."

"Walk me through this, Al."

"Tanner sent a crew into Petri's apartment. Thanks to *my* arm-twisting, I might mention . . . On one point you were right on the money: Gordon's prints are all over the place. There's no doubt in anyone's mind that he tossed Petri from the terrace . . . But Gordon never found what he was looking for."

"And that is . . . ?"

"A safe-deposit box key. One of Tanner's boys picked it up with a metal detector. It was in the freezer, buried in a pint of Häagen-Dazs ice cream—Rum Raisin. Mike Petri may have had a weakness for cheap vodka, but he drew the line at cheap ice cream."

"I'm still not with you. What was in the safe-deposit box?"

"Petri's insurance policy, so to speak . . . a nice little case history of his relationship with one Alex Gordon of Far Yukon Industries—dating back over fifteen years. Obviously, it was the only way Petri could keep Gordon from killing him."

"It doesn't sound like the plan worked any too well."

"Well, it did for fifteen years . . . What we're now piecing together is that Mike decided it was time to check out—as in permanently. Maybe he'd reached the end of his rope emotion-wise; maybe a doctor hadn't given him a clean bill of health . . . Whatever the situation, as near as we can guess, Petri got himself liquored up, phoned Gordon, and handed him the *wrong* safe-deposit box key, which sent his sometime boss on a wild-goose chase—and then into a nasty rage . . . Basically, Petri knew he was committing suicide, but—and here's the big *but;* he had a legit life insurance policy from Mass Casualty. For one million smacks . . . Of course the sticker with these policies is: they don't pay off if you do the deed yourself."

"A million dollars . . ."

"That's what I said, Poly—crates. You and me definitely got into the wrong business."

"Who was the beneficiary?"

"The Franklin Park Zoo—damn near across the street from Far Yukon Industries."

"You're kidding!"

"Nope."

Another sharp pain shot through Rosco's ribs; he groaned into the phone.

"Do you want me to explain all this to Belle?" Lever asked. "Sounds like you're having a rough time of it."

"No, I'm okay . . . So, why does Petri phone me in the first place? Then leave a message stating he's going to call back— when he knows he won't be alive?"

"I figure it's all part of the setup. He's got to get someone to prove he didn't kill himself or that policy doesn't pay off. With his reputation, he knew he couldn't count on Tanner— or anyone else in Boston PD for that matter—so he gets you involved. Mr. Insurance Investigator himself."

"And I take it this 'case history' of Petri's maintains the body in Taneysville isn't the first Mrs. Gordon."

"In a way, yes . . . See, Petri *did* kill the business partner and Wife Number One fifteen years ago—on orders from Gordon—but he buried the bodies in a field off Route 24 near Lake Nippenicket. The location's very specific in his letter. Abe Jones and the Boston ME made a positive I.D. on both of them a little over an hour ago."

"That was quick—even for Abe."

"Petri buried them with their driver's licenses sealed in plastic zip-lock bags. He was very thorough, even clean, you might say. Too bad he didn't stay on the right side of the law."

"But I'm not making the Taneysville connection," Rosco said, coughing slightly and following up with another pained groan. "If Gordon had no idea where the bodies were buried, then he bought that Quigley property as a legitimate second home . . . My question is: How could Petri possibly have convinced him it was the same place he'd buried the bodies fifteen years ago? No one would ever swallow a coincidence like that."

Rosco could hear Lever lighting a cigarette on the other end.

"Al, it hurts my lungs just listening to you do that."

"Tough." Lever inhaled deeply. "It's my office. I run it my way." He sucked in additional smoke and continued. "Gordon said that Petri had told him he'd *dumped* the body on the Quigley site, i.e., Mike moved it *after* Gordon purchased the land . . . Apparently, that little conversation occurred right after the press released the story about mystery remains being unearthed . . . The idea was that if Gordon didn't make a major payoff, Petri would ensure that the business partner's corpse would *also* arrive in Taneysville . . . Don't forget Gordon didn't have any of Jones's findings, so he believed everything Mike told him."

"I gather Gordon's talking up a storm. Surprise, surprise."

"He's trying to cut a deal. We'll see about that."

Rosco nodded, winced, and coughed. "So Wife Number Three really did want to move the addition to the north side of the site after all?"

"You got it . . . You know, it's amazing . . ."

There was a long pause, so Rosco said, "What? What's amazing?"

"Petri. He orchestrated this whole show. Did it all from the grave, so to speak. He set up Gordon like a kingpin and bowled him right over. Sort of his way of making it right in the end."

"He set me up pretty well, too."

"That he did, my friend."

"And I'm right back where I started—except for the two broken ribs and no more Jeep. At least I have *something* to show for my efforts."

Lever laughed. "Ribs heal."

"Thank you for that piece of wisdom, O Great Philosopher of the Twenty-first Century."

"I see where your buddy Tree Hoffmeyer is sinking like a stone in the polls. It's remarkable how fast a lead like his can evaporate. Just shows-to-go-ya what a little adverse publicity can do. Too bad, I would've liked to have seen a change down in D.C."

"We still have a few days."

"Right. Don't hold your breath." Lever laughed again. "The eternal optimist . . . Keep me posted."

Rosco hung up the phone, then walked to Belle's home office, eased himself into a chair, and related what Lever had told him. She listened in silence then walked to his side.

"How do your ribs feel?" She kissed him on the cheek—lightly.

"Hey, we can do better than that," was his mock-wounded response. "Actually the ribs feel a heck of a lot better than they did. It's amazing what a couple of days can do." Then almost to himself he added, "Where do we go from here?"

"I'm wondering the same thing . . . Right now, we're back at square one, except for one thing—we have four crosswords. And an anonymous constructor who—" Belle was interrupted by the sound of Kit's frantic barking. "Rosco, I think you and your dog need a little training session."

He smiled. "How come every time she makes a racket, digs in the garden, or chews something beyond recognition, she's *my* dog? But then she . . . You're right. Time for a serious conversation with dad. Bring on the choke collar, the stern commands. Tough love's my middle name."

"I must have overlooked that part of your personality." Belle laughed, walked to the living room, knelt down, gave Kit a loving and lengthy pat, then retrieved the mail from the box on the porch. When she returned to the office, she found Rosco spreading the four crosswords on her desk, and grunting with the effort.

"Don't you think you should stay put and let the pros have at it?"

"Uh-huh . . ." he mumbled absentmindedly. ". . . Okay, here's puzzle number one, two, three, and four—"

Belle placed an opened envelope beside him and said, "And let's not forget number five."

Across

1. L × L
4. Heave
8. Come together
12. Air; comb. form
14. Raves' partner
16. Entreaty
17. 1989 Robert Downey film
19. That girl's
20. Essential oil
21. Congregation
23. ____-wit
24. Had been
25. Film in which Ronald Colman won an Oscar
29. Love letter letters
30. Serf
31. "____boy!"
34. Butt
36. Certain cat
40. Classic Hitchcock film
44. Theme
45. Before
46. And the rest
47. Veni-vici link
50. ____-back
52. Gaynor, Garland or Streisand vehicle
56. "None____the Brave"
59. ____Hagen
60. An Adams
61. Nose; comb. form
63. Guided by truth
65. Classic Grant/Lombard film
68. "Do____to others . . ."
69. Friendlier
70. Comic strip dog
71. Dance maneuver
72. Not this
73. EST part

Down

1. Certain parrot
2. Zubin____
3. "Darn!"
4. Tuscan three
5. Org. formed in 1948
6. Glitch
7. Flash
8. Dashboard info
9. 1985 Peter Yates film
10. Letter tip?
11. Waste maker
13. "I'm____roll"
15. Hawks
18. Things can get stuck in it
22. Tooth; comb. form
26. Kashmiri tongue
27. "Fine"
28. Rented
29. Spit
31. PIN spot?
32. Notwithstanding
33. Asian holiday
35. MLB award
37. Common preservative
38. ____Lillie
39. Fashion inits.
41. 57-Down's opposite
42. ____Guthrie
43. Close
48. Killed
49. Makes the final cut
51. In the matter of
52. Prime rib topper
53. Trick
54. Panache
55. Winner of 35-Down in '70 & '72
56. Ties
57. Like a cold oven
58. Played with

READ BETWEEN THE LINES

62. _____-ha

64. "_____ Hat"

66. Stage union; abbr.

67. "Rocky III" opponent

CHAPTER

37

"But it's so obvious, Rosco! Anyone can see this!" Belle's hands danced in the air as she spoke, while her hair sprang about as if spiked with electrical currents.

"I don't know, Belle. It's a big, big leap . . . And I'm not so sure this idea of—" He bent over her desk examining the five crosswords. "Ooof . . . yikes, that smarts."

Belle was immediate concern and action. She reached toward his shoulders as if she intended to physically remove him to a more comfortable location. "You shouldn't be standing like that. I'll get you a—"

"No. I *should* be standing . . . and walking around, and working this out . . . taking deep breaths, yelling at TV sportscasters, and doing all the normal things *real men* do." He tried to laugh, and swallowed a grimace of pain. "It only hurts when I try to think."

Belle cocked an eyebrow. "I'm not even *considering* going there."

"Hmmm . . . I have a feeling I'm going to regret that last statement."

"You mean *thinking* being one of the things *real men* don't do? Is it because you macho types find it too painful, so you try to avoid it?"

"It was a joke."

Belle looked at him. "Actually, it *is* a funny notion." She smiled, then returned her focus to the gathered crosswords. "Okay . . . puzzle number one, entitled *A Burning Question*—"

"But logic keeps telling me that refers to the fire—"

"It *could,* Rosco. It *could* . . . which is obviously what I initially believed—just as I'd imagined Gordon was at the center of the puzzles . . . But after putting the five together . . . well, look: first crossword. Here the constructor is trying to get our attention. *Question*—a la the title: Whose body is buried in Taneysville? Answer: SMOKESCREEN . . . SMOKE AND MIRRORS; i.e., we're dealing with a trick of some sort—"

"But the fire was real."

"I grant you that . . . And we certainly have Gordon's shifty business dealings to contend with, but the remains don't belong to his wife. Therefore, my intuition *strongly* suggests I've been barking up the wrong tree—"

"To borrow a phrase from Kit's activity book."

This time it was Belle who groaned; she gave Rosco a look. "Okay . . . crossword number two: CHANGE OF HEART spelled out at 35-Across . . . which is the same phrase as the title to puzzle number four—"

"But—"

"Hear me out . . . What does CHANGE OF HEART say to you, Rosco? . . . Doesn't it say that someone's unhappy with—"

"Unhappy with a decision and is revising it—"

"Precisely! In this case, we have an old person . . . someone who most probably witnessed the crime—"

"Hold on. I'm not seeing anything about witnessing—"

"Well, what else can the constructor be suggesting? We have anonymity, meaning fear of disclosure, fear of retaliation . . . So the assumption . . . the only *logical* assumption is that whoever created these puzzles not only knows *who* was buried in Taneysville but also *when* they were buried, and *who* committed the crime . . . Also, we're probably dealing with someone who's had a name change—directly referencing the need to remain anonymous . . . Look at the other solutions to the second crossword: WHAT'S IN A NAME at 19-Across . . . NAME OF THE GAME at 42-Across. I admit I assumed the puzzler meant Gordon, but obviously—"

"Belle, this is pure conjecture—"

She stared at him. "I know that, Rosco . . . I do . . . But I *feel* I'm right. Instinct tells me I am."

"So, your supposition is that our mystery constructor is still afraid of revealing an identity—?"

"Exactly! And you know why? Because the murderer is still *alive*—"

The phone rang at that moment. Belle yelped in frustration while simultaneously grabbing the receiver.

"My dear girl," she heard, "wait until you hear this. I've made such an important discovery."

"So have I," was Belle's hurried reply, but Sara seemed not to have heard her.

"Do you remember dear Rosco saying I had a 'bee in my bonnet' when we drove him home from the hospital?"

Belle's impatient fingers tapped across the crosswords. "Yes, Sara, I do."

"Well, that got me thinking about the letter *B* . . . and then one thing led to another and I began considering those somewhat archaic puzzle solutions we were discussing in my car on the ride out to Taneysville: NICKELODEON, PENNY ARCADE, FIVE AND DIME . . . You recall that I told you they'd piqued my curiosity?"

Belle hadn't a clue where this conversation was headed. She stifled a sigh and said, "Yes, Sara, I do remember that."

"Well, silly me. They're movie titles! 'B' movies, they would have been called back in the fifties when they were made . . . *COIN A PHRASE* . . . *THE QUARTERBACK* . . . Anyway, the reason I made note of them at the time was that a local girl appeared in all of them. She was one of the actresses."

". . . Paula Flynn." Belle's voice was a whisper.

Sara, on the other end of the line, responded with an equally subdued and astonished, "Why, yes. You've heard of her?"

Rosco uttered an impatient, "What's going on?"

Belle pointed to 17-Across in the fifth crossword and began to read aloud, "*Read between the Lines* . . . CHANCES ARE . . . HERS . . . WAS . . . A DOUBLE LIFE . . . THE LADY VANISHES . . . A STAR IS BORN . . . BUT . . . JUST . . . IN NAME ONLY . . ." She stopped and stared at Rosco. "There it is, as plain as day."

"Are you suggesting Paula Flynn is our mystery puzzler?" he asked. "Could she still be alive?"

Before Belle could answer, Sara's perplexed voice crackled through the receiver. "What about Paula Flynn?"

"I think she's the one who constructed the puzzles, Sara! No . . . no, I'm *certain* of it. She's our 'old person.' Our 'local person'—"

Sara interrupted with a matter of fact: "I'm afraid I have to agree with Rosco; I doubt the poor woman's still alive. I remember reading somewhere that she'd fallen on exceedingly hard times after her stint in Hollywood—"

"No, Sara. She's trying to tell us something, and she has

been hoping to do so clandestinely . . . It's Katie Vanovski, a.k.a. Paula Flynn. She must have returned to the area. She must be living somewhere nearby—"

"But, my dear, surely the press would have—"

"Not if she'd fallen on hard times, Sara. She wouldn't be news any longer—" The words stopped in Belle's throat. She gasped as the next idea hit her. "That's why Katie never went home during all those years! That's why she couldn't keep up with her niece and nephews. She was afraid. She must have witnessed the crime just before she left . . . and that's what she's been attempting to tell us. She knows who the murderer is! And she knows the person's still around!"

Sara's response was a vigorous: "Well, we'll have to find her, won't we?"

C H A P T E R

38

"Maurice Williams Talent Agency," the woman on the other end of the telephone line announced in a pronounced New York accent. Her tone was devoid of anything that could remotely be deemed friendly—or even polite.

"Yes," Rosco said, "is Mr. Williams in?"

The voice sighed. Mightily. "Mr. Williams died in 1963. Look, fella, we take no unsolicited phone calls, screenplays, or performer's pictures and resumés in this office, so—"

"No, no," Rosco interrupted, "I'm just trying to get a little information on one of your clients."

"Are you with the press?"

Rosco realized that the simple truth was going to get him nowhere with this woman, so he moved to plan B—the lie:

"My name's Jerry Sharpless and I work for Paramount Pictures? In L.A.? Anyway, I'm in the accounting department out here, and I just phoned the Screen Actors Guild and they informed me that the Morris Williams Talent Agency represented an actress by the name of Paula Flynn?"

"Paula Flynn . . . ? That was centuries ago. Even I wasn't with this office then."

"Well, the guild still has your agency's phone number listed as Miss Flynn's contact."

Rosco could hear the secretary tapping on her computer keys. After a moment she said, "Huh? Yep, she's still in here. Who woulda guessed it?"

"Well, I've got a residual check for her here. We used a clip from *The Quarterback* in our latest Schwarzenegger epic, and—"

"Just send it to our office here in New York and we'll process it out to her."

"It's for three dollars and ten cents."

"You're kidding me."

"Apparently it's a silent bit. All of her lines have been cut."

"That's not even worth the postage."

"That's what I figured you'd say. Do you want me to send the check directly to her house instead of having your people deal with it?"

The woman remained quiet, so Rosco pushed on. "Our office out here is gonna need to fill in a new W-4 form for her, and also enter her address into our data bank so we can process a W-2 in January."

The woman sighed. Again mightily. "Hold on, let me get her back up on my screen." After a few seconds she said, "Paula Flynn, Paula Flynn . . . okay, here we go: she's at the Bayshore Retirement Home, 717 Cherry Hill Lane. That's in Newcastle. It's up in Massachusetts—zip: 02744."

"Thank you very much. Have a nice day."

"Liar, liar, pants on fire," Belle said after Rosco hung up the phone. "I'm going to have to watch myself with you. You're very slick."

"Please, don't make me laugh."

Belle picked up the slip of paper on which Rosco had jotted

down the address. "Not the toniest section of the city."

"I know." He stood and took a step toward the front door. "Let's go."

"Don't you think we should call first? You don't want to just barge right in, do you?"

"Absolutely. There's no point in giving her time to think over her answers. Your theory may be right; it may be wrong; but remember, Paula—or rather, Katie—is an actress. We don't want to give her time to rehearse."

The Bayshore Retirement Home was on Newcastle's south side, and was a facility built in the early 1930s before the area's rampant development. Originally intended to sit amid bucolic woodlands and open spaces, it was now surrounded by four-lane roads and strip malls. There wasn't even so much as a garden for the elderly residents to stroll, and the only trees were spindly specimens that had been planted by the highway department and then left to brave the depredations of salted winter pavements, careless delivery truck drivers, and summer droughts.

"Pretty grim," Belle said as she parked in a spot marked VISITORS ONLY and turned off the engine.

"I was thinking the same thing," was Rosco's quiet response. "A long way from the glory days in Hollywood."

They sat for a moment pondering the singular life of the old woman they were about to meet—and the fear that had been driving her.

"What if we're not allowed to see her?" Belle's question was tinged with the vague hope that she and Rosco could go home before actually confronting the woman who had once been Katie Vanovski.

"We walk in as if we're expected and know exactly where

we're going. These places are all understaffed. No one will say boo."

"But how will we find her if we don't ask?"

"I imagine the residents' names are inserted in plaques outside their doors . . . We'll find her, don't worry. And if anyone questions where we're going, we just say Miss Flynn is expecting us . . . We can say it's business—that we spoke to her talent agent—which isn't a *complete* lie."

Belle sighed. "I kind of wish we didn't have to do this . . . We may be putting her in danger—"

"No. What we're doing is getting her *out* of trouble by finally putting a killer behind bars."

A s Rosco had predicted, no one stopped them or even spoke. They passed directly in front of a reception desk—devoid of personnel—and into a common area dotted with wheelchairs and their dozing occupants, and wall-mounted TVs that no one seemed to be watching. A staircase and two overworked elevators led to a second floor. There wasn't an inch of carpeting to be seen, or a single decorative pillow, ornamental plant, or vase of plastic flowers. *Institutional* seemed a word invented for places like Bayshore.

Belle and Rosco traversed the first floor, climbed the stairs, and were confronted by two long and utterly cheerless corridors. Rosco had been correct: residents' names were affixed beside each bedroom door. Paula Flynn was among them.

"Poor thing . . ." Belle whispered. She took a breath, knocked on the door, received no response, then looked at Rosco, who gently eased the door open. "Miss Flynn?" they murmured in respectful unison.

Hunched crookedly in a battered armchair and sitting with her back to them, Paula Flynn made no reply. Instead, she seemed to be staring at the window while the reflected daylight illumined her birdlike body as if from within—as if she were undergoing a continuous round of X rays. Her skin looked transparent; her scalp shone through her thin white hair; even the blue hospital blanket that hung from her shoulders seemed as thin as tissue paper.

Belle opened her mouth to speak again, but no words came. Instead she gazed about the room: the hospital bed, the shabby dresser, a table on wheels on which sat a plastic water pitcher and Styrofoam cups. The sole source of color came from three movie posters hung on the wall above the bed. Designed in classic fifties Hollywood style, each boasted large letters shaded in fiery red and orange that provided a jolting 3-D effect. *NICKELODEON, starring Ronald Harmon and Paula Flynn . . . PENNY ARCADE, with Sterling Sanders and Paula Flynn . . . Rock Mason and Paula Flynn in THE QUARTERBACK.* It was hard to imagine the gorgeous young female depicted in the artwork was the same Paula Flynn.

As Belle and Rosco stood in silence debating the best way to introduce themselves, Paula Flynn spoke, although her body remained turned toward the window. "You weren't supposed to find me, Miss Graham."

Rosco and Belle shared a glance but didn't reply.

"I can see your reflection in the window . . . Your photograph in the *Crier* doesn't do you justice. You're a beautiful young woman."

"Thank you," was all Belle could think to say.

"And I gather this is your husband . . . ? Mr. Polycrates? The camera-shy private investigator."

"I find it helps my line of work to keep my mug out of the papers." He stepped around to face Paula. "But, please, Miss Flynn, call me Rosco."

She studied him. "You've done well for yourself, Miss Graham." She nodded her tiny head toward the movie posters. "You remind me of Sterling Sanders, Rosco; however, I would guess you still have the teeth you were born with."

"Yes . . . Please forgive our intrusion, Miss Flynn, but I don't see how we could have solved this case without your—"

"My puzzles explained everything. All you needed to do was expose the guilty party—"

Belle stepped forward. "But only you know who that is."

The old eyes stared, the old face almost immobile. "Pardon me?"

"Rosco has friends in the police department, Miss Flynn. You won't be in danger if you share your information. The killer will be arrested. He'll be off the streets."

"There's no statute of limitations on murder cases," Rosco added. "You'll have nothing to fear."

Paula Flynn returned her gaze to the window. "But I . . . I don't understand . . ."

"We need you to tell us the name of the person who killed the girl in Taneysville," Rosco said. He tried to fold his arms across his chest, but a sharp pain from his rib cage stopped him midway. He opted to keep his hands at his sides. "Miss Flynn, by withholding this information, you continue to put yourself in danger."

"Danger? But I . . . I . . ." Paula Flynn looked at Belle and frowned in dismay.

"You did witness the crime, didn't you?" Belle asked.

Again, the ancient actress frowned. "No . . . No, I have no idea who murdered the woman . . . I only know her identity."

CHAPTER

39

Rosco had retrieved two folding chairs from the Bayshore Retirement Home's dining area on the assumption that Paula Flynn's explanation was going to take longer than expected. Belle had used his absence to relay her theory as to what had occurred those many years ago in Taneysville, but as Rosco set up the chairs, Paula startled them by stating an emphatic: "You couldn't be more wrong. I've never been to Taneysville in my life."

"But . . . but . . ." Belle stuttered, "the local library has a scrapbook of all your successes . . . Photos . . . magazine interviews . . ." She paused to collect herself, then continued in a gentler tone. "Miss Flynn . . . Rosco and I know your real name. We know why you left home as abruptly as you did . . . and why you were never able to return."

Paula remained motionless for a long moment. Eventually she whispered a nearly inaudible: "I'm not Katie Vanovski. I never have been. And I've never been to Taneysville."

Belle looked at Rosco, who raised his eyebrows in disbelief.

Both were silent, pondering how to deal with what they knew was a total falsehood, invented by an aging and rather traumatized mind.

"I understand," Belle finally answered. "You've seen something terrible, and you don't want to discuss it . . . That's okay . . . It is . . . but Rosco and I . . . well, we just want to see you out of danger. Whoever murdered—"

"I'm not—"

Belle reached out her hand and touched the bony arm. "I know . . . You're Paula Flynn now."

The old lady's head sagged while a brief and bitter laugh rose from her hollow chest. "Not even close."

Again Rosco and Belle regarded each other; this time Rosco was the first to speak.

"But you did send Belle the crosswords—?"

"And the name outside your door says—"

"TRADING PLACES . . . SMOKE AND MIRRORS . . . LOOK FOR A SWITCH . . . That's what I was trying to tell you in the puzzles. I stole Katie's identity. I—"

"You did what—?" Belle made no attempt to hide her confusion.

" 'Borrowed' it, I guess you might say . . . At least at first . . ." The woman who called herself Paula Flynn seemed to drift into a trance. A thin smile crept across her wizened face. "In Boston, in 1951, some Hollywood producers came through on what they called a 'talent hunt' . . . I'd been to plenty of contests like it before. They were usually no more than a bunch of dirty old men ogling the young girls—trying to use the 'casting couch' routine . . . Anyway, I was twenty-six years old by then and I'd learned how to gauge who was on the up-and-up and who wasn't . . . The Bijou Theater, that's where the contest was held . . . It's where I met Katie . . ."

"The Boston contest . . ." Rosco's words were more confirmation than question. He looked at Belle, who returned his gaze in utter silence.

The old actress's voice continued. "It was amazing how much we looked like each other . . . Of course, Katie was a brunette and I was blond. Naturally blond; not a bottle blond." The smile grew then abruptly receded.

"But the newspaper articles out in Taneysville indicated Katie was sixteen when she got her big break," was Belle's perplexed response. "That would have made her ten years younger than you."

"Katie acted a good deal older than her years. And I always looked young for my age. I could pass for a college girl until I was well into my thirties." The shoulders hunched. "She'd had an awful time of it at home. She *and* her sister—"

Belle was about to ask another question, but the old lady's words drifted off in a different direction. "It was on a Friday afternoon . . . a wet day in early spring. The building's heat was either on the fritz or the owners were being cheap. Whatever the case, we were all chilled and damp and pretty wilted. That on top of bad cases of nerves and not having much in our stomachs . . . There were about fifty of us. All types of girls . . . Katie and I gravitated to one another because we looked so much alike I guess—same height, build, everything. We could have been twins, except for our hair . . . And we'd obviously traveled down the same unpleasant roadways.

"Anyway, the talent scouts were on the level that day—that is, unless you consider the studio contract they roped me into, and the six years it took me to get them to 'release' me . . . That and the 'favors' I had to do for certain directors in order to get 'meatier' parts in their films.

"But back then everything seemed golden. The five winning girls were going to be taken out to Hollywood for a screen test—all expenses paid. In those days you had to be able to sing and dance as well as act; not like today when . . .

well, no matter . . . Anyway, we all auditioned, and were told to come back on Monday for the final decision—meaning forty-five girls were going to return just to be told to 'take a hike.' I offered to let Katie bunk in with me. I had a small flat in Boston, and that way she wouldn't have to go home. But she said she was leaving home no matter what—win or lose, come hell or high water—and needed to pack her belongings. She was really desperate for a way out of Taneysville—"

"But she didn't win, did she." Belle interjected, more as a statement than a question.

"Oh, she did! Of course she did. Katie was a talented kid."

"Now I'm the one who's confused," Rosco said.

"On Monday we returned to the Bijou—all of us contestants sitting in the audience, and the talent scouts arranged behind a long table up on the stage. Katie was nowhere to be seen, so I assumed she'd missed her bus or something. I thought she'd fly through the doors at any moment . . . As the men began calling off the winners there were screams and hollers . . . I remember my fingers were crossed so tightly they went numb. Or maybe it was the cold . . . Then a man said, 'And the fifth girl is . . . Katie Vanovski.' And my heart sank. I wanted to be one of those five so badly."

"But Katie still wasn't there."

"No . . . There was this heavy silence. I looked around . . . We all did. All of us in our hats and dress coats holding our breath and clutching our purses. He repeated the name, and by the way he said it, I knew he wasn't prepared to wait, that he'd assume Katie had gotten cold feet—which would be a sure indication she'd never make it in the movies . . . So I jumped up and said, 'Here I am . . . Here I am! Katie!' "

"And these guys believed you?"

"We were a bunch of amateurs; we didn't have pictures or resumés for them to look at; no one filmed the auditions; and there were so many of us of us to keep track of. 'Well, Katie Cat-Got-Your-Tongue Vanovski, this is your lucky day,' the man said as I walked toward the table. I remember him grinning at the notion that I was too excited to know my own name, but his only question was to ask what had happened to my hair. I told him I'd bleached it over the weekend, and he grinned again and said, 'I like it better this way, Katie. You're going to go somewhere, kiddo.' "

"When did they take you to California for your screen test?" Rosco asked.

"We were on the train the next morning. It turned out the studio was desperate for women with Boston accents for a Katharine Hepburn film, and all five of us got contracts." Paula's eyes misted over. "I really only did it to save Katie's spot. I would have admitted the truth if she'd shown up . . . even out in Hollywood . . . but she never did. And after a while I managed to fool myself into believing she really had gotten a case of cold feet, and that she wouldn't have lasted two seconds with the wolves and lowlifes that lurk around every studio . . . In the back of my mind, though, I always guessed there had been a problem."

"And so Paula Flynn's your real name?" Belle asked at length.

"Oh, no . . . The studio invented it. If Katie had been at the Bijou that day, she would have been renamed Paula Flynn instead of me . . . And I would have spent my life—well, doing what I'd been doing before."

The three were quiet for several long minutes, but Rosco wanted to hear the obvious, so he asked, "And you have reason to believe the body found in Taneysville is Katie Vanovski's?"

The old head nodded. "I have no real proof; just an old woman's intuition. As soon as I read the story in the newspaper—that's when it all hit me. Although, I guess . . . I guess I'd always suspected Katie had been killed . . . Because

290 • NERO BLANC

if she was so desperate to leave home, why didn't she show up to hear the results of the contest—?"

"But she didn't know she'd won—"

"And later on, when I was in California . . . when I was, well, when I was lying and telling folks I was born and raised in Taneysville . . . Why didn't she challenge me then? Why did she just stay silent? Year after year . . . ?"

Belle frowned. "After you'd become a star you could have told the truth. You could have revealed your own story."

A weary sigh greeted this remark. "No, I couldn't. My past was . . . well, let's just say it wasn't all that squeaky-clean. I needed to be someone exactly like Katie. People didn't need to know who I really was . . . or what I'd been."

"But there's no proof the remains are actually hers," Belle offered after another few moments of silence.

"That's simple enough for Abe Jones to determine," Rosco replied. "If his DNA samples match up with the Bazinnes'— that solves half the mystery. As to who the murderer is . . . or was—"

"That's what I wanted you both to figure out," Paula interrupted with some vehemence. "Instead of tracking me down . . . When the body showed up, everything came back to me: everything Katie said—and everything she was too scared to tell me about what her brother-in-law was doing to her."

"Jacques Bazinne," Belle finally said. "Also deceased . . . The father of three middle-aged offspring who are convinced their famous aunt deserted them." She looked at Rosco. "How do you tell someone their dad may have been a murderer?"

CHAPTER

40

"So . . ." Belle said as she and Rosco settled into the front seat of her car, "what next? I feel we have an obligation to share what we've learned with the Bazinne family."

"Absolutely. I agree." Rosco drew in a troubled breath. "It's not going to be easy, though."

Belle was silent, thinking. "Well, we can't do it over the phone, that's for certain . . . I've met Jeanne . . . Maybe I should drive out there now and talk to her—"

"It's going to be a tough conversation, my love."

"I know . . . but what other choice do we have?"

". . . Okay." After a beat he added, "But I should be with you."

Belle considered the suggestion for a moment. "I'd love to have the company, Rosco . . . And I know I'm really going to need it on the return trip . . . However, I have a feeling it will be better to approach her as one woman to another."

Rosco also remained quiet as he considered this. Then said, "I hate to make you face this alone, but I think you're probably right . . . I'll tell you what, though: Why don't you leave me at Hoffmeyer's store first, and then pick me up after your conversation with Jeanne. That way you'll have company on the ride home."

Belle nodded brief agreement as she started the engine. "No time like the present . . . I guess."

Rosco removed his cell phone from his jacket and began punching in a series of numbers. "Before we go running off to Taneysville, I should bring Tree Hoffmeyer up to date. I'm sure he's going to want to formulate some sort of press release."

As Belle left the Bayshore Retirement Home's parking lot and began driving west, Rosco did just that, concluding with a subdued: "Of course, the odds of ever knowing conclusively who killed Katie Vanovski are next to nil."

Tree's response was businesslike. "That's probably beside the point at this juncture. The salient fact is that the murder occurred more than fifty years ago, dispelling all speculation about 'mobsters dumping bodies' and 'dirty laundry,' et cetera. We're looking at ancient history; the fact that a movie star had some connection to the event will only increase voter recognition. I feel sorry for this Katie Vanovski, I do, but in the long run, I hate to say it, but this is a best-case scenario for my campaign . . . I really appreciate all the hard work you've been putting in, Rosco, and I'd like to talk longer, but I should schedule a news conference right away—"

"Ahhh," Rosco said in an attempt to slow him down, "could you hold off on that for a while? We're on our way to Taneysville right now. It's only fair to notify the Bazinne family before they hear the news on the radio or TV."

In the silence at the other end of the line, Rosco could hear impatience and compassion vying with one another. "It's Friday afternoon. I've got only four days before the election. This information has to get—"

"Just give me a couple hours, that's all I'm asking. You'll still have time to make the evening news."

Hoffmeyer took a few moments to answer, but eventually said, "I'll wait for your call. Just don't hang me up on this, okay?"

Rosco clicked off and slid the phone back into his jacket. "Politics isn't the nicest game in the world."

On the drive to Taneysville, Belle and Rosco decided they should also inform the elder Hoffmeyers—a duty Rosco would handle while Belle explained the situation to Jeanne Bazinne. Pulling up in front of the general store, Belle tried for a lighthearted: "Watch out for the pork rinds," while Rosco also attempted a pseudo-sunny:

"What you don't know won't hurt you."

Both sallies fell flat. Then Belle turned her car toward Lonnie Tucker's gas station.

She parked, took a deep breath which was intended to banish the complex sensation of pity mingled with outrage, then stepped from the car. Gloom, sorrow, and anger walked beside her as she entered the garage office, where Lonnie greeted her in pleasant unconcern as he tallied up some figures in his accounting books. "Jeanne's in the trench working on an oil change," he said. He seemed totally unconcerned about Belle's motives in seeking out his mechanic. As Belle began crossing the shop's gritty floor, Jeanne had just started to crawl out of a large pit that allowed her access to the underside of the car she'd been servicing.

"You here for a change?" she called out without looking to see who the visitor was.

"Change?"

"Oil change?"

"No . . . Actually, I came here to talk to you, Jeanne . . .

about your father." Jeanne stood in utter silence as myriad expressions began racing over her face.

"He's dead." Jeanne wiped her greasy hands on a rag that was equally embedded with grime, then turned as if to resume her work. Another thought arrested her, however, and she stepped toward Belle. Her lips were tight with unspent fury. "So don't think you or that PI you're married to can accuse him of offing that girl up at Quigleys'."

Belle paused for an infinitesimal second, enough only to wonder what private connection Jeanne had made. "That's quite a leap . . . What makes you imagine we'd be considering that?"

"Blaming my pop?" Jeanne snorted. "Why not? Everyone comes lookin' for us Bazinnes if there's trouble. Fire up at the old house? Frank's the bad guy. No one even bothers lookin' for the truth or pays the slightest attention to Big Otto mouthin' off in Eddie's Elbow Room . . . No, sir . . . Otto's the one playin' with matches . . . But it's always the same around here. You got trouble? You hunt up a Bazinne . . ." She threw the rag on a zinc-topped table strewn with wrenches and grease guns. "That's why I 'imagine' you're thinkin' my dad was involved in what happened up at Quigleys'. It was only a matter of time before those goody-goodies up at the church decided he snuffed that girl . . . Makes it a heck of a lot easier with him bein' dead and gone, don't it?"

Belle said nothing, but neither did she back down. She simply stayed put and continued studying the angry woman who in turn seemed to grow larger and more ferocious as she stared defiantly back.

"You're not gettin' me to spill my guts about our glorious, fun-filled childhoods, if that's what you're hopin', doll. And you're not gonna catch Frank or Luke doin' it either . . . And they won't be near as polite as me—"

"It's you I want to talk to, Jeanne. Woman to woman."

"Oh, lady, where are you from? The moon? You and me got nothin' in common. Absolutely nuttin'!" Again, Jeanne made as if to step back into the trench; Belle read rage in the rigid set of her shoulders—as well as some other indecipherable but equally violent emotion.

"Tell me about your aunt, Jeanne."

"Lady, you're not listenin' to me—at all! I don't want to talk. Not to you. Not to anyone."

Belle stood her ground. "Katie didn't desert you, Jeanne."

"What do you call it when someone up and leaves and never looks back? Never sends her sister a birthday hello or a sympathy card when she's dying—"

"Katie didn't go to Hollywood, Jeanne. She didn't act in those—"

"She sure as heck did! She changed her name to Paula Flynn! She was a big star! She was famous. I saw her picture in all those—"

"That wasn't your aunt. That was someone who took Katie's name."

Jeanne rounded on Belle. Beneath the caked dirt, her face was an ugly and threatening red. "You can't steal names!"

"You can if no one protests."

Either the words themselves or the gravity of Belle's tone finally took root in Jeanne's conscious thought. Her heavy shoulders quivered ever so slightly, but the emotional change this small physical gesture revealed was immense. "What do you mean?" The voice was now hesitant and uncertain.

"I mean the actress known as Paula Flynn isn't your aunt. I met her today . . . Paula Flynn . . . She told me all about the talent contest that she and your aunt attended—"

"Before I was born—"

"That's right. In the spring of 1951. And yes, your aunt Katie won . . . She won the chance to go to Hollywood and take a screen test, but she wasn't there to claim her prize . . .

She'd returned to Taneysville to pack. She never made it back to the theater in Boston."

Jeanne's bewildered gaze fell to the floor. "But Mom said . . . I mean, Aunt Katie had already moved out of our house when she did that contest . . . She'd rented the room over Hoffmeyer's store . . . on accounta . . . on accounta . . . well, Mom said Pop used to get real mad at Katie. Didn't like her gettin' fancy ideas . . . didn't like her wearin' fancy clothes . . . showin' off to all the guys . . ." Jeanne's fists swiped at eyes that were suddenly brimming with tears. "But Pop wouldn't have . . . I don't think Pop would have . . . He wouldn't have hurt her like that." She shook her large head. Belle reached out her hand, but Jeanne flinched away.

"I don't want to talk to you anymore, lady. And I don't want you talkin' to Luke or Frank either. We got enough troubles without people makin' up stories about things that happened half a century ago."

"How did your mother die, Jeanne?"

"If you're askin' if Pop beat her up, he didn't! . . . She got cancer—just like other people do . . . And I called out to Hollywood. I tried findin' where Aunt Katie lived . . ."

Belle took a deep breath. She knew her next piece of news would be the hardest to bear. "It's almost certain that the body found near the Quigley house belonged to your aunt. DNA testing will prove it conclusively."

"But Katie went to *Hollywood.* She left this dump and never once looked back—" Jeanne's face crumpled. "My pop had nothing to do with this! I swear he didn't."

M ilt Hoffmeyer Sr. hadn't been in his store when Belle had dropped off Rosco. Unable to immediately perform his part of the assignment, he'd purchased a large bag of pork rinds—"to share" he'd told the girl minding the cash register—as well as a copy of *Newsweek,* both of which he'd carried outside to the wooden bench that sat beside the store's main entrance. There, Rosco had settled down to wait.

After twenty minutes, Milt stepped onto the porch, looked down at Rosco, and said, "I guess you're waiting for me." His heavy face looked both serious and sad, and Rosco felt some annoyance that Hoffmeyer's grandson hadn't kept his end of the bargain but had obviously called his grandparents to tell them the news.

Rosco nodded. "That's right."

Milt also sat on the bench. "Ever since Gordon bought that property . . ." he began. "First John and the vestry, and then that awful fire . . ." The words trailed off while Rosco considered how difficult the situation was going to be for everyone in Taneysville. Whether they'd liked Jacques Bazinne or not, his children were their neighbors, and Katie had once been the town's brightest hope.

"We only put the final pieces together this morning, Milt . . . after a long talk with Paula Flynn—the real Paula Flynn, that is."

"So . . . where do we go from here? What's the next step . . . ?" Again Milt's words faltered. He straightened his spine, then let it sag again. He seemed old and very tired.

Rosco shrugged. "It's all up to the authorities at this point. There's no telling how they plan to proceed, but they won't let it die, you can count on that . . . As far as Tree's concerned, he doesn't seem anxious to have me pursue it any further."

"No. No, I wouldn't think so . . . That's not going to help him." Milt glanced at Rosco, then dropped his gaze to the aged wooden planks that stretched across the porch. "Katie was a headstrong girl. Had big dreams. When she set her mind on something, no one could stop her . . ."

"That's what I understand—and much too young to die. Especially the way she did."

Milt looked at Rosco. "It was an accident; you have to believe that."

Rosco didn't respond, so Milt repeated a more emphatic: "It was an accident . . ."

"Well, yes, given . . . the nature of the wound . . . I would guess that . . . might have been a possibility."

Milt stood and stepped toward the edge of the porch and placed his hands in his pockets. "The moment Gordon," he began, then stopped. "And then that damnable backhoe . . . Well, I'm glad the truth is finally out . . . I really am . . . Lies and secrets are just too, too . . ." He shook his head, and looked back at Rosco again. "I couldn't let her go. I loved her way too much . . . My heart would race just looking at her . . ."

In the utter silence that ensued, Rosco watched the last piece of the puzzle begin to fall into place. "You . . . You and Katie—"

"We were just kids . . . kids in love . . ." Milt's words came out in a rush. "No one knew. Not even our friends . . . I mean, we were so young . . . I was seventeen; she was a year younger; and back then, well . . . times were different . . ." He pulled a handkerchief from his back pocket and wiped at one eye. "You see, Katie had moved out of her sister's house . . . She'd had . . . troubles there . . . My father never liked Jacques Bazinne—considered him a real bully and a brute. The classic example of how abusive some men can be . . . So, Dad let Katie have the room above the store, and hired her to work behind the counter after school."

Rosco thought. "That couldn't have sat well with Bazinne."

"No. No, it didn't. But legally, Jacques couldn't make her stay home because he had no custody over her; she was only his wife's sister . . . But a lot of anger surfaced because of what my dad did . . . Folks took sides . . . and Jacques's wife, she was Katie's older sister, she accused . . . Well, it was an upsetting time. I guess that's why everyone in town was happy to think that Katie had become Paula Flynn, the movie actress. They realized the chances of a Hollywood star coming back to Taneysville wouldn't be likely."

Milt sat back down on the bench. He looked worn out, hunched and enfeebled by decades of secrecy. "I've been living with this heartache nearly all my life. And I'd give just about anything to change what happened." He sighed.

". . . Afterwards, after Katie was . . . Well, I turned kind of wild . . . got into a lot of scrapes . . . turned pretty tough and mean . . . It was May who saved me. It's May who keeps saving me . . . And now I've got to . . ." His head sank toward his chest. He dabbed at his eyes again. Rosco didn't speak or move.

". . . It was the Friday night after that talent contest in Boston . . . Katie told me she'd won. We were meeting secretly—like usual. She said they were sending her out to Hollywood . . . told me she had to pack and return to Boston Monday morning early. I remember thinking how odd it was that she didn't seem more excited . . . I decided it was because she'd already left me—in her mind, anyway. And that felt even worse . . . like I'd been forgotten . . ."

"She hadn't won, Milt—at least not on Friday."

Milt stared at Rosco for a long time. "So that was it . . . That's why she acted so strange." He closed his eyes tight, seeing Katie, seeing the past. "On Saturday night we took a long walk together and ended up at the Quigleys' lane. There were no lights on so we snuck up to the house. It was unlocked—nobody locked their houses back then, not like nowadays." Milt took a deep breath while tears began coursing down his cheeks.

"Did you go in?" Rosco asked.

"I didn't want to but Katie insisted. She wanted to . . . She wanted to, you know . . . I'd never . . . I'd never done it before, but she was . . . She was so bold, so excited about the danger of it all—thinking the Quigleys might come home at any moment . . . And then when it was all over, I . . . I don't know. I was so desperately in love with her, I couldn't bear the idea of her leaving. Not after what we'd just had together."

"What did you do?"

"I begged her not to go away . . . I told her we could get married . . . that someday I'd be taking over my dad's store . . . But she only laughed at me. She said she'd rot if she stayed in Taneysville any longer . . . Then she marched outside—kind of mad and spiteful as if she were angry at herself as well as me. I chased after her and grabbed her shoulders. She pushed me away . . . And then . . . then we were just struggling with each other, not fighting but sort of locked together. The next thing I knew she was falling out of my grasp. She hit her head on a rock . . . There was so much blood . . . It was everywhere. All over the . . . There was nothing I could do."

"And you buried her there?"

"I didn't know what to do; and I just panicked, I guess. I was only a kid. A kid in trouble. And I'd killed the one person I . . ." Milt stifled a sob. "The Quigleys didn't come back. Later, I found out they'd gone up to Maine to visit family. Their garden had been freshly tilled. Nothing showed. I took all Katie's things out of the room upstairs . . . After that, everyone assumed she'd gone to Hollywood, just like she'd promised to do."

"And then Paula Flynn began to appear in movies."

"If I hadn't known the truth, I would have sworn it was Katie—they looked that much alike."

Another sob shook Milt's frame while Rosco placed his hand softly on the old man's shoulder. "You're going to have to be charged, you know that, don't you, Milt? There'll be a trial."

"I know. It's been a long wait, but what I feel now is relief . . . the pure and simple truth is finally . . ." The words died away.

"Do you want me to call Lonnie? Or can I count on you to turn yourself in?"

Milt sat quietly and said nothing. After a few minutes, Rosco said, "Milt?"

"I'd like to tell May first. And Tree. I want them to hear it from me." He stood, stepped off the porch, then turned back to Rosco. "I'm going to go talk to May . . . then I'll call Lonnie."

Milt walked slowly down the street and disappeared around the corner. Rosco remained on the bench for another ten minutes, sitting quietly with his arms folded across his chest and pondering the situation. After a while Belle pulled up. He stood, walked down to the car, and dropped wearily into the passenger's seat.

"What was Milt's reaction to the news about Jacques Bazinne?" she asked.

He didn't answer right away, so she said, "Are you all right?"

He put an arm around her shoulders, then gave her a long and loving kiss. "I think it's time we went home."

Across

1. Trail
5. Echolocation device
10. Work with
14. Sore
15. Senseless
16. Rescue
17. A thought; part 1
19. Leg joint
20. Up and_____, as a starlet
21. Bovine pacifiers
23. Explosive; abbr.
24. Garden tool
25. A thought; part 2
29. Lose one's luster
30. Was once
31. Broadway hit of '68
34. Boy
36. Ties up
40. A thought; part 3
44. Mold
45. Continental divide?
46. Regrets
47. Sch. grp.
49. Like some excuses
51. A thought; part 4
56. "Our Town" subdivision?
59. Chihuahua cheer
60. Greek peak
61. Gawker
63. Hibernia
65. Thinker of the thought
68. "_____Is a Doggone Good Thing"
69. "Married to the Mob" star
70. Ruby and Sandra
71. British gun
72. Belonging to a certain Hardy heroine
73. Finishes

Down

1. Repair
2. Allergic response?
3. Topic
4. Blow up
5. Letter opener?
6. Billfold item
7. Civil rights grp.
8. Void
9. Turn scarlet
10. Question
11. Swahili, Kikuyu, Zulu, et al.
12. Shindig
13. Canine and wisdom
18. Bear in the sky
22. Take the helm
26. At ease
27. Breakfast, lunch, or dinner
28. Horseman of 1775
29. Shaved ice drink
31. Towel word
32. Damper dust
33. Playwright Levin
35. Turn scarlet
37. The Seine, basically
38. Compass point
39. '60's grp.
41. Active lead-in
42. Wood product
43. Russian range
48. Classify
50. Cat call?
51. Cowardly namesakes?
52. "The Radical" writer
53. Enthusiasm
54. It's often in dispute
55. Clubs
56. One of the Woodys
57. Surrendered
58. Lock

POST SCRIPT

62. "Travels in the Congo" author
64. Dusk to Donne

66. Sighs of relief
67. Literary monogram

The Answers

A BURNING QUESTION

1 A	2 D	3 S		4 B	5 E	6 E			7 S	8 A	9 S	10 H	11 E	12 D
13 R	A	M		14 L	A	M	15 B		16 A	D	M	I	R	E
17 R	K	O		18 A	S	I	A		19 L	O	O	K	I	N
20 O	A	K		21 S	T	R	I	22 V	E		23 K	E	N	T
24 W	R	E	25 S	T	S		26 T	E	M	27 P	E			
		28 E	M	S		29 T	A	X		30 A	S	31 S	32 A	33 I
34 A	35 M	M	O		36 W	O	N		37 P	A	C	M	A	N
38 S	M	O	K	39 E	A	N	D	40 M	I	R	R	O	R	S
41 G	L	U	E	R	S		42 S	E	T		43 E	K	E	T
44 D	I	T	S	O		45 O	W	L		46 P	E	I		
		47 I	S	48 I	T	I		49 C	A	N	N	E	50 D	51
52 B	53 I	54 G		55 D	O	T	T	E	D		57 G	L	O	
58 A	T	O	59 N	C	E		60 C	O	L	D		61 G	A	T
62 N	E	V	A	D	A		63 H	A	L	L		64 U	T	E
65 S	M	A	L	L	S		66 D	O	E			67 N	E	D

SWAP MEET

```
 1  2  3      4  5  6           7  8  9 10 11
 S  T  E  ■  O  T  S  ■  ■  ■  S  T  O  R  E
12        13       14    15
 H  E  R  ■  D  I  E  D  ■  S  P  A  Y  E  D
16        17              18
 O  E  R  ■  E  K  E  R  ■  H  A  M  L  E  T
19          20          21
 W  H  A  T  S  I  N  A  N  A  M  E  ■  ■  ■
22              23           24 25 26
 N  E  N  E  S  ■  ■  W  A  R  ■  ■  A  M  O
       27    28 29          30 31
 ■  ■  T  R  A  D  I  N  G  P  L  A  C  E  S
    32       33          34
 ■  S  T  R  ■  O  C  T  ■  ■  Y  M  C  A  S
    35       36          37 38
 ■  C  H  A  N  G  E  O  F  H  E  A  R  T  ■
39          40          41
 G  R  E  C  O  ■  ■  T  E  A  ■  M  U  Y  ■
42          43 44          45
 N  A  M  E  O  F  T  H  E  G  A  M  E  ■  ■
46          47          48          49 50
 U  M  E  ■  ■  A  L  E  ■  ■  T  A  M  P  S
       51 52          53 54
 ■  ■  ■  R  E  D  C  H  A  M  E  L  E  O  N
55 56 57          58          59
 S  T  R  I  P  E  ■  U  S  E  S  ■  N  E  E
60          61          62
 D  R  A  P  E  D  ■  B  E  S  T  ■  T  S  E
63                64          65
 S  E  N  S  E  ■  ■  ■  A  S  S  ■  S  Y  R
```

TWENTY-FOUR SKIDDOO

1 P	2 L	3 E	4 A	⬛	5 B	6 A	7 L	8 M	9 S	⬛	⬛	10 P	11 T	12 A
13 R	O	L	L	14 P	E	W	E	E	S	⬛	⬛	15 L	O	B
16 O	N	E	F	L	E	17 W	E	A	S	T	⬛	18 A	N	N
19 M	I	C	⬛	20 O	R	I	S	S	A	⬛	21 L	I	T	E
⬛	⬛	22 W	A	I	S	T	⬛	⬛	⬛	⬛	23 O	D	O	R
24 O	25 N	E	F	L	E	W	26 W	27 E	28 S	T	⬛	⬛	⬛	⬛
29 S	M	E	E	⬛	30 A	P	S	E	⬛	⬛	⬛	31 A	32 S	33 P
34 L	O	O	K	35 S	36 F	37 O	R	A	S	W	38 I	T	C	H
39 Y	O	N	⬛	40 D	E	A	D	⬛	⬛	⬛	41 R	E	A	D
⬛	⬛	42 O	N	E	F	L	E	43 W	44 O	45 V	E	R	⬛	⬛
46 C	47 A	48 M	P	⬛	49 O	R	A	L	S	⬛	⬛	⬛	⬛	⬛
50 A	B	E	T	⬛	51 G	52 E	O	R	G	E	⬛	53 S	54 O	55 S
56 T	H	E	⬛	57 C	U	C	K	O	O	S	58 N	E	S	T
59 C	O	T	⬛	60 A	S	T	E	R	N	⬛	61 B	E	L	A
62 H	R	S	⬛	63 T	H	O	R	S	⬛	⬛	64 A	N	O	N

"CHANGE" OF HEART

¹P	²I	³P		⁴D	⁵A	⁶M		⁷A	⁸M	⁹A	¹⁰U	¹¹P	¹²S
¹³A	V	E		¹⁴E	V	A		¹⁵G	E	M	¹⁶T	R	A
¹⁷T	E	N		¹⁸N	I	¹⁹C	K	E	L	O	²⁰D	E	O	N
		²¹N	²²A	Y	S	A	Y		²³T	R	U		
²⁴M	²⁵A	Y	I		²⁶O	D	E	²⁷E		²⁸O	²⁹F	³⁰F	³¹S
³²G	R	A	M	³³P	³⁴A		³⁵A	C	E	³⁶C	³⁷E	³⁸I	R	E
³⁹T	A	R	T	A	R		⁴⁰S	C	A	R		⁴¹V	I	A
	⁴²C	O	I	N	⁴³A	P	H	R	A	⁴⁴S	E	
⁴⁵A	⁴⁶G	A		⁴⁷N	I	N	A		⁴⁸O	S	C	A	R	⁴⁹R	⁵⁰S
⁵¹S	O	D		⁵²T	E	D		⁵³B	E	A	N	I	E
⁵⁴S	T	E	⁵⁵M		⁵⁶Y	⁵⁷E	⁵⁸N		⁵⁹R	D	A	S
		⁶⁰A	⁶¹S	⁶²K		⁶³B	⁶⁴E	⁶⁵S	T	E	D
⁶⁶Q	⁶⁷U	⁶⁸A	R	T	E	⁶⁹R	B	A	C	K	⁷⁰I	⁷¹R	⁷²A
⁷³E	R	R		⁷⁴A	N	Y		⁷⁵T	O	O		⁷⁶M	A	D
⁷⁷D	E	C		⁷⁸R	O	E		⁷⁹O	T	S		⁸⁰E	T	E

READ BETWEEN THE LINES

1 M	2 M	3 D		4 T	5 O	6 S	7 S			8 M	9 E	10 S	11 H
12 A	E	R	13 O	14 R	A	N	T	15 S		16 P	L	E	A
17 C	H	A	N	18 C	E	S	A	R	E	19 H	E	R	S
20 A	T	T	A	R			21 F	O	L	D	22 D		23 N	I	T
24 W	A	S		25 A	26 D	27 O	U	B	L	E	28 L	I	F	E
			29 S	W	A	K		30 E	S	N	E			
31 A	32 T	33 T	A	34 R	A	M	35 M		36 T	A	37 B	38 B	39 Y
40 T	H	E	41 L	A	D	Y	V	42 A	43 N	I	S	H	E	S
44 M	O	T	I	F			45 P	R	E		46 E	T	A	L
			47 V	I	48 D	49 I		50 L	A	51 I	D			
52 A	53 S	54 T	A	R	I	S	55 B	O	R	N		56 B	57 U	58 T
59 U	T	A		60 E	D	I	E			61 R	62 H	I	N	O
63 J	U	S	64 T		65 I	N	N	66 A	67 M	E	O	N	L	Y
68 U	N	T	O		69 N	I	C	E	R		70 O	D	I	E
71 S	T	E	P		72 T	H	A	T			73 S	T	D	